"Now you're frowning, Holden." He liked how his name sounded on her lips. Crisp but with a loving roll to it.

"I'm thinking I may owe you an apology."

"Why is that? Are you done?" She nodded at his empty plate, then carried it to the sink when he raised his hands.

"Thanks." He grabbed their mugs and glasses and set them on the counter. "Breakfast was delicious."

"You're welcome." She pulled out latex gloves and he took them from her.

"I'll clean up. You cooked, you're done."

"It's not necessary—"

"Please." He didn't budge, didn't let his gaze drift to where the tank top bared her shoulder and the lone angel drawn on it. An angel the size of a tiny fairy rested on her golden skin, its pink wings and hair unmistakably feminine.

"Fine. But tell me why you're so against reporters while you clean up."

She was so close, her scent teasing him as it had last night. Washing dishes was going to be his most difficult task to date on this case.

At least it kept his hands busy...and off Bella.

* * *

Book Seven of The Coltons of Mustang Valley

* * *

Dear Reader,

It's a delight to welcome you back to Mustang Valley with *Colton's Deadly Disguise* and the thrilling ride journalist Bella Colton and FBI agent Holden St. Clair take us on! Well, with a little help from a scary possible serial killer, and the overriding danger that's sweeping Mustang Valley these days. You know, the usual great elements that are in every Harlequin Romantic Suspense.

Bella and Colton's story was so fun to write. The fact that it takes place during the Ms. Mustang Valley pageant makes it all the more intriguing—what kind of killer goes after pageant contestants? And more importantly, will Bella and Colton be able to catch their breath long enough to realize their sizzling chemistry might be something more?

I'm so happy to be part of another Harlequin Romantic Suspense Coltons series. I also appreciate any chance I have to connect with you, the best reader ever.

Please visit my website and sign up for my newsletter and site news. You can find me on social media, too.

Happy reading!

Peace,

Geri

GeriKrotow.com

Facebook.com/gerikrotow

Instagram.com/geri_krotow

Twitter.com/GeriKrotow

COLTON'S DEADLY DISGUISE

Geri Krotow

HARLEQUIN
ROMANTIC
SUSPENSE

Special thanks and acknowledgment are given to
Geri Krotow for her contribution to
The Coltons of Mustang Valley miniseries.

Recycling programs
for this product may
not exist in your area.

ISBN-13: 978-1-335-62648-6

Colton's Deadly Disguise

Copyright © 2020 by Harlequin Books S.A.

This edition published by arrangement with Harlequin Books S.A.

For questions and comments about the quality of this book, please contact us at CustomerService@Harlequin.com.

Harlequin Enterprises ULC
22 Adelaide St. West, 40th Floor
Toronto, Ontario M5H 4E3, Canada
www.Harlequin.com

Printed in U.S.A.

Former naval intelligence officer and US Naval Academy graduate **Geri Krotow** draws inspiration from the global situations she's experienced. Geri loves to hear from her readers. You can email her via her website and blog, gerikrotow.com.

Books by Geri Krotow

Harlequin Romantic Suspense

The Coltons of Mustang Valley
Colton's Deadly Disguise

The Coltons of Roaring Springs
Colton's Mistaken Identity

Silver Valley P.D.
Her Christmas Protector
Wedding Takedown
Her Secret Christmas Agent
Secret Agent Under Fire
The Fugitive's Secret Child
Reunion Under Fire
Snowbound with the Secret Agent

The Coltons of Red Ridge
The Pregnant Colton Witness

The Coltons of Shadow Creek
The Billionaire's Colton Threat

Visit the Author Profile page at
Harlequin.com for more titles.

To Alex

It's such a joy to see the thoughtful, compassionate man you've become.

Chapter 1

Isabella Colton pulled up to Mustang Valley High School fighting a sense of urgency that wasn't usually her gig. Normally she absorbed every mile of scenery as she drove between her home nestled on the outskirts of Mustang Valley and into the town proper. Saguaro cacti sprinkled spots of green across the southeastern Arizona desert; many of the desert flowers were abloom, their hues of fuchsia, crimson and cream a stark contrast to the constant cactus green. But she'd noticed none of them today, and barely even registered the way the deep blue sky contrasted with the pale coral, violets and browns that made up the sandstone horizon.

Why, when she'd finally settled into her career as a journalist, was she all of a sudden feeling so stressed? Was it because she knew so much was riding on this assignment? Or the fact that she'd deliberately lied to her triplet brothers—Spencer, a Mustang Valley PD sergeant, and Jarvis, a businessman currently working as a ranch hand—when they'd asked why she couldn't meet them today for lunch.

Could it be because you're going against every principle you hold closest to your heart?

Maybe. Choosing to sign up as a contestant in the Ms. Mustang Valley Pageant was certainly out of her wheelhouse. As in, out in space from her true beliefs. But she was willing to do whatever it took to get the story, this story, right.

She'd been a reporter for the Lifestyle section of the *Mustang Valley Gabber* for over three years. It was time to break out, to write about subjects she was passionate about. More than anything, Bella longed to get to the truth of life, subject by subject. This was who she was, and she'd known it ever since she'd lost her parents when she was ten years old. There were a lot of things she couldn't control in life, but when she could, she wanted to get to the bare facts.

Since she'd accepted that reporting was her talent, she didn't want to waste another minute on articles that no longer interested her. It wasn't fair to her readers or to her. She'd written enough lifestyle and fashion pieces for the *Gabber* to last her lifetime.

It was time to make a change. Bella wanted to make a difference.

For years, she'd had to watch her best friend, Gio, do everything to fit what she believed to be the pageant lifestyle; from starving herself to paying thousands of dollars she didn't have for unnecessary collagen and Botox injections that began in her early twenties. Last year, Gio paid the final, irrevocable price when she died due to malnutrition and other effects of her eating disorders. At first glance, deciding to enter the exact culture that had killed Gio seemed counterintuitive. But not when she reminded herself why she was doing this—to out the people who had killed her best friend.

Bella needed the inside dirt on this pageant, and the only way to catch this fly would be with a generous dollop of honey, according to what Gio had told her over the six months before her death, just under a year ago.

Heartache mingled with grief at the reminder of Gio's death and Bella's irretrievable loss. Tears swelled and blurred the view of where the Arizona horizon and blue sky met in Mustang High School's parking lot. Bella's heart constricted at the natural beauty she and Gio had often shared on long hikes through the desert, or to the local lake, next to an abandoned silver mine that they both loved so much. Until Gio's disease weakened her too much to make the treks. Gio's precipitous demise had been a shock, the years of illness finally ending her too-short life.

Bella owed it to Gio and every woman. Too many, including Gio, had suffered from the constant dieting and negative body image that pageants—and society as a whole—had so vilely infected them with. Bella owed it to them to expose the people and institutions that perpetuated their suffering. While she couldn't go after the entire pageant industry, she was able to delve into Ms. Mustang Valley, where Gio's problems, according to her friend, had all began. If she could keep this in mind, instead of her constant grief for her bestie, she'd get this assignment right.

What hurt the most right now was that all Gio had wanted from this particular pageant was the scholarship prize to Mustang Valley Community College. Gio would never go to school again, ever.

"Stop this right now. Pull it together, Colton." She

flipped the decrepit old station wagon's visor down to use the mirror and dabbed at her tears, grateful she'd chosen the makeup with a waterproof label on it. She bolstered her spirits by sniffing the inside of her wrist, where she'd applied her favorite perfume. The soothing floral scent was a signature Parisian brand she'd noted on Kristi Sparkle, the supermodel who'd passed through Mustang Valley just a few weeks ago. It had been a fun gala at Mustang Valley town hall, where Bella had been able to interview the not-yet-thirty-year-old woman for a good fifteen minutes. It had made Bella grateful that in all of her thirty-one years she'd never held a job that required her to be anyone but herself. And while she'd maintained her weight she worked hard to do it. Healthy eating and lots of physical activity. Except when she had a pressing deadline, when Bella's coworkers knew to stay out of the line between her and the chocolate-chip cookies at the local bakery.

Bella's job as a journalist for the paper and blogger for its website afforded her an inside glimpse into the lives of the more affluent citizens of Mustang Valley, Arizona. It often put her in the position of experiencing events she'd only ever seen on television as a child. The only girl of three siblings, her first two decades had been tumultuous with Mom's and Dad's deaths when she and her brothers were only ten. Then, Aunt Amelia had raised them, but she never let them forget that she'd sacrificed *the best years of my life* to do so.

It'd taken a while for Bella to let go of the guilt her relief at Aunt Amelia's passing ten years ago had caused. At twenty-one, Bella hadn't comprehended that her sense of relief was absolutely normal.

Her professors at Arizona State had expressed their sympathy and compassion for her loss, for not having a parental figure at her graduation the following May. But to Bella, Aunt Amelia's death had been when her true life began. When she was able to make her own decisions without the looming negative comments Aunt Amelia doled out like thistles on a hiking trail. Those thorns were able to sneak into the oddest places such as the sole of a shoe or inside the back of a shirt; their sting was always guaranteed.

"Okay. You've got this." She spoke to her reflection, popped the visor back up and got out of the car. It'd been thirteen years, but MVHS still had the aura of countless life lessons about it, including when she'd tried to sneak a cigarette in the girls' restroom and skipped out on lunchtime. In both instances her nemesis Mrs. Maple had caught her and none-too-compassionately marched her down to Principal Kenner's office. Bella grinned, remembering the expression on Aunt Amelia's face when she'd been called in over Bella's truancy. It'd only been over one lunch period, to get a tattoo with her best friend. Bella reached up to rub her shoulder for good luck, where the small angel rested, but stopped herself. She'd put professional concealer over the symbol of her friendship with Gio, as the Ms. Mustang Valley Pageant did not allow visible tattoos. Bella sniffed. Another good reason to eschew the event.

You're doing this for Gio.

The building itself had undergone a recent facelift; bright teal roofing and matching painted trim stood out against the dark bricks and highlighted the elegance of the grand dame of Mustang Valley. Originally the town market during the mid-nineteenth century, the building had been expanded upon and modernized over the last century and a half. It truly was a beautiful piece of Mustang Valley charm. Had she really managed to avoid this place for the better part of ten years?

Bella teetered on the kind of espadrille wedges she probably hadn't worn since high school, either. She bent down to tighten the ankle strap, not needing to make a fool of herself by twisting an ankle before she even submitted her application.

Today was the last day to enter the competition. A quick glance at her phone confirmed that she had a full fifteen minutes to turn in her application with attached résumé, photos and birth certificate. A certificate she'd thought long and hard about forging, but would it really gain her the edge she desired? She was well within the eighteen-to-thirty-five-year-old limit. She'd been working for the *Mustang Valley Gabber* long enough. It'd been Bella's goal for the last couple of years to move out of the *Gabber* and get to a bigger news outlet. If she were ever to be the kind of reporter she believed she could be, this was her most realistic chance.

She had to convince the pageant board that she wanted to do this, for real.

The front entrance of the school was clean and bright, as she always remembered. The relentless Arizona sun beat on her shoulders, bared by the strapless red-and-white-striped top she'd chosen to go with the white capri pants. The outfit was totally out of character for Bella; she preferred simple lines, be it in jeans or a sundress. But she had to come across as a serious contestant, and that meant she had to scream "glamour." She'd even had red highlights woven into her ash-blond locks, something she'd never considered previously. Tattoos, piercings, sure, but her hair was something she'd never dyed before. To her initial chagrin, the highlights had blended into her hair to make it all appear red, a strawberry blond shade. Gio had had red hair, and Bella decided her matching color was a good-luck charm from beyond. Tears again threatened and she sniffed them away, lifted her chin and straightened her spine.

Bella opened the school's front door and walked into the lobby.

She gave herself a moment to take it all in. A lot had changed over the past several years. The first thing her gaze landed on was a metal detector, but before she could assess the rest of the entrance she was stopped by a police officer.

"Excuse me, ma'am. I need to see inside your bag." The man was tall and fit, not unlike Spencer. Dark hair, and what looked like even darker eyes but she couldn't be sure as they were downcast, his gaze following his hand as he moved a stick through her large white leather designer bag. As he searched, she checked his name badge to ask Spencer about him later. Or, maybe strike a conversation now. She was on the clock as far as her undercover report was concerned.

He didn't have a name badge, and a closer look revealed he wasn't MVPD at all but rather, private security. The dark blue uniform was so similar in appearance to Mustang Valley PD's that it was an easy mistake to make.

"I thought MVPD had an officer here at all times." As soon as she spoke her mind she wanted to bite her tongue. She was here on an undercover assignment. Not the time to reveal her knowledge of the local community. Be a pageant contestant, not a blogger.

"When the students are present, yes, they do. But not during weekends and spring break. I'm pageant security."

"Oh." She looked at him and wished she had some

handy banter. He was undeniably attractive, but with an air of stiff reserve. She opened her mouth to start a friendly conversation but he wasn't interested.

"Name?" Cold brown eyes assessed her and she stiffened, fighting the urge to take a step backward. An aura of authority exuded from this man and she couldn't help but wonder if he did something else.

"There's not a visitors' list—no one knows I'm entering." She wasn't about to be intimidated.

He held up a handwritten logbook. "I'm required to enter each name, for the pageant authorities to verify that they have received every application."

"Isabella Colton." His heavy, albeit well-sculpted, brows didn't budge from their place that reflected his intense focus as he wrote her name on what looked like maybe the twentieth line on the page.

Bella ignored her anxiety over how many contestants there might be. More would be better, as it would allow her to blend in more readily. If there were only twenty, she'd have to work at participation while gathering information for her report.

"ID?" He held out his hand without looking back up. She retrieved her Arizona driver's license, placed it carefully on his palm.

"Is this a part-time thing for you?" She smiled as she imagined a beauty contestant would, fluttered her lashes, ignored the two that stuck together. This glamour gig was not as easy as it had looked in the several pageants she'd studied online during her preliminary research. Her research yielded enough ammunition to warrant her entering the pageant. Of all the Arizona pageants, the Ms. Mustang Valley competition reflected the highest number of winners who'd later admitted to having mental illness, an eating disorder, or both.

Most had gone public with their struggles once their year's reign was up, in order to both keep their scholarship intact, yet also provide public outreach to young women who found themselves in the grips of the same vicious diseases.

The security guard cleared his throat and she all but physically shook her head.

Worry about the research later. You're a contestant right now.

She still wasn't certain about which talent she'd choose. It was a sad competition between oratory skills, i.e. reading a Samuel Clemens Langhorne or Mark Twain poem, or performing a Hula hoop routine she'd choreographed in seventh grade with Gio to their favorite bubblegum pop hit.

He handed her ID and bag back, the tips of their fingers briefly making contact. "You can step through the metal detector now. The pageant committee is on the stage, in the theater, through the second doors on your right." His deep voice revealed nothing but professionalism. The security dude wasn't going to be an ally in her quest to uncover this pageant's deepest secrets. At least she knew from the start. She wouldn't waste any more energy on him. There were more important sources to mine.

Bella walked under the metal frame and when the detector didn't sound, she didn't look back. Forward was the only direction to achieve some kind of justice for Gio.

Wondering why the fleeting contact with this man moved her more than it should have wasn't worth her time.

Except, if she found out what else he did for a living, other than work as a pageant security guard, it might make an interesting side item for her investigative piece. She chuckled under her breath as she headed for the auditorium.

FBI Agent Holden St. Clair took a swig of water as he took his post offstage in the high school theater. The area between the side curtains allowed him to watch each contestant as they were interviewed, observe the pageant board members and keep an eye on the contestants who'd already been interviewed but now were seated on the stage, waiting until the entire process was over. The early birds got to see all of the interviews, which he supposed was some kind of pageant advantage. Holden didn't care. His job was to keep the building secure. He'd gone back and forth between here and the school entrance for the last eight hours.

It had been a long day.

After all contestants had finished today they'd be asked to leave and then only the ones who received a callback would return tomorrow for the start of the pageant preparation.

He'd had to stifle a laugh when his supervisor had told him he was assigned to work undercover at the Ms. Mustang Valley Pageant. His life experience to date included serving overseas while still in the army, and several different investigations as an FBI agent, including a few serial killer cases, not working as a security guard—even though he was hunting a murderer now.

Something about Mustang Valley was bothering him, ever since he'd driven into the modest-size town. His assignment was straightforward: observe and protect the pageant from the possibility of a serial killer who'd struck at two previous pageants earlier this year in Arizona. He was doing this undercover, with minimal other

Law Enforcement Agency, LEA, involvement for now. Besides the director of Arizona pageants, who'd hired him, Holden had an inside LEA connection in town: his army buddy Spencer Colton, who worked at Mustang Valley PD with his K-9 companion Boris. After he'd spoken to Spencer on the phone, they'd met up at a restaurant in Tucson, so that Holden's cover as a security guard wouldn't be compromised. Spencer had given him the scoop on Mustang Valley and in particular the high school's blueprints, security footprint and the background on each of the Ms. Mustang Valley Pageant board members. The pageant board included Hannah Rosenstein, a MVHS Spanish teacher, Selina Barnes Colton—Colton Payne's ex and a rabid socialite who frankly, from what he'd read, was going to be a real pain in the neck—and several local business owners. So far he'd not found any reason to suspect any of them of wrongdoing but it was his job to remain alert.

Spending time with Spencer had been great and he'd been delighted to find out Spencer had fallen for a woman he planned to spend the rest of his life with. Spencer teased him, said Holden's turn was coming. Holden blew off Spencer's sentiments. After being so badly burned by his ex he had no room for anything more than short-lived hookups. Working a serial killer case left no time for that, either.

As much as Spencer assured him that he'd be a perfect fit in Mustang Valley, and that the openness of the citizens would hopefully expose the killer sooner, Holden had been on edge ever since he'd driven into Mustang Valley's historical downtown. Surrounded by so much Southwest American history, it was easy to forget he was here to investigate a serial killer who preyed upon beauty contestants, redheads in particular. So far all of the Ms. Mustang Valley contestants had been blonde or brunette, and he'd wondered if this pageant might escape the notice of the predator. Until Isabella Colton walked in with those red streaks in her hair. And green eyes, eyes he'd find attractive if he didn't know they'd be like bull's-eyes to the killer. Both of the previous victims had red hair, and green eyes.

He made a mental note to let Spencer know that Isabella was applying to compete in the pageant. He assumed it was Spencer's sister, Bella, that he'd talked about. While the Colton name was huge throughout the country, and especially in Mustang Valley, where one part of the family had made itself a billion-dollar oil empire, he doubted there were many Bella Coltons in this two-horse town. The pageant director, also a Colton, was a typical rich socialite, and he didn't think she was a close relation to Spencer or his probable sister. Like any other large, extended family, the Coltons had many branches. Spencer was from a modest background, and had been quick to let Holden know it when they were serving together.

"Thank you, Marcie." The pageant committee chair dismissed the second-to-last contestant to make it in by the deadline. Isabella Colton was the only one who remained.

He'd locked the front doors after scanning Isabella through security. All he had left to do today was observe as the last contestant hopefuls submitted their applications, and survived the board's initial interview.

It wasn't an easy task to remain focused. Isabella Colton's appearance made his gut tighten and put his instincts on high alert. Until the minute she walked through Mustang Valley High's doors he'd been hopeful that he'd be able to move on to the next Arizona pageant, scheduled for Scottsdale next month. He knew the serial killer he was after had only ever murdered redheads.

All hope that this pageant might be spared what two smaller towns in Northern Arizona had experienced— the brutal deaths of redheaded contestants—evaporated with the swoosh of the school's front doors behind Isabella Colton.

Holden wished for the first time in his career that he wasn't undercover. That he could snap his fingers and be the real Holden, for just one conversation with the woman who'd just walked into Mustang Valley High School's theater. To warn her away, to tell her that she should find another way to pay for her college or whatever she wanted to do with the winner's prize. But he was undercover, and since his guise was a security guard, his job was to stay quiet and observe. Isabella Colton still had to pass the scrutiny of the pageant review board, so at least there was a chance she'd be turned away either for her age or an incomplete application. She didn't look older than the thirty-five-year limit, but she wasn't too young, either.

"Isabella Colton?" Mimi Kingston, the pageant director, called out for the redhead and Colton couldn't help but do his job thoroughly and make sure he had a good description of Ms. Colton in his mind. At the security checkpoint he'd been focused on the possibility of any of the contestants bringing in a weapon, checking to make sure they weren't a potential suspect. He'd never investigated a female serial killer but the bureau had several over the years. It happened.

"Bella?" Mimi squeaked out the second syllable, clearly surprised to see the other woman.

"Surprises never cease in Mustang Valley. You know

that, Mimi." Bella placed her application packet on the table that was center stage before returning to the single chair, and sat. He didn't see her bag; she must have left it in the theater seats. Since no one was left other than those onstage, all part of the pageant, it'd be secure. He was impressed. Bella Colton looked more put-together than the majority of the other contestants.

Her golden-red hair was tied up behind her head in one of those fancy styles he'd only ever noticed in the movies. What caught his attention was the creamy pale skin of her nape, where a few wispy tendrils curled. Her top bared her shoulders, revealing a prominent but not unhealthy collarbone. His mouth moistened as his tongue practically experienced how smooth it'd feel under it.

Holden bit down on said tongue and reminded himself he was on duty, and Bella Colton was most likely Spencer's sister. Holden's job was to protect the pageant, and if Bella was indeed his buddy's sibling, it raised the stakes on this operation. Since Payne Colton had been targeted, no Colton was safe.

He watched Bella cross her long legs at the ankles and rest her hands in her lap, her shapely knees fitting perfectly together. Her ankle-length pants were form-fitting and brokered no complaints from him. He liked that her nails were short, though painted bright red. Holden wasn't a fan of those long, fake nails, and he wondered what Bella did when she wasn't trying to rustle up a scholarship to Mustang Valley Community College.

"Thank you for your application, Bella. We're taking turns reviewing it." Derek McDougal spoke up, the only male on the board. He rustled the second page. "I see you're a Mustang Valley High graduate. So you've known about the pageant, as this is its thirtieth year." He passed the application packet to the next board member. "While we're reviewing everything to make sure you qualify, please tell us why you're here." Derek looked at Bella as though she were the canary and he the poised house cat.

Holden's sense went on high alert, as while McDougal didn't appear to have any connection with the previous pageants and murders, he was an anomaly. Two of the committee members, the Spanish teacher and Selina Barnes Colton, had been involved with at least one if not both of the ill-fated pageants and while they were automatic suspects, the outliers had to be examined, too.

"Certainly." Bella beamed. If she noticed Derek's leer she didn't show it. "As most of you know, I'm a life-long Mustang Valley resident. I've been lucky enough to go to college, where I received my bachelor's in journalism. It's there on my résumé." She nodded at her application packet, which was being passed down the row of seven pageant board members. "I've fallen on hard financial times lately. I'd use the scholarship to MVCC to begin a new career that would have a more reliable income than freelance writing."

"But you're employed by the *Mustang Valley Gabber*, aren't you?" another board member called out. Holden made a mental note to check up on Bella's supposed dire straits, but all *thoughts* screeched to a halt. Wait—Bella Colton was a reporter? His gut twisted and he knew his mouth probably did, too.

Holden had nothing more than disgust for reporters. Not for the usual reasons he knew other agents detested the media. Holden's distrust of reporters was very personal in origin, thanks to his last girlfriend, someone he'd thought might be with him for the long haul. Nicole, his ex, turned out to be dating him because she'd hoped to glean confidential information about the Coltons from him. This was last summer, when he'd investigated a crime in Roaring Springs, Colorado during its annual film festival. By the time the last film premiered, Nicole admitted her motive for wanting to wait all day in the hotel room for Holden. They were through. In the two years since, he'd dated on and off, but never anyone serious. And the bad taste in his mouth from being duped by a reporter had never washed away.

"I still work at the *Gabber*, but it's a modest wage, supplemented by freelance work that's also been drying up. It's time for me to face facts—I've got to find another type of job or starve." Bella smiled as she continued the interview. Her entire face lit up and dang it, it ignited something deep inside his chest. Holden's breath caught at the exquisite shade of peach on her cheekbones, the bright hue of her irises. But her green eyes didn't sparkle to match the dazzling of her white smile. Instead, Holden had the oddest sensation that Bella Colton was in the midst of a huge act. And the board was her audience. But why?

"With the scholarship to MVCC, I'd be able to become a nurse."

"The medical industry? A Colton?" Maeve Murphy, who'd worked as the school nurse for decades, spoke up.

Bella's foot began to shake at the end of her long, shapely leg, but her smile never faded, her chin remained uplifted. Holden gave her ten points for composure and the pageant had yet to begin, her application yet to be accepted.

"I'm not clear on what being a Colton has to do with a career choice." He heard the challenge in her tone even as she delivered her response so sweetly. It only served to make him admire her more. He really didn't need to admire anyone right now, though, and definitely not a journalist. He was here to find a serial killer.

You still have to live.

Maeve's plump face turned red. "It's just that, you're from a family of lucrative businesspeople. Why medicine, why now?"

Bella leaned forward, never breaking eye contact with Maeve. "I'm sorry—I think you're mistaking me for one of the other line of Coltons, the ones who own Rattlesnake Ridge Ranch and run Colton Oil. My brothers and I are from a different part of the family. In fact, I don't even know most of my Colton cousins very well." Her voice had turned to ice and Holden watched both her and the pageant committee's expressions. Most of the people on the board were career educators, including Maeve, an RN. If Bella was in her late twenties, maybe early thirties, she, Spencer and Jarvis must have gone to school here while Maeve and the others were on staff. They had to know her and her brothers. He'd read that Mustang Valley had a population of ten thousand. In short, Maeve knew Bella and her brothers.

And for some inexplicable reason, he was relieved to receive confirmation she wasn't familiar with the larger branch of her family.

A woman with pouffed-out brunette hair and large dangling earrings raised her heavily braceleted arm, waving at Maeve. "I can personally vouch for Bella and her desire to make something of herself. She's a lifelong resident, as she's stated, and her aunt raised her and her brothers after her parents' deaths in an auto accident. Tragic, I tell you. Yet you've survived the odds and are here to present yourself as a contestant. And, may I add, Bella was the brightest student of her class when I had her. Brava." Hannah Rosenstein nodded in encouragement toward Bella. Hannah was the school Spanish teacher and Holden had witnessed her vouch for exactly one other contestant, also a former student. If she said Bella was solid, he suspected the board would accept her application.

"*Muchas gracias*, Señora Rosenstein." Bella responded in a decent accent.

Senora Rosenstein grinned. "De nada. It's heartwarming to see you've remembered your Spanish."

Holden sat still until Bella's interview was finished and she was released to leave the building. Only after she exited the auditorium's back door did he stand and head for the back of the stage to begin his last inspection of the building before he locked it up for the night. Until next week, when the contestants would be called in to start the pageant prep.

A movement on the other side of the stage caught his attention. A tall figure in dark clothing, his face covered with the shadow from the brim of a baseball cap, the man wasn't anyone Holden had allowed in the building. Holden had memorized the exact number of people who should be here—board members, contestants, plus Bella, who had left the building by now—in the high school. This was a stranger, an interloper.

Holden drew his weapon from its hidden place in an ankle holster and deliberately made his way to the back passage behind the stage, to avoid detection by the suspect. No one was going to be hurt—not on *his* watch.

Chapter 2

Offstage, Bella quickly slipped out of the espadrilles and shoved them into her oversize tote. Her feet made no sound on the old, highly waxed corridor floor that had borne thousands of teenaged feet through the years.

Looking over her shoulder, she made sure that the way-too-intense security guard hadn't followed her, but he'd been pretty settled in his chair on the stage, observing the pageant committee's discussion. The members had been deep in conversation as she and the other contestants exited. Bella had made to leave with the group, then peeled off as the last of the women exited through the main door.

The memory of his gaze on her made her skin heat and her anger rise. Did he think she couldn't see him as the pageant committee grilled her? And what was his job here, exactly? She thought security guards just manned doors and entrances.

Memories swiped at her focus as she ran to the teachers' conference room. She'd been in several musicals during middle and high school, all performed in this very building, on the same stage where she was going to have to pretend to compete for Ms. Mustang Valley. Bella knew these corridors and rooms as well as the house she'd grown up in until their parents had died. Some buildings were imprinted on a heart as firmly as the memories that were created in them. She sighed. Even the not-so-great memories—the ones of Aunt Amelia, who had single-handedly raised Bella and her brothers after the accident—were here. Bella recalled Aunt Amelia at back-to-school nights, frazzled as she found getting to three different class sessions impossible. She'd taken it out on the triplets later, complaining about how her life could have been so much easier if Bella's parents had lived.

Bella hoped that tomorrow she'd be asked to report back to participate in the pageant. She knew it depended on the interview, the personal essays, answers to a total of five written questions that covered her views on charity, community and personal excellence, and her "contestant resume." The resume had to include current contributions to Mustang Valley, her service hours outside of work, and her place of employment. She'd cringed at the glamour portion of the submission package, which required a headshot as well as an "athletic pose." Bella used her tripod to take the photo of herself in yoga pants and workout bra. But it'd all be worth it if she made the cut. She'd learn more about the selection process and any "advice" doled out by the committee that might include starving oneself. She was looking for this kind of evidence against the pageant, but Bella needed more proof that this pageant in particular encouraged the women to be as thin as possible, or any other trigger that would have set off Gio's issues. Gio had mentioned Señora Rosenstein as being particularly snide in her comments about any plus-size contestants, forcing them to weigh in each day, sometimes twice per day. As the pageant's self-appointed volunteer choreographer, Selina had made nasty, derogatory comments to Gio and other contestants more than once, and Gio told her there were transcripts of the actual pageants where Selina cut contestants for such subjective transgressions as not being "dancer-like." Gio's claims weren't enough to write an investigative report with, however. Bella needed to establish a pattern of wrongdoing for as far back as it existed, if possible.

The records of the previous pageants were reportedly stored in a single, locked file cabinet in the corner of the teaching-staff room which doubled as a group dressing room. Gio had gone over all of it with her as she lay dying, her spent body nearing its end on the hospital bed.

Gio's last smile to her had belied her wasted state, and Gio's spirit buoyed her with each step closer to the staff room. Reaching the steel door, she peered through the small, high window, but it had been papered over from the inside. Probably a security move due to the ever-present threat of school shootings. It was a harsh reality Bella's generation had only begun to come to grips with. She sucked in air as quietly as she could, listening for anyone else in the area. It was impossible to tell if someone was in the room until she entered, and she had no idea how much time she had to find what she wanted.

Holding her breath, Bella opened the door and pasted

a smile on her face. If anyone was here, she'd make up a stupid excuse and skedaddle.

No one was in the room and she scanned it with her reporter's-eye view. The worn furniture and wood-paneled walls had been replaced with contemporary ergonometric chairs, sofas and laptop desks. The walls were a pale shade of lime, the white trim of the huge picture windows creating a crisp, clean, calming effect. If she weren't a Mustang Valley native, she'd be stunned by the unparalleled view of the Mustang Valley Mountains.

Bella would have plenty of time to appreciate aesthetics later, while running through the pageant. Right now she needed the files Gio had told her about. The files held the transcripts of previous pageants, priceless evidence. Her chest felt heavy as she remembered Gio's insistence that the Ms. Mustang Valley pageant was the most tortuous, demeaning experience of all the pageants she regularly competed in. Sure, Ms. Mustang Valley held the highest prize—a full, four-year ride to the local college. But it came at such a high price. As part of her prep for going undercover, Bella had interviewed a couple dozen Ms. Mustang Valley pageant entrants from the past decade. She'd found their names in the archives of the local newspapers, as all contestants were announced before the final night.

While all described the competitive environment she'd expected, with the stakes so high, none gave her the specific details Gio had in those last months before she died. Bella needed the pageant's written history, and if she was lucky, she'd find out what Selina Barnes Colton and Hannah Rosenstein had really said to Gio.

Acutely aware that she could be interrupted at any second, Bella searched the room for the file cabinet.

Nothing resembling Gio's description or her memory existed in the staff room. Tears of frustration and rage threatened and she blinked. She refused to have her attempt to find justice for Gio stymied this early into her efforts.

Calm down. Think.

Hands on hips, she took one more look around the room, beginning and ending with the stage door. Her mind's eye saw the stage beyond the double doors, the dressing area to the left—

The dressing room! The space beyond the room divider where the cabinets had been placed. She recalled Gio's offhand comment about how crowded it was in there, with twenty-four women changing for swimsuit and evening-gown competitions.

She slowly opened the double doors to the stage, aware of each tiny creak and squeak. The voices of the pageant board floated through along with the unmistakable scent of the stage. Pinewood, varnish, decades of sweat and joy that had been expended through performance after performance, tryouts and auditions. To her left the sun's rays filtered through dust from the dressing room. Sweat beaded on her upper lip and trickled down her spine, even made her palms wet. Apparently air-conditioning wasn't in the school's weekend and evening budget.

As soon as she could close the doors without a sound, she made haste toward the side room. Before she reached the threshold, her gaze landed on her prize: the old, battered metal file cabinet sat in the far corner of the room, laden with props resting atop its rusty finish.

Yes.

She reached into her pocket for the key that she'd found in the box of treasures Gio had left for her. A favorite pair of earrings Bella had always admired, photographs going back to elementary school, the tickets from a summer concert series they'd scrimped and saved to afford. And a small, sealed envelope.

Gio's mother brought the box over to Bella's home two weeks after her daughter had passed. She expressed again how much Bella had meant to Gio and how much Bella's support helped her during the awful grieving process.

Bella wasn't surprised to find a small note in Gio's unmistakable neat print addressed to her. Her bestie liked to have closure and loved writing letters. The surprise had been the file cabinet key tucked inside the exquisite stationery.

Bella had expected that she'd have to do a lot of digging and research before getting enough evidence to take to the police in the hopes of obtaining a search warrant, to get official access into the files. Gio's claim that certain pageant officials had caused her eating and mental disorders needed to be substantiated.

The pageant files from years past would tell Bella not only who the judges had been, but bear witness to their thought processes and training methods. Methods that Gio thought still existed even today, with all the knowledge about eating disorders and mental illness.

Bella looked at her watch. She figured her time was running short, as the security guard was bound to get up and check the backstage area. Did she have enough time to finish her theft?

No time to worry about it.

The key was in her pocket and she wrestled it out, jiggled it into the lock. For one heart-stopping moment she feared the key might break before she was able to turn the lock as both were practically ancient, the metal spotted with rust.

Finally the lock turned and she grasped the handle, used her thumb to slide the drawer stop to the right.

The sound of fabric against fabric was her only warning before a strong hand clamped over her nose and mouth. She was pulled up against a person behind her. She fought to turn but her attacker was stronger and yanked her hair, hard.

"Don't move or I'll snap your neck." The low, taut voice vibrated with menace and sounded like a horror-film villain's. Spots started to float in front of her vision and she kicked backward with her heel, hoping that the blows against this maniac's shins and feet would make him loosen his hold on her.

He tugged harder on her hair and she cried out in pain but with her air supply cut and in such agony it came out as a whimper.

"You're not being very smart. You'll never win this pageant. If you want to live, you'll quit before you start."

Focus. Observe. She tried every tool she'd ever read about to capture a solid description for the police. And most of all, she fought for her consciousness. Victims who passed out didn't always fare well.

"Stop!" A loud, booming voice echoed through her rapidly fading awareness. Bella tried to hold on to that voice, its strength, its promise of safety.

But her world crashed into nothingness.

"Stop or I'll shoot." Holden had his weapon aimed on the man in black, whom he'd gone after when he saw him in the shadows. The creep held an unconscious, drooping Bella Colton with one arm, her head up next to his as protection from Holden's bullets. At least, Holden hoped she was unconscious and not dead.

"Never." The assailant turned and faced him. He wore a ski mask and sunglasses under the black ball cap. A mouthpiece revealed how he disguised his voice. "I will crush her throat if you don't back off."

Holden stood his ground, praying for extra time. For this suspect to make a mistake, to move enough so that he could get a clear shot without risking Bella's life.

Unless the killer had already claimed his next victim. He risked a quick look at her face and its pink tinge assured him her heart was at least still pumping.

Moving his gaze back on the enemy, he slowly lowered his weapon. The other man had no visible weapon. But the serial killer had poisoned or shot each of the other two victims, so his comment about crushing her throat didn't match. But it might be part of his thrill—using different MOs.

"You'll never get out of here alive. Turn yourself in now and you live." Holden had to be careful to not betray his real identity to this lowlife. The less the killer knew, the better. It wouldn't matter if he could apprehend him right here, right now, but Holden had been in this situation before. Bella's safety came first. He watched the man's hands for any sign of movement toward Bella's throat. Right now his arm held her neck up against him.

"You don't own me, you pathetic excuse for security." The killer's voice sounded like a space alien and that added an extra creepiness to his words. Holden itched to cuff him, to get him to confess to what he'd done.

"What do you have against this woman? Drop her."

"Everyone is not what they seem." He was backing

toward the exit, dragging the still unresponsive Bella with him. "If you were doing your job, I wouldn't have been able to get to her. She's mine."

Not on Holden's life.

Holden took one step toward the assailant and allowed himself to fall forward, as if he'd tripped. The man jerked, saw the clear line Holden had to shoot him and let go of Bella, then ran out the exit. Holden took off after the man, but when he entered the large corridor he was gone. Holden pulled out his cell and called 9-1-1, identifying himself as pageant security to keep his cover. He requested police backup, informed them of Bella's unconscious state and asked for EMT support ASAP. He continued to run through the school in all directions the man could have gone but it was fruitless. And he had to turn back to protect Bella until the other LEA arrived on scene.

The man behind the stage, who'd rendered Bella Colton unconscious, had disappeared as if a stage trapdoor had opened and swallowed him whole.

Sirens sounded and he rounded back to the staff room, to check on Bella. As he neared, he saw EMTs rush in and decided to stay back until they'd treated her. If she regained consciousness here, he didn't want to be the first person she saw. Better to stay in the background of all that had happened. His cover was vital to keeping the pageant contestants safe, especially the single redhead with green eyes, Bella Colton.

He slipped into an empty classroom and called Bud Langston, the Arizona State pageant director, one of the few people who knew about Holden's undercover role besides Holden's handler at the FBI office in Phoenix. Bud had contacted Holden, who got permission from his supervisor to work the case that the FBI began investigating after the second pageant murder. Bud's son had been Holden's college roommate and Bud had jumped at the chance to have Holden work undercover during the Ms. Mustang Valley Pageant. Anything to keep the participants safe.

"Bud."

"Talk to me, Holden."

"It's a rough start to Ms. Mustang Valley, Bud." Holden recapped what had happened.

"Thank God that Bella Colton wasn't harmed—or was she, besides being knocked out?"

"I don't know for certain, but I'll find out and get back to you. She was out the entire time I was there, so there's slim to no chance she knows of my involvement."

"That's something, at least." Bud swore and Holden bit back a grin—Bud was a navy veteran and *salty* came to mind. "I wish you'd caught him."

"I do, too. But, Bud, we can't be certain this is the same man we're looking for. Beauty pageants attract all kinds, and are the perfect target for anyone who's off-balance and looking for a sick thrill." Criminals had all kinds of motives.

"I get that, and I'm glad you're on the case. What will it take to call in more federal agents?"

"That's above my pay grade, but to be honest, we're stretched thin at the moment. Plus, the risk of anyone figuring out we're here will prevent us from operating with the freedom we need to apprehend the suspect." Holden was fairly certain the criminal only saw him as a bumbling security guard, which was how he wanted it. It might make Holden the man's first target, if and when he came back. Holden would be ready for him.

"Thanks for what you did today, and please keep me informed." Bud's sincerity was tangible in his voice.

"Will do." When Holden disconnected, he put in a call to his FBI supervisor, who expressed the same disappointment that Holden hadn't apprehended the criminal, and added an additional task that Holden had already figured into his work in Mustang Valley. He'd call Spencer later, after he got out of here. Spencer and he had agreed to not communicate unless absolutely necessary while Holden was on this case, undercover. And now his buddy's sister was smack dab in the middle of the case. She'd been hurt on his watch, not something he relished telling Spencer.

He had to keep tabs on Bella Colton at all costs, without her figuring out he was FBI. Holden had trailed suspects and victims alike, all in the line of duty as an agent.

So why did the prospect of keeping her safe fill him both with anticipation and dread?

Chapter 3

Bella squinted against the bright light the ER doctor shone to measure her pupils' responses. "I'm fine, really. I think he knocked me out with one of those pinches, you know, to my jugular." She felt silly, especially after she'd realized the ER doc was none other than Shawn Trembly, a boy she'd briefly dated in high school. They parted ways after school and ended up being friends. "It's great that you were able to fulfill your dream, Shawn. You know, to be a doctor."

"You mean a sleeper hold, a choke hold." Shawn nodded as he kept to business, evidently not as ready to dismiss Bella's attack and loss of consciousness as anything near normal. "That could be true, and the bruises at the base of your neck support it, but I want an MRI to confirm. You hit your head when he dropped you, and there isn't a lot of swelling at the contact spot. We need to rule out a concussion. And yes, I got to follow my dream. But I'm not a doctor, I'm a physician's assistant with a specialty in trauma."

"That's still great." Could he talk about anything other than how she'd been knocked out? Bella didn't want to dwell on her attack. She had a case to investigate.

"Let's keep the focus on your treatment, Bella. You've been through a traumatic event." He tapped into a laptop, his expression grave. Shawn was classically handsome, with deep blue eyes and dark hair she remembered being curly, but was now in a tight crew cut. But she felt zero chemistry between them now. And for reasons unknown to her, the mental image of the security guard at MVHS popped into her brain. The man had been so intense. She stiffened. Could he have been the person who attacked her?

In truth, it could be anybody. It gave powerlessness a whole new dimension, and she'd thought she'd already been through it after watching her best friend die.

Anxiety rushed over her, and she knew one thing. She had to get the heck out of this hospital. Researching the guard was her first priority. Maybe he wasn't on the payroll for the protection of the contestants but to keep the pageant's legacy intact by guarding that file cabinet.

"I'm not nauseous, or dizzy, and I don't remember seeing stars."

"But you were unconscious. Give me the benefit of the doubt, Bella." Shawn wasn't going to budge and she let out a long sigh.

"Fine." Sometimes giving in was the quickest way to a vital goal. Bella had to get to the bottom of this pageant's history and apparently continued abhorrent ways, and she was running out of time. She had the length of the pageant to bring this investigation to fruition. And

Bella had to get back to those files before they disappeared. Her gut sank at the thought. By getting caught trying to open them, she may have alerted the bad guys that they needed to destroy them, or at least hide them elsewhere. And who used paper files anymore these days, anyway?

She needed to get back to the school and into the staff room when the rehearsals weren't in session, and when no security was on premises. It was the school's break, but certainly the principal and senior staff had to come in to take care of administrative duties? She could pose as herself, doing an article on MVHS and how it had changed over the years. A profile on Shawn, from being her high school physics lab partner to becoming a trauma/ER physician's assistant, would be a great cover.

The sense of dread in her stomach lessened, but not when she thought of walking back into MVHS.

Bella wasn't a gambler, but she'd bet that the mysterious security guard was definitely a key to finding answers.

Two hours later and with assurances that she didn't have a concussion, Bella pushed through the hospital exit doors and ran smack into a tall, hard mass of man in a blue uniform.

"Spencer!"

Her brother was almost a foot taller than her and kept himself in top shape as a sergeant for MVPD. In uniform, he usually exuded authority, a no-nonsense countenance. Since he was her triplet and she knew him better than most anyone, save their brother Jarvis, Bella could tell Spencer had more on his mind than police business.

"What the heck, Bella?" His blue eyes sparked with

concern and not a small dose of frustration. He looked at her, then pulled her to him in a big-brother-style hug. Which technically was correct as he'd been born two minutes ahead of her. "I about flipped when I found out you'd been brought in."

Bella soaked up the love, as her brothers were her closest friends and only immediate family. Despite the Colton name and the hundreds of distant relatives who shared it, Bella and her brothers had only ever been able to rely on one another, as had their parents before they died over twenty years ago.

"I'm fine." She pushed back and looked into Spencer's eyes. "Seriously. I had a scare, by some jerk who's probably involved with the Ms. Mustang Valley Pageant. He knocked me out with one of those Vulcan-grip maneuvers."

"Do you mean a choke hold?" His worry was evident. "What were you doing at the high school, Bella?"

"Where's Boris?" She sought to distract her brother as she looked around for his K-9 partner, a beautiful chocolate lab they all considered part of the family.

"With Katrina. They're working on some more indepth maneuvers. And stop trying to avoid my question." Spencer might be in overprotective-big-brother mode, but it didn't stop the warmth in his eyes from blossoming at the mention of his love and local dog trainer, Katrina. They'd recently fallen in love and gotten engaged.

"Let's talk while you drive me home."

"You don't have another ride arranged?"

She shrugged as they headed for the police K-9 SUV parked in front of the entrance. "I was going to call for a ride with my app." Actually, she'd planned to walk back to the high school to retrieve her vehicle and maybe manage to sneak back inside. Nothing she'd willingly share with her cop brother.

"Why wouldn't you call me or Jarvis? We're your family, Bella."

"I know, but you're also both a bit controlling about what you think I should be doing with my life."

"It's no secret that something's afoot in Mustang Valley." He got behind the wheel and moved a laptop out of the passenger side. She slid onto the leather seat and realized how hot it was.

"Air, please."

"Sure thing." He flicked on the engine and put the SUV in Drive. "Where to? The high school?"

"Yes. I left my car there earlier."

"And why exactly were you there?" Spencer's attitude was all casual but she knew it was from years of experience interviewing victims and criminals. Her brother could be as patient as needed when he wanted information.

Bella sucked in a breath, held it and slowly released it. The technique was part of her daily meditation to keep her tendency toward anxiety at bay. If the day's events hadn't triggered her, she'd bet Spencer's reaction was about to.

"Don't get mad. The last thing I need right now, after such a, a traumatic experience," she silently thanked Shawn for the description, "is you coming down hard on me. I'm doing an undercover exposé of the local beauty-pageant circuit and I need to participate to get my story. But no one can know about this, Spencer. You can't tell anyone at work. Promise me."

"Of course I won't." She knew he would though, if he thought her safety or anyone else's depended on the information. "Why would you do this, Bella? Is it about Gio?"

Her throat tightened and she squeezed her eyes shut. This was going to be more difficult than she foresaw, the constant reminder that her best friend and confidante of twenty-five years, ever since first grade, was gone.

"Partly, yes. Mostly I want to dig deep and find out who's really in charge of these things, why they still have categories like evening gown and talent competition. I mean, it's the twenty-first century. What gives, you know?"

"Save the flip tone for your readers. I'm your brother and I'm telling you, this is a bad idea. You've heard about the other two pageants in other Arizona counties, right?" He took the slow way to the high school, through the back part of Mustang Valley that cut through pastures and gave the best views of the mountains in whose shadows they'd grown up.

"I have heard. But the murders are unrelated. One was poison and the other a gunshot. Probably disgruntled boyfriends or overzealous competitors."

"They haven't found the killer in either instance. You need to be very, very careful, Bella."

"There's a security guard employed by the pageant. He'll keep it safe. According to the EMTs who took care of me, he's the one who called it in."

She wondered if he'd found her on the floor, unconscious, or if he'd gone after her attacker—or both. As fit and strong as the mysterious guard appeared, bottom line was that he was a civilian, nothing more. He hadn't prevented her attack.

"There is, and he's got a superb résumé from what Chief tells me, but it's not good enough for me at this point. Since you won't carry your own protection, Bella, you need to consider dropping out of the competition. Can't you get the information you need by interviewing the contestants?"

"No. Not the same. Look, I don't tell you how to police. I appreciate your input, but don't tell me how to do investigative reporting. I promise I'll let you know the minute anything fishy turns up. But I have to be able to do my job, Spencer."

"I hear you're in financial trouble."

"What? From the interview the board did?" Anger spun in her stomach like a heavy rug in her dryer. "Is nothing confidential in this tiny town?"

Spencer laughed and she wondered what amused her brother. Of course, he'd been a lot happier lately, and smiled more than she'd ever remembered. "Not a whole lot, I'll give you that." He pulled into the high school parking lot and up to her car. "Just do me a favor and be extra careful."

"I will. I promise." She said goodbye and got into her vehicle. There was no chance of Spencer departing before she pulled out, and he'd no doubt follow her for a bit to make sure she not only drove capably but got home safe and sound.

Sometimes having a big brother put a big, wet damper on her investigative reporting.

Holden carefully followed the K-9 SUV through Mustang Valley back roads, promising himself he'd take a bike ride out here when the case wrapped up. Not if, but when, because he had to catch the Pageant Killer before anyone else got hurt.

He'd pulled up Bella's bio, then her blog, then had his colleague back at the Phoenix field office do a background search on Bella. She was smart about her security protocol, but his agency had ways of ferreting information. Holden already knew that Spencer was a highly decorated police officer, but he hadn't heard that Spencer had recntly saved his fiancée from certain death with the help of his K-9, a chocolate lab named Boris. Boris, along with the other MVPD K-9s, had his own Facebook fan page. As an FBI agent Holden stayed off social media, but he knew it was an important way that the local LEA could communicate with their community.

Holden suspected that Spencer had no idea that his sister had entered the pageant. Finding her in the staff room after she'd made it look like she'd left the building raised all kinds of red flags.

As the car dipped around a bend, he realized they were heading back to the school. As he'd predicted, Spencer was taking Bella to get her vehicle. Was he really going to allow his sister to drive after such a traumatic event?

Not that it was his problem. Keeping Bella safe from the killer was all he was tasked to do. Besides finding and arresting the murderer.

Holden continued to follow Spencer but couldn't help the flashback images that he associated with the words *traumatic event*. He'd worked a case in which a serial killer that the agency had tracked for nearly a year had taken him hostage. In what he'd expected to be his first successful apprehension, he'd miscalculated and the killer had trapped him in an abandoned silver mine in southeastern Arizona, not far from Mustang Valley. He'd still caught the killer, but it had taken its toll. The experience had been harrowing and life changing. Instead of deterring his desire to do investigative work, fortified it.

Spencer signaled a left turn into the school drive and Holden quickly turned right, down a side street where he wouldn't be detected by either Colton. He'd taken the time to change out of his security-guard uniform and into plain street clothes—cargo shorts, dark T-shirt, running shoes and ball cap—as soon as Bella had been taken away by the EMTs. He hated not being completely open with Spencer about this, but he had to figure out what Bella Colton was about.

He'd also had to accept that the attacker had gotten away. For now. If indeed Bella's attacker *was* the killer.

Holden knew that since he traded his security uniform for street clothes right after he left MVHS, he wouldn't be readily recognizable by most people he'd worked with earlier today. He didn't want to have to explain why the pageant security guard was hanging out around the school after hours.

He parked his car on a quiet street and got out, hoping to appear as much a part of the scenery as possible. Lucky for him there was a walking path that ran past the subdivision, the school and out to the desert beyond. Mustang Valley gave every appearance of being a beautiful place to live, to settle, to raise a family.

Except for the possible serial killer who stalked the pageant.

Holden walked until he was close enough to make out Spencer's SUV cruiser, which was parked next to the most beat-up, ugly station wagon he'd ever seen.

Bella Colton must not have been telling a total lie when she'd informed the pageant committee about her dire financial situation. No one with a decent paycheck would drive such a jalopy. He wondered how it passed inspection, then remembered her brother was a cop. His handler in Phoenix had filled him in on Bella sporadically over the last couple of hours. The psychological profile he was steadily building of her didn't fit a person who'd cheat on her auto inspection, though.

Bella had a decent blogging career in hand, but much of her freelance work reflected the expertise of someone with a lot more talent than just writing for the local, small-town blog. Holden's colleague was female and apparently Bella's articles were receiving a lot of play on social media and had even found their way into print here and there.

From all indications, Isabella Colton was a woman on the verge of a career breakout. Holden knew the feeling. If he nailed this case, he'd be that much closer to his next rank. Not only would it be a pay raise, but he'd be achieving the goal he'd set out for right after graduating from the academy in Quantico, Virginia. Holden wanted to be career FBI.

The white stripes on Bella's top reflected the lowering sun, and turned her hair a golden shade of copper that reminded him of the pots and pans his grandmother polished and hung over her wide farm stove in Kansas. Grandma St. Clair had served as a WASP—a Woman Airforce Service Pilot—in World War II and she was his most ardent supporter when he'd been selected for Army ROTC at Kansas State. Grandma had sent him letters the entire time in the army, and had attended his promotion to captain two years before he resigned his commission to become an FBI agent. Sadly she'd passed before he'd left Quantico but she'd known the path he'd chosen. Like Grandma St. Clair, Holden wanted to make a difference in the world. Protect it at all costs from the most evil acts.

Bella walked the short distance to her car, and gave her brother a quick wave before getting behind the wheel.

Please don't follow her home.

If Spencer trailed Bella, Holden would be unable to tag along at all this evening. He couldn't risk Spencer spotting him, as his army best friend would recognize him immediately. Bella shouldn't see him either, to be on the safe side. He had no reason to think Bella had the military background Spencer did but in truth had no idea if Bella had ever served or engaged in any kind of LEA training. The background information he had wasn't complete.

You could confront them both, let Bella know who you really are.

He wasn't ready to. Not yet. His gut was telling him to lay low. Besides, Spencer was going to be angry when he found out that Bella had been attacked on Holden's watch. Holden deserved the rancor but wasn't going to let it be a distraction. Not until he figured out what Bella Colton was up to. She wasn't just a regular pageant contestant. She'd better hope the committee didn't read too many of her articles or they'd question her motives for competing, too.

Holden turned and walked the short distance back to his car. As he did, he heard a siren. By the time he was in his car and at the corner of the side street, he saw Spencer's unit fly around onto the main street and head away from the school, siren flashing. Counting to five, Holden pulled out and slowly drove by the school. He expected to see Bella's car heading out of the parking lot but instead saw the back end of her vehicle as she drove toward the school, then turned left onto the inside perimeter road.

Bella Colton chose to come back onto school property after surviving a close call with a possible serial killer. Not that she knew about the serial killer, but she'd been attacked. Why would she do that?

Holden knew only one way to find out.

Chapter 4

Bella's head pounded and she grabbed her water bottle from the worn adjustable holder she'd found at the dollar store.

"Yuck," she spoke to herself at how warm the liquid was, but at least it was some kind of hydration. Thank goodness the hospital had told her she didn't have a concussion, or she wouldn't be able to return so soon. If she was accepted into the pageant, she'd get an email or phone call tonight and have to report again tomorrow morning for the indoctrination process. It'd be too late to search the file cabinet by then, with so many people around.

As she drove past the main building and then around to the backstage parking lot entrance, she let out a huge breath of relief. Yes! The first responders had all left, so she didn't have to either lie or sneak her way back in. The stage entrance loading dock stood out, the massive concrete block reminding her of the piers she'd once seen when she and her brothers went to the Pacific Ocean with their aunt. Aunt Amelia hadn't been a very loving or demonstrative woman, and in fact had made it clear that she'd been saddled with raising Bella and the boys at the most inconvenient time of her life. Bella had wanted to tell her aunt, even when she was only ten, that there probably wasn't ever a good time to have your sibling up and die and leave you with triplets, but she'd thought better of it. Aunt Amelia had a short fuse and Bella never liked to be on the receiving end of her verbal lashes. And at least Aunt Amelia did love travel and they made yearly pilgrimages to places she had visited as a young woman, fresh out of college.

Since the school's rear lot was completely empty, she turned her car around and backed in, butt against the loading dock, to facilitate a quick exit if necessary.

Please let me get in and out of here okay.

She was prepared this time, as she shoved her cell phone in a back pocket with one hand and held her pepper spray in the other. No one would sneak up on her again if she had anything to do with it.

The pavement under her wedge heels had cooled and a soft breeze came in from the mountains, a gift. When she looked north she saw why—a cloud bank held tight over the range, promising rain in the next day or so.

She smiled and despite the attack, made a conscious decision to stay positive. This was all about exposing a vast, far-reaching, decades-deep pageant practice that had left too many young women with very adult mental and physical illnesses, from body dysmorphia to eating disorders. A sliver of doubt niggled at her premise and she tried to brush it away. In her research she'd discovered that it was widely believed that eating disorders, like addictions, occurred in people predisposed to such diseases. That might mean that Bella wouldn't be able to definitively blame a particular pageant board member or group. Gio's mother had admitted their family members suffered from mental illness for as long as she could remember. But the pageant board had planted the seeds for Gio's disorder to sink its claws in deep, hadn't they? Would she be able to definitively state that the pageant triggered Gio's genetic tendencies? She decided to not worry about it in this moment, and focus on getting back inside the building. More information could clarify Gio's nightmare.

Bella hadn't thought about the prospect of climbing atop the loading dock. The back garage-type door was her only way in, from what her reporter's group informed her. Her editor-in-chief and supervising editor knew what she was up to, as did her closest reporter friend, Fred Jameson. Fred had never let her down, was always there for her and didn't hesitate to speak up if Bella was crossing a boundary. Like the time she'd tried to stake out the local drugstore to catch underage teens purchasing vaping paraphernalia. She'd nearly been arrested as the shop owner wasn't impressed with her credentials and positive motives. Fred had given her the passcode for the loading dock's security pad, procured from "a friend of a friend." Bella suspected Fred had paid someone off for the information but didn't ask for details.

She silently thanked the years of video workouts she'd done as she climbed atop her car and then leaped up to the loading dock, no small feat in capris and sandals. Euphoria began to sing in her veins until she eyed the keypad lock next to the sliding door. Her colleagues had failed to mention this. It must be a new addition.

Still, she was this far. Bella decided to go for it and pressed the main button, hoping that maybe she'd luck out and the door would rise at once. All she got was a "please enter the passcode now" message, given in a disembodied female voice.

"Drat. Drat. Drat." She muttered as she looked over her notes and emails from her trusted reporter circle. There, in bold letters, was the password that Fred had insisted she write down.

MUSTANG#1

Without hesitation she punched in the code. Hitting Enter, she held her breath. Until the grinding gears engaged and the door rolled up.

Bella hunched to get inside as quickly as possible, and once past the entrance hit the close button, ensuring no one would see the open door and call the police. That's all she needed, to be caught breaking into the very school she'd been attacked in mere hours earlier.

Darkness immediately surrounded her so she pulled out her Mag-Lite and made her way through to the staff room, behind the stage. There hadn't been any cars in the front lot where Spencer dropped her, and none back here, so she was comfortable in the thought of being alone. For now.

She still had to be careful. Not that being a journalist didn't involve a modicum of wariness each day, but this time it felt different. Not only because she was attacked. She was getting herself more embedded than she ever had before, and the stakes were higher, now that she knew Spencer suspected the two pageant murders were related. His belief had been written all over his face.

No one would blame her if she decided to quit.

Never. This was for Gio's sake.

Light still came through the staff-room windows and

allowed her to see what she'd tried to breach before—
the antiquated file cabinet. Except something was off.
She squinted, tried to deny what she saw. Each and
every drawer was open. Rushing to the cabinet, she
couldn't keep her groan from morphing into a cry as
she saw all of the drawers had been emptied. If anything
had ever been in there at all. Grasping the corners of
the rusty metal cabinet, she bowed her head and for the
first time since Gio's funeral allowed herself to weep.

After a good cry, she'd be ready to make an even
better plan. No one or nothing was going to keep her
from justice for Gio.

Holden gave Bella Colton credit. The woman was
as intrepid as any agent he'd ever met. As much as he
wanted to discredit her motives due to her job description, he couldn't. She wanted something in the school,
most likely the staff room, and wasn't going to let a
mere attack get in her way.

He waited to see her disappear through the cargo entrance before he used his fob to enter the building. It'd
show up on the security system as him, as the guard,
and he'd explain it as having seen the cargo door being
opened after hours. If Bella had a key code she might
have some kind of legit reason for entering. But if she
were entering the school again for a valid reason, why
wouldn't she use the front entrance? His internal radar
wasn't happy with what he'd witnessed. It was time for
Bella Colton to answer some questions.

It took him a few minutes to get to the stage, as he
had to move quietly. He drew his weapon as a precaution against the attacker returning, not to protect himself from Bella. She was an aggressive reporter but had
no criminal record. Once again he thanked his lucky

stars for his investigative team at the Bureau and the training he'd received. This case was growing more complicated by the second, as if the evil surrounding it was molten lava seeping into every crack and crevice of Mustang Valley.

An odd sound made him halt backstage, behind the curtain that allowed for undetected passage from stage left to stage right. The sound was from the staff room, he was certain. But he had to get closer, to make sure it was only Bella in there. As he crept along the cinderblock wall, the black curtain to his left, he heard his breathing, his heartbeat. But no more sound from offstage. Had Bella already left?

He cleared the curtain and saw the light pour out of the staff room a.k.a. stage dressing area. A few more steps and he'd put Bella's journalistic snooping to a quick end.

But when he looked into the room, cleared left and right, it was empty. He stepped inside the open door and saw that the LEAs had done their job—swept for fingerprints, opened all drawers and file systems to rule out explosives, left everything as they'd had to.

The attacker had held an unconscious Bella near the old file cabinet, before he'd dragged her to the side exit and made his escape. Holden holstered his weapon and walked to the cabinet, the dusty behemoth's four deep drawers wide open.

"Stay right where you are or I'll spray!"

Female voice, to his rear, dead center. Voice—Bella Colton.

Crap.

Holding up his arms, he spoke. "You're safe. I'm the security guard."

"Don't turn around or reach for your gun. I will take

you down. You're not in uniform." She paused and he wondered if she was calling the police.

"This is Bella Colton. I want to speak to my bro—"

"Heck no!" He turned and faced her, ready to explain why he was here and find out why the hell she was. "You're okay, I'm—"

Wet liquid heat hit his face, his eyes, his nostrils and then his mouth. And oh, by the love of heaven, it burned. As if microscopic shards of glass were cutting his face wide open.

Bella Colton had just pepper sprayed him. He, an FBI agent, had been bested by a reporter.

Again.

Chapter 5

Bella watched the security guard, in plain clothes, wince against the sting, while his hand reached into his back pocket. She kept her grip on the spray canister, ready to hit again.

"Hands in front." But he didn't pull out another weapon, and his pistol remained holstered. He held out what she thought was his wallet, until it flipped open, displaying a badge and credentials.

"Holden St. Clair, FBI." His voice was remarkably steady for someone who'd just been hit with burning pepper-oil solution.

"Really." She leaned forward and grabbed the ID holder from him. It looked real enough. "I'm going to verify this through my brother." She called Spencer's cell.

"Go ahead. Tell him you're with me."

"Bella, you there?" Spencer's voice broadcast over her phone's speakers, from the side table where she'd thrown it when she decided to use the pepper spray. No longer seeing Holden as a threat, she grabbed her phone and turned the speaker off.

Spencer sounded stressed. A twinge of guilt made her feel like the bossy sister he teased her about being.

"Do you know an FBI agent named Holden St. Clair?"

"Maybe. Why are you asking?" Spencer's voice was guarded.

"I just pepper sprayed him."

"For crying out loud, Bella, he's on our side." Still, Spencer didn't say how he knew Holden, if he did. Or why.

"What do you mean by that?"

"Put him on the line, Bella."

Grudgingly she handed her phone to Holden. "He wants to talk to you."

Holden took her phone and she absently noted she'd have to clean it, so that she didn't get any pepper oil on her.

"Holden here." He looked at her but it was short-lived as he squinted his eyes closed again, tears pouring from them.

"Yes, I'm with her. She's safe. Uh-huh. Yes, it's true. She did. I'm buying next time. I'll let you know." Holden's one-sided conversation with her brother was impossible to follow, but she thought she heard the roar of Spencer's deep belly laugh when Holden said *Yes, it's true*. Apparently she'd brought down a Goliath with the pepper spray.

"Trust me, Spencer. Thank you." He handed the phone back to her. She gingerly held it to her ear, careful not to touch it directly on her skin until she cleaned it. Holden's hands were probably full of pepper oil.

"Yeah?"

"Listen, Bella." Spencer's voice was lighter, but still serious. "For once in your life you have to follow everything someone else tells you. Holden is the real deal—we served together."

"Wait—he's *that* friend Holden?" Shock pulsed through her. Spencer had mentioned a Holden, the man who'd saved them both from certain death during one training mission gone wrong. Spencer always spoke with awe when he talked about Holden. "As in your bestie, your army buddy?"

"Yeah."

She'd just pepper sprayed her brother's best friend, and a war hero.

Way to begin your investigative journalism career.

"Did you know he was working the pageant? Why didn't you tell me?" Bella knew her face was red. At least Holden's eyes were too sore to notice.

"Why didn't you tell me or Jarvis you were getting involved in the pageant, much less entering it? You don't tell me a whole heck of a lot about what you're working on, Bella. You let us think that you're doing home-decorating stories." Her brother's frustration was tangible over the phone's connection.

"Give me some credit, Spencer. I do more than lifestyle pieces." Although his comment left a stinging barb. She was doing this article precisely to get away from her current kind of story. But it was secondary to finding clarity on, and maybe even the original triggers for, Gio's eating disorders and mental illness.

His sigh would have bounced off the walls of the arroyo they played near as kids. "Just listen to whatever Holden says, Bella."

"Will do. I've got to help him out with the pepper

spray cleanup, then I'll turn in for an early evening to binge-watch my favorite shows. All safe and sound."

"Bella…"

Holden had moved to the staff refrigerator, and she saw his large, strong hand grab a quart of iced tea instead of what she assumed he wanted, the quart of milk next to it. "I've got to go now, Spencer. Thanks for verifying Holden's identity and you have a good evening."

Bella disconnected and looked around the staff room. No sign of her previous attacker, or anyone else. They were alone, she and Holden. His low groan drew her back to him. The man was in a lot of pain but she supposed he was swallowing most of it, keeping up some stoic front he'd learned in the military and perfected in the FBI.

"Wait, let me help you." She took the quart of tea from him and handed him a bunch of napkins from the pile on the counter. "You grabbed the iced tea. I think you want milk, am I right? Come here, I'll fix you right up."

"Sure you will. Just like you sprayed me?" His words came between pants, indicating the depth of his discomfort. Regret tugged at her but she brushed it aside. Nothing she could do to change the past, but she could help Holden now.

She set the milk on the counter and grasped his forearms and ignored the warmth that emanated from his skin. It had nothing to do with physical attraction or any notion of romantic chemistry. The heat was his reaction to being attacked by a nasty chemical, right in the face.

"Here, kneel down with your back against the counter, and lay your head back on the edge of the sink. I'm going to pour the milk directly on your eyes. You're going to have to open them."

"And I should trust you because..." He lowered to the floor, his discomfort obvious but he was for the most part quiet. As much as one can be when tears and mucus were running like an Arizona spring rainstorm. As soon as his head tilted back, she opened the milk.

"Okay, here's the first dose." She poured the white liquid over his forehead, eyes, nose, mouth, then dabbed at his face with more napkins. She had no desire to get the oil on her hands. "Now, open your eyes as soon as you feel the milk again. We have to get it on your eyeballs."

"Got it. Hit me." His grim expression as he braced himself for the next round was almost comical. She bit her lip.

"This will make it feel better, promise." She poured directly on the bridge of his nose, and when he lifted his lids she splashed milk into each eye, and he made sure he blinked several times instead of screwing his eyes shut again. "You've done this before, Agent St. Clair."

"There are a lot of things I've done before, Bella Colton."

"I'm talking about the milk, and pepper spray." Her hands shook and he didn't think it was from the weight of the carton. She was the wrong woman during the wrong investigation, or he'd enjoy the thrill of knowing he'd gotten under her skin.

Thank goodness she'd insisted on helping him with the milk. His eyes still hurt but at least it didn't feel like fire ants were crawling over them and up his nose any longer.

"To answer your question, I've had training in countermeasures for everything from pepper spray to chemical warfare. Where did you learn the milk antidote?"

"My brother, of course. Lean back again." She waited until he was in position and then poured more of the cold elixir on his eyes, his skin. "I made him tell me about everything he learned at the police academy, and he still fills me in about his more interesting cases, as much as he's able. He doesn't reveal any confidential material, of course. He had to take tear gas and pepper spray at the police academy. Do you do the same at the FBI Academy?"

"Yes, in Quantico. Virginia. But your brother and I went through a lot of combat training together in the military, and in particular we did the tear-gas training at the same time." He remembered meeting Spencer and admiring how cool he stayed under high-pressure situations. They'd both gone on to reach US Army captain, before leaving for their respective careers in law enforcement.

"I know where Quantico is. I visited an old boyfriend there once, to see him finish Officer Basic. He was a marine."

"Uh, I know who else trains at Quantico." He couldn't help the tiny dig. "What happened to him?" He hadn't missed her *old*-boyfriend reference.

"He deployed overseas for nearly two years. I waited, but by the time he came back we were kaput. Too young to survive that many miles for so long. Plus, I happen to have two very overprotective brothers. No man has gotten past their scrutiny yet."

Holden shook his head, wiped his face with the paper towels she handed him, letting the last of the milk drip off him and into the sink. He lifted his head, stood up and took ahold of the milk. "Thank you." He looked at her with a clear gaze for the first time. And saw her brilliant green eyes wide and…aware. Of his every move. Heat roiled in his gut.

Can it. She's Spencer's sister.

"No problem." She threw the empty milk container out, cleaned up the sink. He moved to help but she waved him away. "Are you going to tell me why you're on assignment here, during the Ms. Mustang Valley Pageant?"

His eyes were calming down and he couldn't stop his gaze from resting on her. And imagining the direction this conversation would go if they hadn't met in the middle of a probable serial-killer case, if she wasn't related to the one man he trusted with his life. He couldn't give any woman more than today, not after how his ex, Nicole, had burned him. Long-term love wasn't in his cards.

And Bella Colton was the kind of woman you didn't mess around with to ease an itch. Bella struck him as a forever woman—either you gave her everything, or didn't start anything.

Holden knew where that left him.

Holden's silence unnerved Bella as she threw the last of the wet paper towels away, the scent of milk still clinging to the staff-room air. But how could she blame him? He'd survived a pepper-spray attack only minutes before yet he was already in control of himself, and clearly demanded control of their discussion. Bella wanted to be annoyed, angry, furious at this stranger who, in some ways, knew her brother better than she did. Yet Holden exuded a sense of realness, a grounded energy she hadn't experienced with another man. As if he was a man she could truly trust.

Whoa, girl, back it up.

Bella trusted no man besides her brothers. She didn't know Holden from a hole in an Arizona butte. Just because being alone with an attractive man wasn't something she'd done in a long while didn't mean she could let her physical needs dictate her reaction to him.

"Don't make me ask again, Holden. Please."

"Tell me why you entered the contest first." He volleyed the query with complete equanimity. Oh, yeah, Holden St. Clair was a man with his stuff in one sock.

She blinked, ignored the shiver of awareness that was getting too familiar around him. "Why do you think? You heard my interview. I need the scholarship prize."

"So you said. To go to nursing school. And as much as you just handled my injuries with ease, need I remind you that you inflicted them? I'd think someone who wanted to go into any kind of medicine wouldn't want to hurt a fly."

"You were stalking me."

"I was protecting you from your attacker."

"Give me a break, Holden. If that's true, you must have seen me earlier with Spencer. You knew he'd keep me safe. Yet you followed me in here. That's pretty creepy, if you ask me." Her hands began to shake and she didn't have to question why. The mere mention of the attack must be triggering an unconscious memory.

"I was going to call Spencer and tell him that I was concerned about your personal safety. Today, in fact. But I, ah, was waylaid by a person very competent with pepper spray."

"Wait a minute—my attacker, did you see him again? Around here?" Fear continued to rise in her gut and she tried to squelch it but couldn't stop the tremor that rolled through her skeleton.

Holden's hand was on her shoulder, warm, protective. And she didn't bristle, but accepted it with a smile that she knew must look wan at best. Exhaustion poured over her and she sank onto the nearest seat, a sofa cushion.

"No, and if I did, I would have already had you out of here. I'm sorry I didn't catch him earlier." A tendon on the side of his jaw clenched and she knew he was annoyed. At her, at losing track of the attacker, probably both.

"I thought it might be you." Except she'd heard his voice telling the attacker to stop. His voice had steadied her, even in the grips of a probable killer.

He chuckled. "I don't blame you. No, it wasn't me. You can verify with your brother or any other MVPD officer. I called in the incident as soon as your attacker took off."

"After you made him let go of me."

"I can't take credit for that. It was the circumstances."

"Of you forcing him to flee. My brother told me when he brought me back to my car. All of MVPD is in awe of how you handled the situation. You stayed cool and forced the attacker's hand."

She regarded him, liked how he didn't so much as twitch under her scrutiny. "You followed us from the hospital, didn't you? I knew I saw you there." She saw him again in her mind's eye, how he'd leaned up against the nurses' station and kept his face averted as she'd walked out of the hospital. But she hadn't trusted her memory, not so soon after being knocked out.

Holden nodded. "I did."

"How did he knock me out?"

"You don't remember?"

She shook her head. "One minute I was at the file

cabinet and the next I heard this awful voice, then all went black."

"He had a voice box on, over a facemask and hoodie. I saw it."

"Terrifying." But it didn't answer how he knocked her out.

"He used a sleeper hold on you. I saw it as I came into the room. You were already out—there was nothing I could do to protect you from being knocked unconscious."

"You kept me from a lot worse."

"Maybe."

He was being modest but she wasn't going to call him on it. Not yet, not until she figured out why he was here, now. The FBI was interested in the pageant, confirming her suspicions that there was more going on here than a scholarship contest.

"I'm a reporter. I'm not hiding my motives for being here from you. Unlike you." She knew she really needed to back off the accusatory attitude but it was hard. Federal agents had a reputation of not looking fondly upon the media.

"True on all accounts. Answer my question, Bella. Why are you here?"

She ran over all the reasons to not tell him but they didn't make sense. Not when she was looking up at him, the red, blotchy skin of his face a reminder that he'd calmly taken an all-out attack from her, yet remained cool and calm. The ultimate professional. No wonder having him as a security guard had seemed like overkill. He looked and acted like he was tops in his field at the Bureau. Whatever Holden was, he appeared to be a man who got what he wanted.

"I'm doing an undercover report on pageant practices, specifically Ms. Mustang Valley. Not just this year's, but the last ten pageants or so." The time span that Gio had participated. Before eating disorders and resultant poor health had taken her, too soon.

"What kind of 'practices'?"

"I want to find out if they ever made, or still do make, the contestants diet or be a certain size or weight. If they encourage any kind of unhealthy behavior that had a long-term effect on the contestants."

"You look down in the dumps about it. I can't say that I'd find that surprising. Would you?" His astuteness rattled her. How did a stranger see right through her?

"I, I'm doing it because I lost a friend who spent half of her life competing in pageants, including this one. She never won, but never gave up. And it killed her."

"What killed her? Exactly?" His voice, low and deadly, unexpectedly buoyed her. Holden was a man who sought justice every day, who probably understood her motives better than she did.

"It wasn't foul play, if that's what you're asking. Not with a visible weapon, anyhow. To be fair, I don't know what really took her. In the end it was classified as malnutrition due to an eating disorder. No matter what the death certificate said, she's gone forever and while I blame the pageant industry as a whole, I'm especially furious at Ms. Mustang Valley. I can't rest until I know the persons who tortured her the most, who bullied her to turn herself into someone she wasn't by alternatively bingeing and starving herself. I suspect the pageant board and maybe some of the judges are to blame."

"Do you have any idea exactly who? Names?" Holden's interest buoyed her. Maybe she would get her answers more quickly with his help.

"Gio mentioned both Selina Barnes Colton, and Hannah Rosenstein. And I want to state, for the record, that I'm no relation to Selina, not by blood, anyway. And that branch of the Coltons hasn't had anything to do with me or my brothers in decades." Vulnerability flared but relief that someone else believed her suspicions, didn't think she was stringing together random events, outweighed any sense of risk.

Holden watched her for a long moment, then walked to the sofa and pointed at the spot next to her. "May I?"

"Of course." She shifted to the side a bit, but there wasn't a lot of room on the two-cushion sofa. As she realized that she didn't mind being so close to the man she'd been wary of all day, the man she'd attacked, the silliness of the situation hit her. Laughter bubbled up and she let it out.

Holden looked at her and a wide grin split his face, swollen, red-rimmed eyes and all. His pepper-spray injuries didn't keep her from seeing the spark in his dark irises, though.

"I'm so sorry I pepper sprayed you. I'm not known for being the most gentle of persons around these parts, but I don't usually attack complete strangers."

"I'm not a stranger. I'm a federal law enforcement agent who needs answers. It sounds like you do, too. We can accomplish a lot more together than we can separately."

Anxiety rumbled in her gut. She was a reporter first, not some kind of wannabe cop. "I'm working on an article, a report. Wouldn't it be a conflict of interest for us to work side by side?"

"Only if you plan on breaking the law, or to keep anything from me that legally I need to pursue my case. I'm ignoring how you got back into the school tonight, of course."

She considered it, considered him, blew her bangs out of her face. "Fine. But I don't want you restricting my participation in the pageant at all. I need to be able to function as a regular contestant, to get into all the events." She groaned as she thought of evening-gown competition.

"To be clear, you're trying to pin your friend's death on a particular person on the pageant board? And right now you've got Selina and Hannah as suspects?"

"Yes. No. I don't know." She hated this part, the fact that she really didn't even know what she was searching for. It stirred up her worst fears—that she'd never find out why Gio had to die. "What I'm trying to do is expose this pageant's culture for what it is. Find out what triggered a beautiful young woman to turn to a life of self-mutilation and experience severe body dysmorphia at such a young, malleable age."

"You aren't going to find any one person to blame, Bella. You don't really believe that you will, do you?"

Holden's gaze cut through her and she shivered, then was awash in heat. Yeah, there was chemistry here. The kind that could and would not only derail her undercover investigation, but get her heart into deep waters. But something more played out between them. Holden was taking her seriously, not mocking her for entering the pageant.

He seemed to respect her, even though he gave off waves of disdain whenever she said the words *reporter* or *story*.

"I don't know what I believe right now. I won't until I read the pageant archives. Which I may never find now." She cast a glance at the empty file cabinet.

"Fair enough. But I'd hate to see you risking your safety to find there's no answer that will satisfy your need for closure. Trust me on this, Bella. Sometimes we don't get all of the answers." The loneliness in his tone wrapped around her. She wondered if he was talking about the service but didn't want to go there, not with someone she'd just met.

"Where do you live, Holden? When you're not out investigating beauty pageants?"

He blinked, caught off guard by her change of subject. She liked that she did that to him, made him think on his feet. Or on the sofa. Most men didn't reveal that she'd made them do a mental double take.

"Right now I'm staying at the Dales Inn, much to the consternation of my boss." He grinned and it was as if he really did consider her a trusted colleague, adding oxygen to the warm glow in her belly. "We don't usually get put up at luxury hotels on our government budget. But there wasn't any other place to stay, not close enough to do my job well. When I'm not on the road for a case, I live in Phoenix. I work out of the field office there, and fly back to DC as needed to give reports."

"Are you an agent or a profiler?"

"Agent. Profilers don't generally work in the field, not on an active case, unless it's exceptional and has involved a larger number of victims. Why do you ask?"

"I already know why you're here, Holden. There were two deaths in two previous Arizona pageants this year. They're under the same promotions-company umbrella. You must think they're related, and that Ms. Mustang Valley is next on the list. Am I right? Don't worry, I'm not putting any of this in my exposé."

He stared at her for a second before looking away, out the window at the setting sun. "Partially. But I'm not privy to talk about all of it."

"What, you want me to work with you but you're not

going to fill me in on what you find? That's not a good deal for me. Spencer told me more in a three-minute car ride than you have over the last half hour." She stood up.

"Bella, wait." He grasped her hand and she looked down at the sight of their hands together. It should feel wrong, or out of place, considering their stations in life and here, now, in the pageant. Yet it felt right.

Bella tugged her hand free. Falling for an FBI agent was not the path to getting what she needed for her exposé. No matter how much her brother trusted him.

Chapter 6

"I'm sorry." Holden wasn't fond of apologizing and the fact that he was doing so to someone who'd been no more than a stranger only hours earlier should concern him. But a serial killer was on the loose. He knew Bella's brother, a man he would trust with his life during lethal missions. All of that, combined with having witnessed what Bella had suffered through so far today made polite social conventions superfluous. There wasn't time to "get to know" her. Holden was committed to keeping her alive.

She turned, her narrowed eyes flashing jade fire. "Sorry for what?"

He sucked in a quick breath. "For sounding like a jerk. Large parts of the investigation, of my job, are classified. I know you understand this, since Spencer is your brother. He can't tell you all of his police business."

She nodded. "I do understand. And you must understand that since I'm back here, today, willing to risk running into the suspect who knocked me out earlier, I mean business, too. I'm willing to do whatever it takes to split this pageant wide open."

"It's at the risk of your life, if we're dealing with the same killer."

Her eyes shimmered and he caught a wave of grief as it pulsed off her. "I don't expect this story to come without a price."

"Nothing worthwhile ever does. But is it worth it for a story?" His phone buzzed and he checked the text. His supervisor. "I have to take this. Will you wait for me, let me take you to dinner? We can talk this over and come up with an actionable plan that will suit both of us." And keep her safe.

Bella's wariness couldn't be more evident in the way she eyed him as if he were her worst enemy. "Fine. But it's dessert, not dinner. At the local diner downtown. The one with the hitching post out front. Do you know it?"

He nodded, held up his index finger. "Right. Do not leave until I do." He took the call. "St. Clair."

"What's going on? I've got MVPD reports in front of me that an assailant attacked one of the pageant contestants?" His boss, in Phoenix, didn't sound pleased.

"Yes. I'm on it. With the victim now."

"Who is she? And you shouldn't be with her, Holden—she needs to be in protective custody until we catch this killer."

He turned his back to Bella, searching for a modicum of privacy. "Agreed. She's a reporter on undercover assignment, entered the pageant for her story on another topic entirely."

"That makes this even more dangerous, Holden."

"Or it'll bring it to a close sooner." He looked over his shoulder and saw that Bella was talking to someone on her phone, using earbuds. "I will make sure she's safe, boss. Her brother is the only other civilian, besides the statewide pageant director, who knows my identity. Spencer Colton and I served in the army together. I can't convince her to quit, and if being knocked out and almost abducted didn't do it, we're better off having her on our side." His gut churned at the memory of his ex and how he'd been duped by her journalistic goals. At least Bella was up-front about why she was here, and unapologetic about her career goals.

"I completely trust your judgment. It's just that we've got a very intelligent killer this time, Holden. He's willing to use different methods as long as he gets his victim."

Holden didn't have to be reminded that a killer who didn't stick to their own protocol, who kept changing things up, was the most dangerous and hardest to catch. A vision of Bella, bloody and inert, forced its way through his logic and he had to fight to stay present, in the reality that she was safe and he'd keep her that way.

"All the more reason for me to keep a close eye on Ms. Colton."

"What is she investigating, by the way?" His supervisor's question was tinged with impatience edged with curiosity.

"Pageant methods, possibly their influence over young women at critical ages, how the methods can encourage eating disorders."

His supervisor let out a low whistle. "That's a tall order from just one competition."

"Not for this reporter." It was natural to defend Bella and her work.

Another red flag. He was too close to making this case personal. Or had it been personal from the moment he'd realized the killer's number-one target was his buddy's sister?

Bella agreed to allow Holden to inspect her car for any intruders and explosives, and only after he was certain she was safely locked inside, the engine running, did he get in his vehicle. He followed her to the rustic Western diner that was off the town's tourist path, a place she often came to work on her laptop when the *Gabber*'s offices were too busy or she needed to be out of her house. Bella prided herself on her independence, to a fault. It surprised her that she found comfort in knowing Holden was behind her, that if the attacker jumped out from in back of one of the many parked cars around the diner, Holden would be there.

The attack, remembered or not, must have shook her more than she realized. Vulnerability choked her ability to think as clearly as she needed for this job.

Once inside they sat at a booth in a far corner of the restaurant, able to see patrons arrive without unnecessarily exposing themselves.

"Are you sure you just want dessert? I'm starving and plan to have a full meal." Holden was courteous in the way she'd seen other LEAs behave, including her brother. Holden seemed to see her as part of his case, although his demeanor toward her had an icy frosting to it she couldn't put her finger on. Yet.

Her stomach grumbled and she let go of her stubbornness. "You're right. I could use a decent meal. It's been a long day." Her admission came easily. It was the first time since earlier today that she'd been hungry. The events over the last several hours had doused her appetite.

"You're probably coming off the adrenaline rush of surviving the assault. It's your body's natural reaction to what you went through."

A laugh escaped her. "Your words are so compassionate, agent."

He scowled. "Don't refer to me as anything other than my name. That's for both our safety. And I'm sorry if my manners need polishing. I'm hungry."

"More like hangry."

"Excuse me?"

"Hungry, angry, mix in tired, and you get hangry."

His scowl deepened but then miraculously morphed into a grin. "Heck, I've been called worse, I suppose."

"Hi, ya'll. What'll you have?" Angelina, a woman Bella had gone to school with, stood at their table.

"Hey, Angelina." She gave the waitress her order. "Are you still in law school?"

Angelina grinned. "I am. Getting ready to graduate and take the bar. I'm working here at night to help out my parents." Angelina's family owned the successful and cherished local.

"That's wonderful! Congrats."

"I'm Holden. I'm a friend of Bella's." He was polite and Angelina evidently thought he was hot, too, from the way she arched her brow and shot Bella a grin. "I'll have your biggest hangry burger and fries, with a strawberry milkshake on the side." Holden flashed a wide smile at Angelina. "I've been told I'm hangry."

Angelina snorted. "I'm hangry all the time." She winked at Bella. "Hank and I just found out we're going to be having twins."

"Oh my goodness, I had no idea you were pregnant! Congratulations."

"Thanks. We're pretty excited. I hope I can pass the bar before the baby comes." She smiled at Holden. "And I'm hangry by the end of each shift. I'll ask the cook to give you an extra helping of fries."

"Thanks."

Holden conversed with Angelina as if he'd known her as long as Bella had instead of for the last three minutes. As she checked him out, Bella's first impressions of Holden stood; he was strong, poised and exuded confidence that could be intimidating if the one facing him didn't have a spine. But he was kind and didn't seem to think being an FBI agent made him better than anyone else. The opposite, in fact. Holden had a healthy humility she found very attractive.

She sat straighter on the red-leather-padded bench. One thing Bella prided herself on was her strength of character, no matter who she was sitting across from. As he asked for mayonnaise instead of ketchup for his fries, he smiled at Angelina again and the flash of white stirred something Bella had kept quiet for a while, since she'd helped Gio through her sickness and those last awful weeks. Bella's last boyfriend hadn't been able to handle her needing a break to care for her best friend and she'd flat out dumped him.

"I'll be right back with your drinks. Nice to see you, Bella."

"You too, Angelina." She smiled at the expectant mother. It must be baby season for MVHS alumnae. Angelina was the third in two weeks she'd heard was having a child. It stirred something in Bella that she knew to be her biological clock ticking. She wouldn't mind kids someday, but only after she found the right man, and was certain she was up to the task. Being orphaned and left with Aunt Amelia so young had left a stamp of reality on any urge for family, save for her brothers.

"You know the waitress, I take it? Is this the kind of town where everyone knows one another?"

"She and I are high school classmates. We haven't kept in close touch, but yeah, it's a fairly tight-knit community. To a point. It's not like I'd be able to tell you how her marriage really is, whether or not she's living her dream."

"Meaning?" Holden's expression was back to badass FBI agent. She felt as though she was being inspected, and realized she was.

"Let's get something straight, Holden. I'm willing to work with you, even help your investigation if I can, but I'm not beholden to you because you work for some big government LEA."

"Fair enough."

"And it's pretty clear you have some issues with me, though you're not saying what."

His brows rose and she knew she'd surprised him.

"I don't care for reporters. I find your profession revolting." His words didn't surprise her. What stunned her was that he flat out admitted it.

"Then why the heck are you looking to work together? I'm in the pageant solely for my story. I haven't misled you about that." She'd taken a risk by telling him anything to begin with. It was too late for self-recrimination, though.

"To keep this aboveboard, between us, you need to understand that the pageant may be shut down at any point."

"I'm kind of surprised that you haven't done that

already." She smiled at Angelina when she slid a large diet soda in front of her.

"I don't know who it was who attacked you. If I did, and if I could prove it was the same killer from the other two pageants, I'd do it in a heartbeat."

"Would you, though?" Anger simmered low and hot in her belly. "You want to catch a killer. Take away Ms. Mustang Valley and you have no bait, no means of attracting him."

"Tell me about the files you were looking for."

"Pageant records. They've been in that old file cabinet since I went to Mustang Valley High."

"The drawers were empty. You saw that."

"I assumed that MVPD took them. For evidence." She spoke to him as professionally as she could muster this late in a day that had included her first physical attack, ever. It was a blessing she had little memory of any of it, other than the creepy voice behind her before she was knocked out.

"The person who attacked me—did you see him?"

"I did. But he was completely disguised."

"His voice sounded odd."

Lines appeared between his brows and on the bridge of his nose and her fingers twitched. It'd be so easy to reach across the table and smooth those out for him.

What was she thinking? She shoved her hand under her thigh.

"The voice disguiser… That's pretty high-tech, isn't it?" It sounded like a seriously committed criminal to her, to have special disguise equipment.

"Not at all. You can buy them from five dollars on upward to hundreds of dollars. They're available in party stores for Halloween, and online. There are even apps that do it for you."

A shiver ran up her spine and down her front. She crossed her arms against the involuntary response. "I can't see someone trying to protect the pageant files going to such lengths."

"Nor can I, unless…"

"Here you go." Angelina was back and set their platters down in front of them. The aroma of her hot meal made Bella's stomach growl. Holden's surprised glance, then that quick grin, let her know he'd heard it, too. Red-hot embarrassment assaulted her cheeks but she kept a smile pasted on her face until Angelina left.

"I haven't eaten since early this morning, over fourteen hours ago. I'm allowed a stomach noise or two."

"Hey, I'm not saying anything." But the grin was still there.

"You were saying why you think my attacker used a voice disguiser?"

He chewed his hamburger for several moments, wiped his mouth, took a sip of iced tea. "It's not just the voice disguise—it's the lengths he went to, to completely hide his identity. It points to someone local, and if it's someone from Mustang Valley, it could be related to the pageant. Who holds this competition so dear that they'd hurt others to keep it running?"

"That's my question to answer, isn't it?" She munched on a fry. "I'm keeping all avenues open. My first thoughts are to find the evidence for the extreme weight and diet restrictions that Gio told me were assigned as a matter of course for every contestant. I'd hoped to have that in hand already, in those files."

"You don't. So until you get the files?" He didn't miss a beat.

"I have to keep going, play along as if I'm really a legitimate contestant."

"Which you are. Does it bother you, the lying?"

"Not as much as my trust being compromised."

"How so?" One brow up, his intense chocolate gaze on her. Did his lids lower a smidge as he checked out her lips?

She shivered, but not from temperature. This chemistry had to be in her imagination. Maybe it was part of surviving the attack. She may have been unconscious but her brain had witnessed all of it; isn't that what her friends in medicine told her?

"Cold?" He'd seen her shudder.

Bella shook her head. "No. Annoyed is more like it. I told you what I was working on in confidence. And then you told someone during your phone conversation. I couldn't help but overhear it."

"That was my supervisor—I'm obligated to keep him informed about all aspects of this op, especially since I'm working solo here. It won't go any further."

"You're forgetting an important detail, Agent St. Clair."

"What's that?"

"You're not alone. We're in this together, remember?" She couldn't say why but she relished the look of what she interpreted as disgust crossing his face. He hated reporters? Great. She'd be sure to not disappoint.

"Speaking of that, there's something we have to absolutely agree on or I'll be required to disqualify you from the pageant."

Bella's blood stilled, and she swore it lowered in temperature. "Are you threatening me, Agent St. Clair?"

"No, but I'm going to have to make you promise to allow me to protect you."

"I don't ne—"

"Hold it." He held up his hand, a smear of ketchup

on his palm. This man enjoyed his meals as much as she did. "Before you spout off about your brother being able to take care of you and provide security, forget it. We might be facing two criminals in my estimation. A possible serial killer, and someone additional, someone who wants the pageant's workings protected at all costs. If it's all just one criminal, that's enough. MVPD is already strapped to the max with its current investigation, and as a Colton you're that much more visible. You either need to hire 'round-the-clock security with the utmost credentials, or trust my expertise in keeping you safe through the pageant."

"Or else." She waited until he met her eyes again. "Let me guess, ultimatums come in your job description." Her vision narrowed in on his gaze, his confidence prickling her self-esteem. Anger simmered in her gut although it wasn't at Holden, but herself.

Isn't it your ego, your pride that's being hurt?

She ignored her conscience. She had to. Otherwise she'd have to admit that she found the prospect of allowing FBI agent Holden St. Clair to guard her at the least interesting, and at the most, sexually exciting.

"Actually, no. I don't hand out ultimatums or live in the black and white as much as you might think. Criminal investigations are messy, and rarely do they move in a straight line. Do I find the bad guy? Yes, most of the time. And it's pretty straightforward, as far as who a killer is. But getting there, uncovering the evidence, that's different each time."

"Don't expect me to commiserate with you. Reporting—accurate, with verifiable sources, protected or not—is always difficult. When it isn't, I know the subject matter isn't what I'm supposed to be doing."

"You'll get no commiseration from me on journalistic technique." He finished the last of his burger and eyed her over the votive that Angelina lit when she brought their drinks.

If she saw a flicker of humanity in his gaze, she credited the candle. Holden St. Clair was as hard-boiled as any LEA she'd met in her job, and as stoic as her brother. His demeanor was what really frightened her, though. As tough as his statements and matching views were, he spoke without animosity or judgement. He was calm, the strength of his personality driven by integrity, if she had to guess.

Just like her long-deceased father. Not a day went by that Bella didn't think of her parents and the awful loss she and her brothers and okay, even her not-so-dear old Aunt Amelia, had suffered. But she had a feeling that while she was in Holden's company she was going to be remembering Dad a lot more.

Thinking about her dad and the years she'd lost with him only ever accomplished one thing. It made her vulnerable.

Bella didn't do vulnerable—not again, anyway.

Chapter 7

Holden watched the light play across her face, narrowly illuminated by the tiny candle. This greasy spoon was a far cry from the linen tablecloths he was used to sharing with beautiful women, in Phoenix. Yet he couldn't remember having a meal with anyone as attractive as Bella in eons. Not in the physical or chemical way, but intellectually. And maybe a bit more. Bella's intelligence was reflected in her keen wit, dry sense of humor—which he adored—and her willingness to totally submerse herself in the pageant.

"Are you pro beauty pageant or not?" He'd learned long ago it was best to be direct if he wanted the truth. "I can't tell if you're supportive of the other contestants or silently judging them."

"I would have answered this differently, immediately after Gio passed away." She weighed her words. "I have nothing against the pageants that have a valid award, like the scholarship with Ms. Mustang Valley. I absolutely don't support requiring women to adhere to a construct of beauty or certain physical attributes, though." Again, doubt tugged on her conscience. The possibility that Gio's eating disorders had been triggered but not caused by the pageant was something she was going to have to reckon with by the time she finished her exposé.

"Yet this pageant's prize is scholarship driven, as you've mentioned."

She nodded. "It is. Which is why I'm able to stomach entering. Trust me, if the prize had been no more than a tiara and sash to wear in the annual Mustang Valley parade, I'd still have had to consider it to get to the bottom of my investigation. But it would have come at a much higher price. Plus no one would have believed me, or trusted my motive for entering. With the scholarship prize it's easy to pose as a legit competitor."

"Thank you for being so honest in your response. I appreciate that you didn't just give me a politically correct line." He didn't want to hold her feet to the fire as he rather enjoyed their conversation and getting answers meant it would end sooner than later. But Bella Colton was a woman of substance and integrity—he imagined she'd never settle for anything less than complete transparency—and from what he'd already witnessed, wouldn't waste time squandering her energy on circular questioning.

"It's hard to not be in awe of the contestants. They appear incredibly vested in the process," Bella said. As did the pageant board, which he was watching closely, and now knew she was, too.

As if she were a balloon and he held the air passage,

he heard the long swish of breath as it left her lungs, her chest raising and falling in sync.

"That's what's so difficult in this case. When the other pageant contestants, and especially the board, find out I did this for an investigative report, they're never going to forgive me. And I don't blame them. I'm not responsible for anyone else's feelings but my own. Yet I saw the other applicants all waiting for what I was going to say, when I came in the school and they were in the folding chairs just off the stage. They weren't only waiting for me to screw up, which I'm sure most of them were—I'd expect that in any competition. What was different is I felt as though they were cheering me on, showing me that I can do it, that my goals matter. And most of them don't even know me."

"You believe they're supportive of you, even though they'd do anything to win the scholarship themselves?"

"Yes." Her head tilted slightly and revealed the length of her neck that her ponytail bared. She'd put the long locks up before they came in the diner and he longed to see her hair down around her shoulders again.

Definitely not a thought an FBI agent should be entertaining during a lethal investigation.

"You sound like you were surprised."

"Of course I was! You were there—didn't it seem a little bizarre, to have the other contestants see my interview, watch for my weaknesses, yet give a big show of support?"

"No." His one-syllable reply sounded harsh and even though it wasn't his concern, he wanted her to know that he understood her observations. He'd had them, too. "Yes, the fact that they were so ready to cheer you on seemed odd to me, when only one person is going to win that scholarship. Which, may I observe, is a hefty amount of change. It's local, a community college, but still, that's got to be worth at least several thousand dollars."

She named the figure without hesitation and a warmth lit his insides. Bella wasn't a fly-by-night reporter or blogger; she'd done her homework.

"It's enough to either pay for the full four years at Mustang Valley Community College, MVCC, or at least four semesters at the closest Arizona state school."

"I did find it odd that you were in financial straits after working in your field for so long." He didn't want to give away how much he knew about reporters, not to this beautiful woman who didn't remind him one bit of his ex, save for her job description. He still felt foolish that he'd allowed his ex, Nicole, to lead him on for as long as she had, all for a story.

"I'm not in bad financial straits, not really." She grinned. "I'm not stupid. If they research my earnings over the last two years they'll see a significant drop-off from the *Mustang Valley Gabber*—like all newspapers and blogs, we're struggling. I've relied on extra freelance work beyond my full-time *Gabber* position, and it's enabled me to put a good amount in savings over the last five or six years."

"Any reason why?"

She shrugged. "Why not? I'm single and I came up with enough to put a down payment on a house. My mortgage is manageable and I live pretty simply."

He couldn't help check out her clothes, still the same striped top and white pants from earlier. The sparkling jewelry. She seemed as though she was doing more than getting by paycheck to paycheck.

"Hey, don't judge me on how I appear now. Or how

I looked earlier—it's been a rough day, right?" She let out a throaty laugh and he felt it shoot right to his crotch.

Yeah, working with Bella Colton was going to be a challenge. Not the working part—the keeping it to business only piece.

"I have to ask how far you're willing to go for your writing, Bella."

"What do you mean? Haven't I already showed you I'm willing to do just about anything to get the answers I want?"

"Are you willing to have me protect you, offer to be your bodyguard, for the duration of the pageant?"

"Sure. I mean, that's why we're meeting here and now, right? To agree to share information."

"I need more from you, Bella. I can't let you out of my sight until we apprehend the suspect."

"I'm not going to your hotel room with you. So where will you stay?" She was so determined, and he found her independence incredibly sexy. But as he took in her beauty he didn't miss the bright red highlights in her hair—bullseyes to the killer.

"No, you're not coming to the hotel with me." She'd figure out his intention to not leave her side soon enough. "I've been hotel hopping, up until the last couple of days, as I've spent more time in Mustang Valley." He wasn't going to share that he was a naturalist who counted a night under the stars with no edifice to block them more luxurious than the swankiest hotel on the planet. He'd be able to keep her safe in a tent.

She nodded. "Makes sense. So that no one catches on to your routine. You're the one who's supposed to be determining patterns, right?"

"Exactly."

"We'll exchange phone numbers, and I'll text you

each time I leave my house, and tell you where I'm going." She pulled out her phone and her fingers hovered over the face. "Give me your number and I'll call, then we'll have one another's info."

He went along with it, until his phone vibrated, her number illuminating. The buzz went farther than his hand where he held his cell but he'd worry about his attraction to her later. He had to keep Bella Colton safe.

"There you go." She slid her purse onto her shoulder. He reached out and stilled her by touching her forearm.

"Wait."

She stared at him and when their eyes met the claws of her searching need reached him in places he didn't know he'd opened to her. Bella wasn't just another woman or citizen he was trying to protect. There was something more between them. Something he'd been missing in his life for a long time.

"You keep asking me to slow down, Agent St. Clair. I'm concerned you're not going to be happy until I stop my investigating entirely." He heard the threat in her words. Not a frivolous barb, but a show of her steely strength, the determination to do right by her best friend.

"I have to be with you, Bella." As soon as the words left his mouth he saw her eyes widen, her lips part. And darn it, he looked down at where her breasts pressed against her shirt, the hard nipples pushing her response through the thin material.

"That sounds like a personal issue, Agent St. Clair."

"No, I don't mean it that way. I mean yes, there's clearly some chemistry here, which is to be expected. I mean, we're adults, both single, on an intense case." As he bumbled he watched her and instead of being revolted by his faux pas she appeared…delighted. Bella

Colton let out a belly laugh that proved her lack of self-consciousness and her ability to live in the present moment. Good traits for someone who was a potential target of a serial killer.

"You're refreshing, Holden. I've no doubt you're a crack agent or you wouldn't have been sent here. But you're real. I like that."

He ignored his embarrassment, the racing thoughts that he'd never be worthy of this woman's attention. Holden considered himself too devoted to his job to deserve a woman like Bella, a woman who deserved a man who'd give her nothing less than one-hundred percent. He stopped his thoughts with expertise gained from years of investigative work that required complete focus. Had he forgotten that she was a reporter, just like his ex?

You're on the clock, man. Get it done.

"You're a target, Bella. The killer likes women with red hair and green eyes, and you're the only one with both."

"I have blond—" She fingered her ponytail and her face crumpled. "Crap. I forgot. I do have red hair. I thought it'd help me stand out from all the other contestants, especially the blondes."

He nodded. "It does. And it was smart, for the pageant. Except you may have drawn the attention of the killer already."

"I'd say I did by getting attacked." She spoke matter-of-factly and he let it go. It wasn't the time or place to remind her that he wasn't so sure her attacker was the serial killer. The killer's modus operandi was to lay low until he either poisoned or shot his victim. It made Holden think that the killer didn't seem to care how his quarry died, just that they did. Something he wasn't going to let happen to Bella.

"The truth is, Bella—I need to stay with you. At your house, and possibly elsewhere if we decide you need to move. It'll probably amount to nothing more than me sleeping on your floor by the front door for the next few weeks, with no further interruption from any bad guy. But we can't take the risk that they know your identity or where you live."

Her face stilled, then she laughed again. "Oh, just wait until Spencer finds out that his buddy is sleeping with me."

"Ah, not with you, specifically—" All he needed was Spencer coming down on him for moving in on his sister.

"Chill out, Holden, and let me have my sibling fantasy. My brother means well, but he's always telling me how to stay safe and live my life. He's absolutely livid I signed up for the pageant, as I'm sure you figured out already."

"I don't blame him. There are a lot of moving parts here. And another thing—you can't tell your work colleagues or supervisor who I am, or that you're working with me. No one but you, Spence, and the state pageant director know I'm on the case. No one on the Ms. Mustang Valley Pageant board knows who I am. I'm deep undercover here."

"Not so deep, Agent. I know who you are and I'm a member of the press, remember?" She looked away, lost in thought for several moments. He let her process his request. It was a lot. Sure, she'd seen his badge, Spencer had vouched for him, they'd survived a possible abduction attempt already.

He'd helped her—she knew that. But she was about

to let a strange man into her home, no matter that he was Spencer's army friend. Holden wasn't her friend, nor could he ever be, not during this investigation, anyhow. It would compromise his work, because he'd want to trust she was telling him all she discovered with the pageant and that just wasn't reality. Not with a reporter. He'd already learned that lesson.

Holden had his priorities, and Bella had hers.

"If there was another way to do this, instead of having to be with you 24/7 and staying at your place, I'd make it happen." He needed her to know that he wasn't taking the easy way out at her inconvenience.

Steady green eyes met his. "I know." Her mouth was a half-smile and she let out a sigh of surrender. "I've got one brother who's a rancher and one who's a cop. They both deal in reality every day, as do I. If I'm doing my job right, anyhow. You can stay with me, and I'll do my best to stay in your sights or whatever you need for my security. Because it's not just about me, Holden. This is about the pageant, its contestants, the women who really need the scholarship. I'm doing it for them."

"And for your best friend."

She nodded and he saw the glisten of tears in her eyes, but she didn't let one fall. Add stubborn to independent, passionate, intriguing.

"Yes. For Gio."

Bella didn't like that in the span of six short hours she'd gone from being completely undercover, working her report as part of the pageant, to Holden knowing so much about what she was trying to accomplish. But after being attacked, warned off the pageant and now being unable to shake the sense of someone watching her, she gave in to what her brothers called her killer instinct. She had a gut instinct for a story and was good at sizing up character. Holden might never appreciate her vocation or support her article, but he wanted what she did. Answers, and no more people hurt.

"Let's get into your vehicle." He took charge the minute they left the diner. "We'll come back in the morning for mine. This way if anyone's trailing you we'll make it look like—"

"Like I'm picking up a stranger in the local greasy spoon." She unlocked the passenger door with her keys.

"This car is the oldest running antique I've ever seen." Holden's observation brought a smile to her face but she didn't reply until they were both inside her beloved twenty-year-old station wagon.

"This was my mother's car. She and Dad were killed in his car, in a crash. One of their family friends bought this one from our aunt and kept it in his garage until my brothers and I were sixteen, and the day we got our driver's licenses he drove it up to the house." She couldn't stop the giggle as she moved the gear, on the steering wheel, into Reverse. "Our aunt Amelia was fit to be tied, because she didn't want us being that independent so soon, but when she realized we'd be asking her for a lot fewer rides, she gave in."

"Sounds like your aunt had her own issues."

Bella nodded. "She did. I had little to do with her after moving out, when I went to college, but now looking back… I don't know. It couldn't have been easy for her, losing a sibling and gaining three kids, age ten, ready to head into the tween and teenage years, all at once. She wasn't much older than me when it happened."

"I saw on your license when you checked in at the high school that you're thirty-one. That surprised me.

I mean, I know you're Spencer's age, but it still seems unbelievable."

"Why?" She turned onto the main drag through town and headed west, toward the small, quiet subdivision where she lived in an adobe-style midcentury house.

"You look about ten years younger."

"Until I open my mouth, right?" She shot a quick glance at his profile in time to see the quick grin. "I've been told I sound like an old soul, and my deep voice sure doesn't sound youthful."

"I think your voice is sexy as hell."

Heat that had shimmered on the surface of her awareness ignited and spread to her center, pooling in her most sensitive spots. "Uh, Agent? I don't think that's something you're allowed to notice."

"It's not. Sorry. Are you a smoker?"

"Nope, never have been. My voice was froggy as a kid, and I never outgrew it. Supposedly it's similar to my mother's, but I have no way of knowing. I don't remember her voice a whole lot anymore."

"Spencer shared about losing his folks, your parents. That's an awful break in life, to lose them so early."

"Yeah, it wasn't fun. What about you, are your parents still here?"

"Yes, they're happy empty nesters in Kansas City, Kansas. My mother is an engineer and works at the state power authority. My father is a government contractor. I grew up there, in Kansas, with my two brothers. We have that in common, two brothers."

"That's neat. Sounds like you had the perfect childhood." She tried to keep the envy out of her voice, but it was there in the tightening of her chest. Dang, the attack must be making her more emotional.

"Perfect? Wondering if either parent was going to

lose their job as the economy swung up and down? Watching one of my brothers turn to drugs when we were teens?" He spoke matter-of-factly, not with an iota of self-pity. She liked that Holden knew himself well enough to be able to do that, that he knew he wasn't the sum total of some of his life experiences. "It wasn't perfect, no, but it was pretty darn wonderful at times. Our parents always did the best they could for us, and now that my brother's sober we all get together a couple of times a year to hang out."

"That's pretty cool, if you ask me. Kansas City sounds appealing, being a larger city. Living in a small place like Mustang Valley can be a bit like being in a cultural bubble. Except we're lucky that Mustang Valley is in Arizona. By that I mean we have a confluence of cultures, including Native American and Hispanic. I learned Spanish in school from kindergarten."

"I wish I'd studied a second language sooner. I took German in high school, then Spanish in college. I'm not a natural at languages. I imagine since you're a writer, you are."

"I do okay. I haven't had the opportunities you have to see the world, though. That would be neat."

"Can't you do international reporting?" His query hit a sensitive spot in her belly, a vulnerable piece of herself she wasn't ready to reveal. If she landed this piece with the pageant, she'd very well receive the attention her work needed to propel her to the next level, which she hoped would be on a more national and eventually international stage.

"It's not that simple. It'll take me a while to get there."

He let it go and she relaxed her clenched jaw. Her

street sign appeared and she made the left onto the wide paved road.

"I didn't picture you in a standard suburban neighborhood."

"Don't count on it. Why do you say that, though?" She took her time driving around the park that she worked out in. Walking or running proved much less expensive than a gym, and she had a set of weights in her small home's second bedroom that served as her office, workout room and crafting space. It was a guest room, too, but since her brothers lived close by, no one stayed with her, except if her college friends were visiting. No one really had, except Gio.

"You strike me as independent and preferring your own space to having a next-door neighbor."

Darn it, he had a true talent. "You're a natural at profiling, Holden. I mean it." She turned onto a graveled road that lead through a grove of huge cacti.

"Are you taking us out into the desert?"

She laughed. "In case you haven't noticed it, you're in the middle of the desert. It's called Arizona." Bella took the last S-turn and pulled up in front of her house, then shut off the engine. She watched Holden, tried to see the view through his eyes, but it was dark back here as the sun had lowered to below her home's roofline, and the house looked like a dark rectangle surrounded by the glowing golden rays of the last of the day.

"Are you the only one out here?"

"Do you mean my house? Yes. I'm still on city water and utilities, but I get the sense of being out in the country. It's really not that far to the nearest neighbors, no more than a quarter mile in each direction. But I like how it feels more rural. It's a nice break from running around Mustang Valley and beyond each day, chasing down stories."

Holden turned and looked at her. "I didn't mention it because I didn't want to put you on edge, but I've been checking the rearview and side-view mirrors since we left the diner. No one followed us, which is a good sign."

Relief unfurled and the attraction her fear had tamped down surged. This was the first time she'd been alone in her car with a man in…she didn't even remember. The few men she'd dated on and off over the last several years had either driven, claiming their vehicles were more comfortable, or she'd met them out for a meal or other date.

"Yes, that's good news." She watched him, or rather, felt him in the dark. Her dash light had burned out over a year ago and she'd been too busy to replace it.

"So now I'm going to have to ask to do something you're not going to like, Bella." His deep baritone wove a sexy spell around her and she tipped her head back, just a bit. In case he was noticing her lips.

"Okay. What is it?" She smiled in the velvet night, liking the direction things were going.

"I've got to go through your house first, to clear it. Protocol." He opened his door and slid out of the car before Bella's tingling lips had a chance to realize she wasn't getting propositioned.

She scrambled out of the car and walked up behind him as he strode toward her front door, his handgun out and reflecting the porch light, which she had on a solar timer. Good thing she didn't want their relationship to be anything more than business.

Chapter 8

Holden couldn't get out of the jalopy soon enough, away from the temptation he'd been fighting every. Single. Minute. Of this case. It was no use pretending the attraction wasn't there, because it was, in spades. Bella Colton hit all his physical buttons and worse, she had a terrific sense of humor.

Nowhere else to go but forward. He pulled out his weapon and heard Bella's approach behind him.

"Stay behind me, to the right, if you're not going to remain in your car."

"Of course I'm not. What if the killer is out here, and attacks me while you're clearing my house?"

He gritted his teeth. "No talking. Let me work."

She complied but he gave her thirty seconds. Her naturally curious nature wouldn't allow her to not ask questions, he'd bet.

The sandy gravel underfoot gave way to smooth red

tiles that led to the front porch area, which was really a front patio. A small table and a chair looked untouched, as did the ground around the house. He used his phone's flashlight to see if there were any footprints or other evidence of a recent unwanted visitor.

"The front looks fine. Give me your key." He faced her, saw the resistance in her stance.

"I can unlock my own door."

"Bella." He stood in front of her, his hand out. "Our deal."

"Whatever." She grumbled the last, held out the small ring of keys and dropped them in his palm. Was she careful to ensure they didn't have any skin contact or was he reading too much into it? The fact that he was turned on by her didn't mean Bella had any such desire for him. Nor should she—he was here to protect her, find a murderer and then he'd be back to Phoenix. Where he had his life, his job, and no troublesome undercover reporter questioning his every move.

"Stay back until I get the door open and clear the first room. Do you have a front hallway or does it open directly into a room?" He scanned her front windows, all two of them, to try to see what the inside looked like.

"I have a foyer with a skylight, and then it opens into the great room. The kitchen, morning breakfast room and living room all flow into each other. I don't have a lot of interior walls save for the outer ones."

"Where's your bedroom?"

"There are two. The guest room is off the kitchen and the master bedroom is behind that, down a short hall. This is a ranch-style home, one level." She spoke as if he were a grade-school kid and he couldn't blame her. He was asking pretty obvious questions for a person who lived in Arizona. The homes were often ranch-style, meaning one level, to help with keeping them cool through the long, hot days. Even with air-conditioning it was impossible to keep a home livable when the temperatures soared well over one-hundred-degrees Fahrenheit. The local joke was that it was a "dry" heat. When the temperature hit triple digits, it was too hot.

"Got it, thanks. I'll be right back." He closed the few yards between them and the front door, unlocked it and slowly pushed it open, his pistol ready to fire. As the door swung open, inch by inch, he shone his flashlight inside until he reached around and hit the wall light switch. Sconces on either side of a mission-style framed mirror lit up, throwing a pale golden hue into the room. Bella had done her work and made the place a home, if the various decor touches were any indication. A fluffy white throw draped over a white fabric chaise lounge; in another corner a love seat boasted a spillover of throw pillows, all printed in bright, gregarious colors.

No sign of an intruder. But Holden didn't allow relief to take away the weight of responsibility from his shoulders. Not yet. Not until they caught and apprehended the suspect.

He methodically cleared out each room, confirming the house was indeed empty, before returning to where Bella stood on the porch. "All clear." He motioned for her to come inside. "Let's lock up the front door and you're free to move about. I'm going to check the back of the house to be sure you're safe."

She watched his retreating backside and only then did she allow herself to sag against the kitchen pantry door. She'd been surprised at how hard Spencer and his K-9 Boris worked situations before, how very tedious and exacting law enforcement was, done right; but this revealed a whole new level of ignorance on her part that Bella hadn't anticipated. How many times had she heard Spencer say it wasn't about the firearms, or the physicality of the cop, but the intelligence? The ability to conduct their job under any circumstance?

Holden St. Clair knew what he was doing, displaying a tenacity for doing what was right, no matter that they both were bone weary and dog tired. He could have dropped her off, assumed she'd be fine until the pageant began tomorrow, but instead Holden was conducting an investigation of her home security as if it were the beginning of the day and he had all the energy to be as thorough as when he first woke.

She watched the light beam flash outside the windows, first near the living area and then around to the kitchen, before it disappeared as Holden walked the perimeter of her house. Bella tried to stay focused on the present and what she needed to do to prepare for tomorrow, but her mind and her body couldn't stop flashing back to moments ago in her car.

Embarrassment washed over her. She'd really thought he was going to kiss her. Had she misread his signals? The glances, held a heartbeat longer than with just any other colleague, the quick drop of his gaze to her lips? And the electric current of attraction she'd experienced when their fingers touched, was it even possible that something so potent on her part was one-sided?

"Bella!" His shout made her stand straight and cleared her mind of what she knew were inescapable personal rabbit holes. "Come here."

"Coming." She made for the back door, which he must have opened with the key.

He stood under the pale glow of the moon as it filtered through her pergola on the back patio. A quick glance at her large cushioned swing, myriad planters filled with cacti and other succulents, and her different garden sculptures showed nothing amiss.

"What is it?"

"Over here." He led them with the phone light to her air-conditioning unit. "Have you had maintenance or repair on your AC recently?"

"No."

"What about this crack to your foundation?" A long, jagged line ran from the stucco under her bathroom window and disappeared below the ground.

"It's from the earthquake."

"That's right—it didn't hit us in Phoenix as it did here. And the epicenter was close to the Colton Oil industrial area, am I correct?"

"Yes." Annoyance mingled with fear. Would Holden just get to the point?

"Any reason these footprints should be here?" He spotlighted several sets of large prints in the sandy earth around the unit's concrete-slab platform. Her gut heaved and she wanted to blame it on being tired but she knew fear when it hit her.

"Those have to be recent or they'd be gone already." Nothing stayed the same in the desert, not for long and not during a time that included enough breeze at night to blow away the fine sand. "Why would someone come here, though, to an air-conditioning unit?"

Holden snapped several photos of the prints, a few with his feet in the shot for sizing perspective. "I don't know. Unless—" He shone the light up to the three-foot-tall unit, and revealed that there was a good amount of dust atop the grate where the fan blew out hot air from the house.

"He climbed on top to look into that window." She finished his speculation and looked up to the high windows that lined her master bathroom. "Even if someone could get up that high without a ladder, no one could fit through those windows." They weren't more than six inches tall, tops, though very long to allow maximum light in.

Holden pulled latex gloves from his jeans' pockets and she laughed.

"You've got to be kidding me."

"No joke intended. Just part of my job." He pushed hard on the top of the AC unit before hauling himself up. She watched from the ground as he felt along the edges of the windows as far as he could reach. His movement stilled as his fingers rested on the same spot he had paused the first time he visually examined the frame.

"What is it?" Shivers raced down her spine and she crossed her arms in front of her, looked around them at the surrounding garden and wild property that backed up against her neighbors on either side, and acres of empty desert to the rear of the house. It had been her safe haven ever since she'd saved enough for the down payment to purchase the house a few years ago. She'd never felt vulnerable or at risk here.

Until tonight.

Holden tugged on something, then fisted his palm and jumped to the ground, far away from the footprints. "I need to look at this inside, in proper lighting, but I'd say someone is very interested in catching glimpses of you in your shower." He opened his hand to reveal a tiny box with a lens.

"I'm going to be sick." She said it before thinking. "I mean, not really, but the thought of this—I can't do this right now."

His firm, gloved hand grasped her forearm. "Hang on, Bella. It's okay. You're not alone—I'm here. And the good news is that your stalker is nowhere near here right now, most likely. If they wanted to watch you in person there wouldn't be a camera and I'd have found them inside or lurking on the property. I'm going to call Spencer and have him and his K-9 inspect the area for scent, but we should be good to go for tonight."

"Meaning?"

"We'll be able to spend the night here, and then head to the pageant in the morning. It's already past eleven, and I need to be at the school a full hour before the contestants arrive at eight."

"I don't even know if I'm a contestant yet." She'd forgotten to check her inbox; the pageant director, Mimi, had told them they'd find out whether they qualified by nine o'clock tonight. A quick dive into her emails on her phone revealed a message. Her hands shook.

"Well?" Holden stood patiently next to her, as if whether she got into the pageant was important to him, too. Of course, she figured she'd be the best kind of bait for the serial killer, if there was one and if he'd now focused his sights on Ms. Mustang Valley.

She clicked the message open, skimmed the preliminary niceties, and let out a whoop. Relief and a sense of euphoria she did not expect washed over her, easing some of the tension that finding out about the camera had incurred.

"I take it you're in?" His enthusiastic tone was as surprising as her reaction.

"I am. And you're correct, I report at eight o'clock."

"Then we'd best get your beauty sleep going."

"You're crazy to do this, Bella." Jarvis sat at her kitchen island later that night, his hair gleaming under the pendant lights.

"As crazy as Spencer was to call you out here tonight? Really, you two don't need to babysit me. I already have a federal agent at my beck and call." Holden was outside taking evidence as Spencer and Boris patrolled her backyard. It was half past midnight and Bella wanted to sleep for a day.

"You should always let us know what you're up to, sis. You know we're going to find out one way or the other. Word doesn't take long to travel in Mustang Valley." Jarvis ran his fingers through his hair. "And you're working fast even for you if you've already got this agent doing your bidding." His words were harsh but Jarvis's tone was kind, loving even. He was the best brother, as was Spencer, and Bella didn't for one minute take either of them for granted. Yet she had, by not mentioning her intention to run for Ms. Mustang Valley.

"I'm sorry, Jarvis. It's best for me to keep things as low key as possible when I'm doing investigative work."

"I know that, sis, but Spencer and I are your only family. We need to know, so that we can be on the lookout for anything suspicious."

She poured them each a tall glass of ice water, and filled glasses for Holden and Spence, a mixing bowl for Boris that she placed on the floor. "I appreciate that, but this is a very insular community I'm delving into. Gio's passing made me realize that a lot of my grief is over not having been able to prevent her death."

"So you think digging up the past will help you with that?"

She shook her head. "It's not about me. We can learn from the past. If I do this right, I'll find evidence that this pageant committee and board have been negatively influencing young women's health and eating habits and shut that behavior down."

Jarvis's brow went up, the way it did when she tried to get one over on him in a board game. Whereas Spencer would blatantly call her out on anything he thought she was lying about, Jarvis took a more circumspect view of things. Of life, especially.

"That's a tall order, sis, even by your standards. Let's say you do find evidence—though what that'll look like is beyond me, short of finding a memo that states, 'Starve yourself or get kicked out.'"

"I have to do this, Jarvis. Gio deserves it. All the women who enter these contests deserve to know the truth about what they're participating in."

"It seems to me someone isn't happy about you getting involved."

"No one knows I'm doing this as a reporter, except for Spencer's friend Holden, whom you met when you came in."

"He's a good guy, Holden St. Clair."

"You know him?" A thread of self-pity wound its way around her heart. "Why didn't anyone tell me about him, who he was?"

Jarvis smiled. "Spencer did. You knew the name once you met him, didn't you? How did you meet, at the school?"

She nodded. "Yes. He was the security guard when I checked in. I didn't realize he was Spencer's friend, though. He's undercover. I guess I shouldn't have said that to you." The familiar heat rushed her cheeks and she prayed Jarvis didn't notice, or if he did, that he'd take it for her regret at spilling the beans. Not because she was already thinking of Holden as much more than her brother's friend.

Jarvis chuckled. "I'd have loved to see that. And don't worry about telling me—I'm a vault."

"You are."

"What do you wish you'd seen, and what are you a vault about?" Spencer looked at Jarvis as he, K-9 Boris and Holden walked into the kitchen. Spencer removed his hat and placed it on the counter. "Boris, drink." The dog's lapping filled the quiet.

"Oh, nothing. Just how Bella's getting away with being a pageant contestant when we both know how much she hates pretending to be anything other than herself."

She risked a glance at Holden and found another reason to blush in the way their gazes locked, as if they'd been working together for longer than a day. As if…as if there was something happening between them they weren't ready to acknowledge.

Holden blinked, shuttering the desire she'd seen in his eyes. He let out a laugh and the other two men joined in. The masculine rumble at once grated on Bella's nerves and comforted her. She knew her brothers only wanted her safety but they tended to lean over into the minding-her-business category. Holden had already told her he was going to basically be her bodyguard and protector for the duration of the pageant. A need to establish her turf twisted up through her exhaustion.

"Give me a break. Going undercover for this piece is the same way I get any story. It's called doing my job." She emphasized her words, hoping her brothers took her words at face value. Holden, too. He couldn't find out how much he'd affected her since they'd first met. How much he distracted her now, standing in her kitchen close to midnight, a day's worth of beard on his impossibly square chin. At least it didn't highlight his cleft as much, one of his more annoying features. "And while I truly appreciate all three of you looking out for me, I'm a grown woman with a concealed-weapon permit." She walked over to the far kitchen cabinet, opened it to reveal her gun safe.

"Your weapon's in there?" Holden spoke first.

"Yes." She nodded. Let him chew on that. "I'm a perfect shot, too."

"She is," Spencer chimed in. "We thought Bella was going to join MVPD at one point."

"Maybe you should, if you're putting yourself in this kind of danger with your journalism." Jarvis nodded sagely and she wanted to punch both of her brothers on the arm.

"I'm glad you have weapons training, Bella, but no weapon will defend you locked in a safe." Holden's observation came just as she realized the same.

"You're right. Are you suggesting I carry it while working the pageant?"

"Ah, no. I'll be on-site the entire time you're there. Or anywhere."

"I'm counting on you, Holden," Spencer spoke up.

"We both are," Jarvis joined in.

Bella watched the testosterone exchange between her brothers and Holden and decided it was all too much, too late. She picked up her phone for a distraction and saw the email, sent only minutes earlier, from the pageant director. After she read it, she interrupted the men's ongoing discussion on how best to keep her safe.

"Uh, guys?" She held up her phone for them to see the email. "I have to be onstage tomorrow morning at eight. Which gives me a six-o'clock wake-up. You all decide what you need to do to save me, whatever, but I'm going to bed. Night-night."

She turned and left, hoping that no one would tell her

she couldn't sleep in her own bed tonight. More than at any other time, Bella needed the comfort of the familiar.

As her head hit the pillow she realized that Holden felt way too familiar to her. And she'd only known him for one day.

This was going to be her toughest investigative report to date, and it had little to do with a serial killer or the loss of her best friend.

Chapter 9

"You decided to let me stay in my own home. Why?" She greeted Holden as he walked in from the backyard, none the worse for sleeping outside all night. At least, that's where she assumed he'd been, as Jarvis was still sacked out in her guest room.

"If at any time last night or this morning I thought you were in danger, you wouldn't be here. But with your two brothers helping out, we secured your property no problem."

"But you couldn't have gotten much sleep."

He walked over and helped himself to the pot of coffee she'd brewed. "I'm not the one who needed the beauty sleep."

His musky scent mixed with the aroma of the brew and she all but swooned. How easy it was to forget that her two favorite scents—coffee and male—made for a delicious morning wake-up.

Not that kind of wake-up, though. Hadn't she learned from the nonkiss last night?

"I don't need it, either." She sat down at her small table and swirled the creamer with a small spoon. "Where did you sleep, by the way?"

"Mostly on the front porch. Your hammock is a perfect spot, and I only heard a few critters roaming about."

"Did you notice the prairie dogs at dawn? There's a family of them in my front yard."

"I didn't, but I'm guessing Boris warned them off."

"Hmm, yes." She'd forgotten that Spencer and Boris had made their rounds last night. It'd be easy to blame it on the late hour, long day, being attacked; but she didn't waste the energy kidding herself. Holden St. Clair was the distracting factor.

Holden took the seat across from her at the bistro set and she almost laughed. His large frame barely fit on the wrought iron chair, and the table seemed to shrink in his presence. Unlike her awareness of him.

"Let's go over the ground rules again, Bella."

"Rules?"

He nodded, sipped his black coffee. "Yes. For me to agree to your participation in the pageant. And the guidelines your brother agreed to."

"Spencer isn't my keeper." She blew a strand of hair from her eyes. "I appreciate that he's law enforcement. He and Jarvis have always been protective of me, a great thing for a sister. But we're all adults and there's nothing legally stopping me from competing."

"There is if I expose your motive for entering the pageant."

"You wouldn't." But looking into his dark eyes, noting he'd shaved and the cleft on his chin seemed sexier than she'd remembered, she knew he would. "I'll never get the truth about this pageant—which could have bigger significance, legally—if you give me away."

"I'm not going to do that, Bella, but we have to agree to the precautions that will keep you alive."

"You make it sound so dire." She was trying to be casual, to appear as though she could take whatever pageant involvement threw at her. But she couldn't ignore the quivering in her belly, the wobbly feel to her knees. Bella was scared.

"It is. Or will be, soon enough."

"How can you be so certain? You don't even know if the man who attacked me is the same person who murdered those other women. Or if those victims were killed by the same person."

"Actually, we've had DNA evidence begin to trickle in." It'd been a month since the last murder, in Tucson, and they had some evidence being revealed. "There was matching DNA at both murder sites."

"One a poisoning and one gunshot, right?" She recalled reading the initial reports of each murder as they came across the local online paper's front page.

"You're informed."

"It's my job. Plus I've been paying attention to the pageant scene over the last several months."

"When did your friend pass?"

He remembered their conversation in the staff room. It meant he hadn't been treading water, using the time to win her over to his point of view, or reveal what she knew only for his benefit. It might even mean he cared.

Scratch that—it's his job to remember. To observe.

"Almost a year ago." It felt like yesterday and ten years ago at the same time. "She was very sick for the last year, and dragging for the previous five. I can honestly say I haven't seen her as the Gio I once knew for at least seven years or so."

"All from malnutrition, due to her eating disorder?"

"Mostly, yes." Bella didn't want to discuss Gio's long battle with mental illness, the struggles to get her friend in to the right professionals, from psychiatrists to therapists, all trained to expertly treat a young woman for the severity of her eating disorders, anxiety and depression. By the time Gio found a treatment center that worked well for her, it was too late. She'd starved herself so much that the nutritional depletion to her brain had destroyed her ability to see herself as she really was and not through the lens of body dysmorphia.

"You must have seen a lot with your friend, while she suffered like that." His compassion brought tears to her eyes.

"You speak as if you understand what Gio went through."

"No, I don't have any experience with eating disorders, but my grandfather had cancer and after over ten years of fighting it, died last year."

"I'm sorry, Holden."

"Thanks. It's always hard losing our loved ones."

"Yes."

They sat in peaceful silence and it didn't escape her that this was what she'd always thought other people had, what they deserved, when they found that one person to go through life with. Quiet and a simple acceptance of one another's presence.

But she had done little in her life to earn a whole lot of quiet moments, and rest wasn't something she wanted. Not until she got to the bottom of what had triggered Gio's life-ending issues.

"You get that there's a killer who's most likely involved in this pageant, and sees you as their next victim, right?" Holden's words underscored the frivolity of her imagination. So much for quiet respite free of worry.

"I do, but frankly, I don't have a lot of memory of being attacked." Her hand went to her throat. "I heard his weird voice, then yours, and then it's a blank spot until I was in the ER."

"It's normal for your mind to block out unpleasant memories. And being attacked is traumatic."

"True." She put her hand on his. "I've got this, Holden. I know you're the security and law enforcement expert. I trust you and I'll do whatever you tell me I need to, to stay safe and help you keep everyone else safe." She removed her hand. "Is that what you wanted to hear from me?"

"Do you mean it? Because I need you to know that it's paramount that you don't go anywhere alone with anyone until we catch the killer."

"I do."

"But?"

But she wasn't going to let anything keep her from getting this piece filed with her boss. She smiled at the man across the table from her. The man who'd spent a night in her home, something few besides her brothers had. A tug of regret deep in her gut reminded her that she'd been neglectful of her romantic life as of late. Time enough for that later.

"No buts." She stood. "I'll tell Jarvis we're leaving, get my bags and then we have ten minutes to drive to the high school."

Holden took her mug from her and walked to the sink, turned on the faucet and rinsed both cups. Bella didn't stay to watch him perform the morning ritual. The last thing she needed was to imprint the image of Holden moving about her kitchen as if he belonged there.

As if they were more than a reporter and FBI agent, both undercover.

This was always the most exciting part of any chase. Well, except for when the victim realized they were going to die and had no way to prevent it.

The grin was impossible to hide, but if anyone from the pageant board noticed, it'd be easy to pass it off as being happy to be involved in the thirtieth Ms. Mustang Valley Pageant.

Yesterday had been scary—it all could have ended because of one stupid move. Fortunately Bella Colton was fine and from all indications it looked like she'd be back today. Bella had made the final cut and was going to be pitted against the twenty-three other beauties, but none as pretty or enticing as the green-eyed woman with fiery red streaks in her hair. It'd be better if she had her whole head of hair in a bright red. Maybe that was something they could remedy as part of her preparation to be sacrificed.

"Ten minutes." The announcement came over the school's antiquated public address system and the voice sounded tinny in the space behind the stage where so far, no one had ventured since yesterday.

It was the perfect vantage point.

"We can't have you walking back and forth on the stage while we're trying to take the girls through their choreography." The woman leading the contestants through their opening-group-number dance steps left nothing to interpretation in her angry voice. Holden had completed his sixth circle of the large room, from the back of the auditorium seats to onstage, behind the several rows of curtains that could hide anyone all too easily.

Holden stopped in his tracks, turned and faced the tall, attractive woman who'd so far as he could tell done nothing but agitate her other pageant board members. Selina Barnes Colton was the ex-wife of Payne Colton, an oil tycoon in charge of the billion-dollar Colton Oil corporation who basically owned Mustang Valley. Selina was still on the Colton Oil Board of Directors as its VP and director of PR, and had zero problem throwing her weight around town according to Spencer, who'd filled him in on every pageant board member and judge.

"Just doing my job, ma'am." He kept to his security dude persona, not wanting to give her the tiniest hint that he had more right to be here than she realized. "I'll stay out of sight as much as I can, and be quiet."

"Not good enough. The girls need to feel safe in this space—am I right, ladies?" Selina tossed her hair over a bared shoulder, her figure model thin in tight-fitting clothes. Two dozen women stood in a group onstage, in various types of dance outfits. He'd memorized all of them, and constantly counted heads to make sure no one had crept off or worse, disappeared. A pair of emerald eyes flashed at him and he had to bite the inside of his cheek to not respond to Bella's wide grin. She was enjoying watching him take on a Colton Titan. But while the other contestants vocally supported Selina with calls of "Yeah, that's right," and "Listen to Ms. Colton," Bella remained silent.

"I'm here at the request of the state pageant director, ma'am."

"You're telling me that Bud Langston hired you directly and you're not here as part of Mustang Valley High School's staff?"

"Yes, ma'am." Holden had no problem playing whatever role he had to in order to get his job done. But Bella's glances communicated her impatience with Selina's trauma-drama tactics. He needed her to remain passive to Selina's theatrics, so that they could both gather as much information and evidence as possible.

"I think having the security guard where we can see him is a good idea. There are a lot of crazies around these days who prey on pretty women." Bella wasn't a mind reader. Or if she was, she'd ignored him.

Selina spun on her too-high heels and faced down Bella. Holden's hand clenched and he forcefully kept himself from stepping forward. He was going to have to handle this protective instinct toward Bella better. His drive to serve and protect was a part of him, but this sense of needing to know that Bella was in no way in any type of danger went deeper. To a place inside himself he didn't want to journey to, not now, maybe not ever.

To the place where he could get his heart broken again.

"That's enough, Ms. Colton." Selina's head swiveled as she addressed the rest of the crowd. "No worries, we are zero relation."

"Distant," Bella contradicted her and Holden wanted to whoop. His stomach constricted. Where was his agent self? He was here to catch a murderer, not cheer a potential victim on as she verbally sparred with a not-so-nice woman who seemed to think the world revolved on an axis named Selina.

"Wait a minute, you're related to one of the judges?" a contestant piped up, clearly annoyed. Her brunette hair was in two ridiculously juvenile pigtails and she wore an incredibly revealing leotard whose V-neck cut to her navel. Holden had thought this pageant was on the more conservative side but not for this contestant. "That's absolutely not fair. I demand that this woman be disqualified. No one related to the pageant board, judges or director is allowed to compete."

"We are not related at all, trust me." Bella spoke with authority, but it was clear to Holden that the belligerent woman wasn't going to let it go.

"What, do you spell *Colton* differently? Because from what I'm reading on both of your name tags, you have the same last name. And everyone knows that if you're a Colton in Mustang Valley or anywhere in Arizona, you get what you want." The overdone-leotard woman was on a roll, and several of the contestants murmured their agreement, nodding their heads and folding their arms in front of them. Holden knew the moment could prove an opportune distraction to detract from a killer, so he kept vigilant, walking slowly around the perimeter of the theater, never letting Bella out of his peripheral sight.

"*Puuullleeeze*, we're from completely different branches of the family, and we're not even blood relatives." Selina didn't want to be associated with a lowly blogger like Bella, it seemed. Holden stopped fighting his emotions and settled for keeping them hidden from the pageant contestants. At least the focus was off him and his job.

Except, he couldn't keep his focus off Bella and it wasn't for pageant reasons. Suddenly she wasn't a potential victim; she was Bella, the woman he was getting too close to, too quickly.

Chapter 10

"Selina's correct—we're not related. The man she used to be married to, Payne Colton, is very distantly related to me on my father's side, but from a different branch of the Coltons. Trust me, I'm from the wrong side of the tracks. Isn't that right, Selina?"

Bella looked at the woman she'd only seen in tabloid stories and at the most prestigious social functions in Arizona. Selina Barnes Colton didn't limit herself to what she'd once called *the hick town* of Mustang Valley any more than she had to. As the second and former wife of the Colton patriarch, she somehow had maintained her pull on the board of Colton Oil and was known for her take-no-prisoners methods with the press. Bella had tried to score an interview with her for the Lifestyle section of the *Mustang Valley Gabber* but Selina's assistant had turned her down flat, stating that *Selina only talks to national syndicates.* Whatever.

"If that doesn't convince everyone here that I'm not going to give any favorite points to Isabella, I don't know what else will." Selina's gaze was hard as coal on Bella but her smile was wide, her expression catering to the other contestants. "I've been involved with the pageant for the last decade, and I assure you my integrity is impeccable."

Several of the contestants mumbled around Bella but she ignored them. All she cared about was the ability to stay in the pageant. She'd barely gotten here and now was threatened with removal because Holden had walked around the stage one too many times. He really needed to chill out with the security-guard routine. She'd talk to him later about it.

"Let's keep the rehearsal going. If any decisions need to be made about our judges or contestants, we'll take care of it at the pageant board level. And from my perspective, there is no conflict of interest here. Let's begin again. Selina, from the top." Señora Rosenstein, whom Bella still saw as her Spanish teacher and not a member of the Ms. Mustang Valley board, tapped her phone and the auditorium was filled with the sounds of seventies disco. The group re-formed into place and for the next hour went through step after step, turn after turn, working the opening number to look like a dance routine from that era. Bella thought it was a lame way to open a pageant but her expertise was reporting, not gyrating the way Selina suggested they all do.

She noticed one of the lighting techs, Ben, off to the side, watching them. He was always sure with a smile, a quick hello. Nothing to concern her, but she made a mental note to mention it to Holden later. Maybe they needed to add Ben to her short list of Señora Rosenstein and Selina Barnes Colton. Everyone was a suspect until the killer was caught.

The music and routine soon became rote and Bella was able to observe each contestant around her, as well as the judges and board members who were present, watching every lift and spin. Somewhere among them was the person or persons who had conjured up the requirements that the winner of Ms. Mustang Valley be impossibly thin, and able to wear a size Bella last saw in middle school, if ever.

"Remember to make eye contact with the judges and smile!" Selina's raspy voice sounded over the music, the microphone taped to her cheek a bit overdone as far as Bella was concerned. Who was the star of the show, the contestants or this demanding woman known for her willingness to shove whomever she had to out of her way to maintain the spotlight?

"Watch it, Colton." It was Bella's only warning before her knees slammed to the floor, thanks to a well-placed leg that tripped her forward. Bella scrambled back up and looked at her bully, whose face was straight ahead as if nothing had happened. Recognition washed over her. Becky Hoskins, her high school nemesis.

"Hey, I'm in the same place as you, Becky. Just trying to win the scholarship." Her mental list of suspects grew to four with Becky's nasty attitude. The woman had bullied both her and Gio in high school. What did they say about bullies—that they rarely changed? But did it mean they became killers?

"Sure you are. We heard your pity story yesterday but give me a break. I've never heard of a poor Colton." Becky's mean-girl attitude hadn't improved since tenth grade. Even her physical appearance was the same; she was a slim brunette with her hair tied up in a high ponytail and exaggerated eyeliner.

The music abruptly ended and the stage was filled with the sound of labored breathing and shuffling feet.

"Hey, in the back, do you two want out of the pageant? Because we can arrange that, pronto."

"Selina's such a—"

"We're fine, Selina. Just making sure we get the steps right." Bella spoke up, knowing that Selina wasn't paying attention to anyone but herself as Bella danced through the number like a pro. Holden stood at the back of the stage and she risked a look back at him. He didn't move a muscle but the sparkle in his eyes conveyed that he was enjoying the show. Heat that had nothing to do with the physical exertion of the last hour crept up her throat, her cheeks; and her backside warmed where she imagined Holden's gaze.

This was not the ideal way to conduct an investigation, or to stay focused on being safe as she'd promised Holden. Not to mention the pact she had with her brothers to always pay attention and be aware of her surroundings. They'd made the promise to one another after their parents died because of their father's reckless driving. Their dad hadn't been known as a great guy; in fact, he'd not made much of himself and had made their mother's life miserable. And theirs. No way was Bella ever going to let her brothers down. Their bond had gotten them all a long way from sad days living under Aunt Amelia's thumb.

"Don't make us stop again. Everyone, take ten and be back here ready to go another hour." Selina's order broke through her conscience inventory and the other Colton woman walked off the stage as if she'd completed a solo dance routine on Broadway, but when she was on the floor in front of Bella she waggled her finger. "Isabella, come with me."

Don't go anywhere alone with anyone.

Holden's words echoed in her mind as she slowly walked to exit the stage. What was she going to do if Selina wanted a private talk elsewhere? It would be too obvious for Holden to follow them. Maybe he was right and she should have carried her weapon. But where would she holster it? There wasn't a concealing place on her as she wore yoga tights and tank top.

Selina stopped a few rows into the theater seats and faced Bella. Relief relaxed Bella's muscles but she tried to at least look halfway interested in what her distant, nonblood relative was about to say.

"What do you need, Selina?"

"I'll tell you what I need, Izzy." Selina's disdainful use of a childish name might have been unintentional, but it sounded mean. "I need you to back off and be quiet. There's no way I'm ever going to show any favoritism toward you. Got it?"

Bella got it, all right. But she couldn't say anything, not outright, not as a contestant, and certainly not while so many pageant personnel were listening.

"I'm sorry if I gave you the impression of expecting anything other than impartiality, Selina. Trust me, I'd never expect special treatment from you. I'm from the other side of the Coltons, remember?"

"How dare you question how I got where I am." Selina's nostrils flared and it wasn't particularly attractive on her already overly made-up face. No amount of contour cream could erase her ugly expression, stamped with anger. "I've earned every bit of my current status. Check the Colton Oil stock value. It's quadrupled since I was appointed to the board, and my PR skills are second to none in Arizona. You know how I got here? Hard work and brains. You should try it yourself, Ms. Mustang Valley Gabber."

Bella bit the inside of her cheek to keep from blurting out that she wasn't here as just another contestant and that Payne had given Selina an in at Colton Oil. "Reporting is a noble and important job, whether it's for the *New York Times* or the *Mustang Valley Gabber*. I'm not going to justify my career to you."

"Just see that you don't make the other girls think you have a leg up. Hmmph." Selina walked away as if Bella was no more than a speck of dust she'd had to flick off her shoulder. It would have been satisfying to inform her that none of the contestants were *girls*, but full-grown, adult women. But she couldn't risk getting kicked out of the pageant before she'd even begun to do her research.

Bella waited until the older woman was out of the auditorium before she headed for the staff room, where many of the contestants were sucking down water.

"What did she say to you, Colton?" One of the contestants sneered at her and Bella pasted the same smile she'd used with Selina on her face.

"She reminded me that this is a fair process and my last name has no effect on my scores."

"Here you go, Bella." Another, kinder contestant with dark hair offered her a water bottle from the refrigerator.

"Thanks." The cold bottle felt great against her forehead, her nape.

"I'm Marcie." She smiled, her patience and kindness a welcome respite from the cattiness of the morning.

"Bella."

"Don't let them get to you." Marcie unscrewed her water top.

"Who do you mean by *them*?"

"The ones who never make it to the top, but manage to ruin every pageant experience they possibly can. Like Selina. She used to compete, years ago, but never got any farther than Mustang Valley."

"How do you handle it, all the criticism?"

"I remember why I'm here. I need the scholarship." She was beautiful, with cornflower-blue eyes. "It's unlikely I'll get it this year, or even next, but my dance routine for the talent portion keeps improving and I get more confident with each try."

Bella wondered if this woman knew Gio, but she'd met most of Gio's pageant friends over the years, all of whom had dropped out by age twenty-five or so. Marcie appeared too young to have run with that crowd.

"How long have you been in pageants?" Bella worked at sounding casual, as if she needed a friend in this tough competition. What she really needed was a good source on the inside.

Marcie's gaze shifted up and to the left as she thought. "Mmm, about three years now. I started right after high school. I've got a great job with Mustang Valley Health First, the insurance company. But I want to do more. Like you, I'd like to become a nurse, or even a physician's assistant."

"Couldn't you apply for a scholarship through your workplace?" As soon as she asked, Bella bit the inside of her cheek. Marcie could throw the question back at her. *You're a contestant.* How did Holden do undercover work all the time? It was one thing to pose as a pageant competitor for this piece, where everyone knew she was also a blogger. But Holden had to pretend to be something he absolutely wasn't. And he'd had to take guff from Selina Colton, the wicked witch of Arizona from all accounts.

Marcie shook her head. "My company only pays fifty percent of tuition. I need to support my mom and younger siblings. My father died two years ago and my mom has MS. She just had a flare so it's been a rough year. I can't afford to lose the hours at work right now." Bella reminded herself that she'd give the scholarship to the runner-up if she found herself in the unlikely position of being crowned Ms. Mustang Valley.

"How are you managing work with the pageant?"

"We're lucky that all the rehearsals and practices are on the weekends and evenings."

Still, doing the mental math and comparing her own heavy work schedule to Marcie's, Bella knew it was a major effort to handle both.

"Don't look now, but you've got a sexy guy heading your way." Before she could reply, Marcie slinked off and Bella turned.

"Can I have a word with you?" Holden's presence filled up the room, or maybe it was her impression only. The rest of the women continued chatting and comparing notes on the day's routine.

"Sure." Was he going to say something about the obvious chemistry between them? She'd felt his gaze on her through the entire morning routine, and now, this close to him her skin tingled with his nearness.

This all had to be due to the high school building. It was saturated with the hormones and pheromones of students past and present, affecting her reaction to Holden.

She followed him out of the staff room and onto the stage, but in the far back, behind the heavy black curtains.

"It's stuffy back here." She made a show of tugging at her tank top, and immediately hated herself for it. Now was not the time to go all girly on Holden.

"What did Selina say to you?"

Sadly, her instinct was on-target. Holden hadn't drawn her away for a quick romantic rendezvous. She ignored the rush of disappointment and let her arms drop to her sides.

"I'm surprised you weren't able to hear the show she put on for everyone. She made it clear that I'm not getting any special favors for being a Colton." She snorted. "I never have, for the record."

"We'll talk about that later. The next time someone asks to speak to you privately, make sure I'm within earshot."

"You're saying you weren't?"

"I couldn't get there soon enough without blowing my cover, or looking like a stalker. I saw you talking, though, and trust me, if I had to get in a shot, I would have."

A chill ran up her spine and it was hard to ascertain if it was fear, awe of his ability to talk about something so deadly with ease, or her unrelenting sexual attraction to him. Bella didn't like mixed romantic signals, even from herself.

"Good to know." She looked at him and his eyes narrowed.

"What?"

"I've added two people to my suspect list. Becky, one of the contestants, bullied both Gio and me in tenth grade. Her attitude hasn't changed. Selina's insistence on running the practices, even though there's a professional choreographer assigned to the numbers seems odd to me. And then, another person caught my attention. It's probably nothing, but one of the lighting techs, Ben, is always smiling at all the women, and he watches us from the side of the stage. I thought lighting techs were supposed to be up on the scaffolding, or in the tech booth?"

"I've noticed him, too. I'm keeping an eye on him, and the other techs, as well. Trust me, Bella. Trust me enough to do as I ask."

"Okay." A warm sense of belonging filled her. But to what? Holden? She hardly knew him.

You know him better than a lot of people.

A series of claps sounded from the other side of the curtain.

"Break time is over, ladies. Back at it now, please." The announcement sounded far off, as the speakers for the school's address system hung facing the theater seats, away from the stage.

"I need to go." She turned away from him, toward stage right.

"Bella, wait." His hands grasped her forearms and she sighed.

"What?" Exasperation tinged her voice and she didn't care. "I've got to get back without anyone seeing me near you."

"Which is why you need to circle back the other way." He tugged and she expected him to move to the side and let her pass through the curtained tunnel, toward the waiting group. Instead he allowed her momentum to bring their bodies against one another.

Shock of the best kind reverberated from where her breasts flattened against his chest, down to her belly, which settled on his pelvis. He let go of her arms and waited, let her decide the next move.

Bella had experienced her fair share of relationships,

had enjoyed the occasional surprise kiss with an attractive man. But no other man made her heartbeat do the tango before he'd ever touched her. She did the next practical thing and wrapped her arms around his neck, pressed her lips to his.

With zero hesitation she was immediately in the embrace of a man whose passion ran deep, if his kiss was any indication. His lips were firm and decisive, his tongue's masterful strokes leaving no question about his intent.

Holden wanted her.

His hands were on her buttocks, lifting her up and to him, and Bella couldn't get close enough to his hard arousal. She pulled back from the most delicious kiss of her life but before she could speak Holden's cheek was against hers, his moist breath against her ear.

"It's not one-way, Bella. We both want it. But it can't happen, not now, not here." A quick soft kiss to her cheek and he turned her around and gently nudged her toward her destination.

The kiss was his best mistake to date, one he couldn't do the postmortem on until the case was over, the killer behind bars. Holden was grateful for the backstage darkness as he'd needed a few minutes to settle himself after that scorching thirty seconds in Bella's arms.

He agreed with Bella that the suspect pool was widening. But he knew from experience they could still be on the wrong scent. Was Bella's attacker someone they hadn't considered yet, someone protecting the Ms. Mustang Valley Pageant?

He couldn't call in to headquarters while he was monitoring the pageant practice. Frustrating, but a reality of his job.

When he got back to the stage area he counted the contestants and came up one short.

Leotard lady.

He immediately swung back around toward the restrooms, thinking she'd taken a quick run before Selina began her drill-sergeant tactics again. But seeing a blonde woman speaking intently to Bella stopped him. It was Leigh, a known member of the Affirmation Alliance, a local group Spencer suspected of shady practices—maybe even a cult. His pulse hammered at his temples as his protective instinct surged. Bella was vulnerable at the moment, having been attacked only yesterday and then having her home invaded by him, Spencer and Jarvis last night. Add MVPD's forensics team working outside, and it could only add to her stress. He took a couple of steps toward the group, then stopped. It would be too obvious to interrupt their conversation now. He'd have to catch Bella at lunch and warn her.

As he kept an eye on Bella and Leigh, he understood how people were attracted to the Affirmation Alliance. Their motto of "be your best you" and the promise of no more worries about anything but success would be tempting to anyone, but especially someone who was in a slump, whether it was due to work, health, or a combination of both. But it was too perfect, offering life satisfaction simply by joining the group. It had all the makings of a cult. Leigh might appear sincere, and maybe she was, but her repeated vacuous statements gave him the creeps. It didn't hurt that Leigh was the perfect image of a blonde bombshell with her platinum hair in curvy lengths around her porcelain, doll-like face, and her curvaceous figure would turn any guy's head.

Except Holden's. He seemed to only have eyes for a certain redhead these days, and worse, she was a reporter.

Chapter 11

"Okay, that's a wrap for the morning." Selina spoke with suffocating authority. She held up her hand. "Hang on a minute, though. I have an announcement from the pageant board. The judges have agreed to allow Bella Colton to remain in the contest since she and I are not related at all, and you all can no doubt already ascertain that I'd never give anyone an unfair advantage. You're all on the same level playing field here."

Several murmurs and a snide glance from Becky played out. Bella remained still, refusing to give in to Becky's emotional immaturity.

Selina clapped her hands together as if applauding herself. "That's that. You have forty-five minutes for lunch, ladies. May I remind you that there are only two weeks until you walk across this stage for the last time, with one of you garnering the crown of Ms. Mustang Valley. Ask yourself if the extra carbs are worth it, my friends."

If Bella had a coconut cream pie in hand she'd plant it on Selina's face. Bella could ignore that the woman was bossing her way around, shoving the choreographer to the side so that she could run the show, so to speak. But the admonishment to basically starve themselves was over the top. Was this how it all started, with a committee member basically telling the pageant contestants not to eat?

"I'm hungry. How about you, Marcie?"

Marcie blinked. "I'm always hungry. But you heard Selina. No pain, there will be a lot of gain." The petite woman looked down woefully at her rounded figure. "If I even look at a slice of bread I gain weight."

"That's not true, Marcie. We all need good nutrition. We're burning a ton of calories with all of this prancing around. C'mon."

Marcie's shorter legs hurried to keep up with Bella, who headed for the staff room. She had her heart set on devouring the turkey on rye she'd packed at zero-dark-thirty this morning.

"Mind if I join you?" Delilah, a willowy platinum blonde, fell into step behind them. "There are some scary ladies in this crowd, let me tell you."

"How do you know we're not two of them?" Bella couldn't help but wonder why the stunning woman who'd given the best reason for needing the scholarship would be intimidated by any other contestant.

"Trust me—I've competed against almost everyone here at one time or another. The nicest people can become ugly when so much money is at stake." Bella admired Delilah's composure and pragmatism. She'd given a heartrending speech about having survived cancer as a child, and needing the scholarship so that she could become a pediatric oncology nurse, her dream job. She'd not been able to attend college right after high school as her family needed her to go to work right away when her father became one-hundred-percent disabled in a mining accident.

"Tell me something, ladies. Does this pageant always encourage its contestants to starve?" Bella had to take this chance to get some answers.

Marcie shook her head. "I don't think they're telling us to starve."

"All pageants suggest eating healthy food, getting rid of the processed." Delilah shrugged. "It's not unique to Ms. Mustang Valley."

"Huh." Bella tried to appear mollified but her mind was doing cartwheels. This added credence to her thoughts that while she was certain Ms. Mustang Valley hadn't helped Gio in anyway, it might not be factual to state that this particular pageant had caused Gio's illness. As with all investigative reporting, she had to accept what appeared to be truth, not bend the facts to her opinion. It didn't make it easy, for sure. Not when Gio had suffered so much.

The other two women took Bella's silence as a sign the conversation was over and they all agreed to take their lunches to the school cafeteria and eat together at one of the long metal tables. A few of the other contestants were there, too, but sat separately and far enough away that conversations couldn't be overheard.

Bella saw Holden from the corner of her eye as he first walked around the cafeteria, checked the exterior doors to make sure they were locked and then lingered in the kitchen area which was visible through the various windows for different food services. It made her feel safe but also concerned her. What if the killer went after someone else while Holden's attention was on her?

"We know one another and have been through what, Marcie, five or six pageants together?" Delilah opened her bag to reveal a huge bowl of lettuce and not a lot else. Looking at the rabbit feast made Bella's stomach rumble.

"Seven if you count the Ms. Mustang Valley Holiday short pageant last year."

Delilah laughed. "When you decorated sugar cookies as your talent."

Marcie groaned and looked at Bella. "It was a total disaster. I thought it'd be easy-peasy. I bought several premade, plain cookies that were shaped like cacti. My plan was to paint them green for Christmas and blue and white for Chanukah, then add appropriately colored sprinkles."

"And?" Bella sipped her water.

"And she didn't realize that someone had put her frosting in the freezer the night before."

"Why would they do that?"

"So that I couldn't spread the frosting quickly, as you can imagine I needed to when we only have three minutes for our talent portion. It was awful. The cookies crumbled under the globs of sticky frosting that behaved more like a big, marshmallowy mess." Marcie's distress was still evident in the downturn of her mouth.

"I'm sorry, Marcie. It's hard doing the talent, I take it."

"It's not about the talent part, or that I failed miserably. What still makes my blood boil is that someone sabotaged me. I've never done anything to keep another contestant from doing her best. It's not my style." Marcie's cheeks were pink and her eyes sparkled. "If I ever figure out who it was, they'll be sorry."

Bella's hand froze over the bag of potato chips she'd

brought as a side dish to her sandwich. "What do you mean?"

"She means she'll give them the Marcie dressing-down." Delilah sprinkled more vinegar on her greens and mixed it all with her plastic fork. "When Marcie gets going, no one's immune."

Marcie giggled and Bella discreetly expelled a breath. Still, she'd have to mention it to Holden. She knew a serial killer could come across as normal. Charming, even.

"I hope it doesn't come down to you telling someone off." Marcie's story had also been touching, about how she wanted to go to the community college to earn a business degree so that she could expand her hair styling job into her own salon.

"It won't. What I didn't say when we were giving our reasons for running for Ms. Mustang Valley is that I escaped an abusive marriage five years ago. I'd planned to go to school and had saved the money, in fact, from taking every extra wedding and prom appointment possible for over three years. My ex took the money and blew it in the casino, and on drugs."

"I'm so sorry, Marcie, that's awful." Bella reached across the table and grasped her hand.

"Delilah helped me get out of my house when my ex was at work."

So that explained the friendly bond she sensed between Delilah and Marcie.

"And you helped me when I was sick."

Guilt sucker punched Bella. "I knew you both in high school but never took the time to get to know you better. I wish I had."

"You didn't need anyone—you had your brothers,

and you were always with Gio. We were all in awe of how protective your brothers were of you."

"I never saw it that way, but it makes sense now. I could have used more girlfriends, as my aunt was difficult at best. But you're right, I was tight with Gio." Darn it if her voice didn't hitch.

"I was so sad when she passed, Bella." Marcie's eyes moistened and reflected compassion. "She was such a sweet soul."

Delilah nodded. "Gio talked me off the ledge more than once. I get stage fright and if not for her I wouldn't still be competing. She was a doll."

"You mentioned earlier that you think Ms. Mustang Valley is like other pageants as far as encouraging the contestants to stay 'healthy.' As in, skinny. Has any other pageant ever suggested to you or someone you competed with that you need to lose weight? I'm trying to keep my mouth shut but I have to admit, with this being my first pageant, it's annoying to have Selina tell me to watch my carbs."

Marcie and Delilah exchanged knowing glances. Bella interpreted it as an understanding that she was clueless as to how the industry worked.

"Honey, when don't pageants tell you how you need to look?" Delilah motioned at her lunch. "Do you think I really like this much arugula?"

Marcie giggled. "I ignore it, as you can see." She nodded at her almost empty bowl of cold pasta salad. "The truth is that most local pageants aren't about physical beauty as much as they are about talent and aspirations."

"Except for Ms. Mustang Valley." Delilah's voice lowered dramatically. Bella's stomach tightened and the hair on her nape rose. She recognized it as her reporter's intuition.

"What do you mean?" She tried to make light of cleaning up her lunch refuse, not wanting either woman to hold back.

Delilah's brow rose. "It's known in Arizona pageant circles to be the worst as far as physical judging goes. And for some insane reason, the women who began their pageant careers with Ms. Mustang Valley hold it up as the holy grail, the one pageant that will make the biggest difference in their lives."

Interesting, but not enough to frame her article. "That makes sense since it's the only one that offers a full four-year scholarship to MVCC." MVCC was the largest community college in the area and boasted almost two dozen four-year career degree programs, while most just offered associate's degrees for two years of study. She'd discovered how much the college had expanded since she'd graduated from high school when she'd done her preliminary research for the Ms. Mustang Valley contest. And almost wished she had a chance of winning, so that she could have the thrill of giving the scholarship to the runner-up.

"It's more than that." Marcie's expression was grave. "It's almost as if they sign some kind of contract when they compete in this pageant."

"We all do." Bella had grimaced at some of the language, but it wasn't as bad as she'd feared.

"No, not the contract you signed for this year's Ms. Mustang Valley. They used to have to sign a lot more away, including any proceeds from commercial deals that came their way as a result of Ms. Mustang Valley, even if they didn't win."

"Isn't that standard?"

"Not at all, not anymore." Delilah kept her voice low. "There was a contestant one year in the same contest as Gio, Marcie and me, at the Ms. Saguaro Cactus pageant. She didn't win the crown but did receive a contract to appear in a national ad campaign for toothpaste—she had the brightest smile! At first she was so excited that she'd be making enough to not only put herself through college but her two sisters. Until—"

"Until the Ms. Mustang Valley contacted her and reminded her that she'd signed away rights to any monies when she'd entered her first contest, the Ms. Mustang Valley the year before." Marcie hadn't been able to contain herself, apparently, as she interrupted Delilah.

"How long ago was this?"

"Almost ten years now, I'd say."

Bella did the mental math. She wasn't positive but she was pretty certain Gio's first pageant had been Ms. Mustang Valley. And the way Gio had emphasized that the evidence of misdeeds was in the paperwork to this particular contest was interesting, but again, not enough to form a true exposé.

"You don't look like you believe us," Delilah spoke up.

"I absolutely believe you. I'm trying to match it with what Gio told me." On this, at least, she could be totally up-front with the women.

"You mean Gio signed one of those first contracts?" Marcie's face scrunched with puzzlement. "I don't remember her ever getting a contract related to the pageant."

"I'm not talking about that, but there was one advertising deal that Gio landed years ago. I'm wondering if something at the Ms. Mustang Valley Pageant, or someone, forced Gio to begin an unhealthy pattern of behavior that led to her eating disorder."

"If you're looking for that, just look around, Bella." Delilah seemed frustrated. "As much as Marcie said the pageants don't care about that impossible beach-body look, Ms. Mustang Valley winners are always very thin and fit a certain profile."

"Like what?"

Marcie nodded. "Yeah, Delilah's right. I've never known anyone with an ounce of extra weight to win this pageant."

"Yet they might win other Arizona pageants, but owe this pageant any financial gains?" Anger surged, making Bella hot and cold all at once. Was this why Gio had never treated herself after landing a lucrative contract that included her face on the bottle of a popular beach-hair-care product? Gio had won the contract from the Ms. Mustang Valley pageant the year she'd been a runner-up for the crown, before the MVCC scholarship had become the sole award. Had she not seen any of the proceeds? As her best friend, Bella felt she should know, but she and Gio didn't talk about their finances much, if at all. Would Gio's parents know?

The implication that Ms. Mustang Valley had contributed much to Gio's pain was clear to Bella, but it still wasn't enough for her report.

"If you're trying to find out why Gio had an eating disorder, that's complicated, honey." Delilah spoke with authority. "I've been there myself, and trust me, it's not a black-and-white situation. Sure, the pageant might encourage a smaller physique, but it always boils down to personal choice."

"Does it, though?" Bella wasn't going to let this sit. "Just as someone with cancer doesn't have a choice about getting it, the person with the eating disorder doesn't have a choice in how their brain chemistry works. If they're encouraged to lose weight in an unhealthy manner, it can trigger a latent tendency." Bella agreed, and saw that combined with not receiving all the money due her from the hair product ad, Gio had myriad reasons to fall into a depression.

"Right. So how can you prove that the pageant caused anyone's body dysmorphia or bulimia or anorexia?" Marcie stood. "We have to get back to the stage."

Bella threw her napkin into her paper bag. "It just sounds odd to me, is all. That the contestants of Ms. Mustang Valley have a higher rate of reported eating disorders than any other pageant in the state."

As soon as she spoke, she realized she'd gone too far. Either woman or both could easily see that she was investigating the pageant. Yet neither so much as batted a false eyelash as they made their way through the wide, dark high school corridors lined with lockers, back to the staff room and attached backstage. Bella supposed they were back in their mental game, rehearsing the dance steps and thinking about what they had to do next to secure the top spot.

They were near the last turn toward the staff room when a locker door burst open and a huge *boom* sounded with a bright white flash, reverberating through the floor and Bella's feet, landing her on her bottom next to Delilah and Marcie, who had also been blown back.

Marcie's scream sounded far away, more like a squeal, but with her ears ringing and almost blinded by the flash, all Bella could think about was getting away from the explosion.

"This way!" Delilah grabbed both of their arms,

tugged them back, away from what Bella now saw was a large cloud. Too late, she realized it was more than an explosion—there was a cloud of something hanging in the air and her eyes began to sting. They'd been gassed.

Holden heard the explosion at the same moment he saw the locker spring open. He'd been trailing the women on their way back from the cafeteria, annoyed that Bella had gone so far away from the main group all for the sake of her story. Nothing was worth her safety, not when she was the target of a serial killer.

He saw the filmy cloud appear from the locker and immediately went into biohazard-emergency mode.

"Don't breathe—hold your breath!" He did the same as he raced toward them, reaching the three just as Marcie's body hit the deck. Bella had scrambled to her feet and begun to run away, along with Delilah, and he pointed toward the end of the hallway as he held his breath and threw Marcie over his shoulder. His eyes burned and teared but he had only to get them to the exit doors, approximately one hundred feet away, and out into the fresh air.

His entire focus should be on the safety of everyone but all he felt in the moment was relief that Bella was okay, or at least would be, once clear of the detonation site. He'd never had such a visceral reaction to a citizen he was supposed to be protecting before.

They barreled through the double doors and an alarm immediately sounded, which he knew would summon MVPD.

Marcie began to cough and sputter as he lowered her to the ground, and Bella immediately supported the woman around her shoulders, squatting down to Marcie's level.

"You're okay, hon. Let it out." Bella looked up at Holden and he wanted to take the anxiety, fear and anger from her. But he couldn't, no one could, until they found the perpetrator. He didn't even know if this was the same criminal who'd attacked Bella, or if it was also the serial killer.

The case grew more tangled with each incident. Not unlike his feelings for the woman whose beseeching glance tore at his insides.

"Are you okay, Bella? Delilah?" He checked each response, and nodded at Marcie. "I'm pretty sure it was tear gas. You'll feel better the longer you're away from it." As he spoke, he became aware of the hot sun beating down on all of them, the lack of breeze. "Let's all move to under the stadium seating." The rest of the pageant contestants and board were pouring out of the staff room. He suspected the gas was tear gas, from all the reactions so far. It'd be difficult for anyone but the US military to obtain anything more toxic. But he wasn't going to allow anyone near the detonation site until he was certain.

"Over here, under the bleachers." He called to them and motioned toward where the other three huddled, in the shade. Sirens sounded and he figured he'd have backup in another minute.

As the women headed toward the football arena he called Spencer.

"Talk to me, Holden."

"Detonation in a hallway locker, right near the staff room. Similar to a flashbang but it shot out of the locker so quickly I couldn't assess it. Gas, most likely tear gas, followed. Bella and two other contestants were the targets. Marcie was knocked out from the percussion but is coming around. Bella and Delilah are safe, and I'm about to take a head count. Send the EMTs to the football stadium. I've directed all evacuees to head under the bleachers for shade."

"We're turning into the school now. Talk to you on-site." Spencer disconnected as Holden spotted the first of the several response vehicles he expected.

Holden counted the personnel as they exited the building. All were accounted for save one. He counted again, matched faces to names, and his stomach sank. While Leotard Lady, real name Debra Juarez, was back, and looking quite shaken, another one of the contestants was missing.

Chapter 12

"Anybody see Becky?" He'd memorized the list and knew the woman who'd given Bella a hard time earlier, about being a Colton, was the missing person. So far, she fit the profile of the killer more than his other suspects, but his training kept him from jumping to any conclusions about anyone.

Selina Colton shook her head, walking over to him. "No, and I haven't seen her since before our lunch break. She and Bella, Marcie and Delilah are missing."

"Bella, Delilah and Marcie are under the bleachers. Marcie's going to need medical attention. Stay with them and wait there for the police and EMTs."

For once Selina didn't argue and walked off toward the rest of the group.

Holden called Spencer.

"I've got to go back inside to find Becky. She's the

missing person. The rest of the pageant contestants, and the board, are at the football field bleachers."

"Wait for backup, Holden."

"I can't—she could be unconscious." Or worse, if the serial killer had something to do with this. Spencer knew it, too. "You're right behind me, anyhow."

"We are. I'll send a team into the school, through the doors you exited. You take the stage and staff room, until we get there. Be careful, Holden. This guy's playing for keeps."

"Roger." He shoved his phone back in his pocket and drew his weapon. The side stage exit door was still wide open and he made sure to prop it with a wedge he found just inside the door. The more air that got into the building, the better. He didn't notice any fire related to the explosion, so that was one stroke of luck in all of this.

It didn't take long to clear the stage and auditorium, followed by the staff room. He didn't go back into the hallway where the tear gas could still linger, as the door between the staff room and corridor was closed and had left the staff room behind the stage clear. Whoever had rigged the locker knew enough to enable a remote detonation. It wouldn't take a rocket scientist but this criminal wasn't unintelligent, either.

Still no sign of Becky, though. There were two spots left, the steps that were used to access below stage for special effects, and the deepest places backstage, where all that normally stood were old props. Holden circled back to them, checking every niche behind the long stage curtains, weapon held in front of him. Satisfied that no one remained on the stage, he crept to the small stairwell nestled at the far right backstage.

And found Becky, her brunette ponytail askew, lying still at the bottom of the seven steps.

* * *

"Drink up, everyone." The EMTs handed out bottles of cold water and Bella gratefully gulped from hers. Marcie was being attended to, and she and Delilah had checked out okay as did the rest of the pageant members.

Except Becky.

"I should have waited until we were all together before we left the stage," Selina verbally berated herself. Selina faced off with Bella. "Did you push her?"

Her words hit Bella in her gut and it took every ounce of her self-control to not verbally lash out at Selina.

"How dare you accuse me! Was it you?" Selina's eyes widened and if she had talons, Bella knew the other woman would have dug them into her. Bella waved her hands in a surrender gesture before Selina's fury erupted.

"Forget I said that. You and I couldn't have hurt Becky, am I right? None of us could have known what happened to Becky—we were nowhere near the backstage stairs, not one of us, right?" Bella made eye contact with each person in the group, contestants and judges alike, as they stood around in a wide circle, eager to hear the dialogue between her and Selina. One by one, they each looked at the person next to them, and shook their head in confirmation that they'd been together. Within a minute, everyone had been accounted for and determined to be nowhere near the backstage doors at the time of the explosion.

Bella nodded. "Exactly. None of us is to blame. It was more important to get everyone out of the building after the explosion than to go back and search. That had to be left to the professionals." Bella hoped Selina got the hint. Bella had no time for her drama. The murderer was giving them enough of it. She knew Holden wouldn't say it was the serial killer for certain, but she had no doubt it was, even though Becky's hair didn't fit the profile. Only hers did, with the red highlights. Why would anyone else put the pageant through all of this? And wouldn't an explosion be the perfect way to distract everyone, especially Holden, enough to kidnap one of the contestants?

But "one of the contestants" was supposed to be Bella. She fingered her hair, which had fallen out of its ponytail. Her red hair was a beacon to the killer. So why hadn't he tried to grab her in the chaos of the explosion and tear gas? Why did he go after Becky?

It impressed her that Holden was so certain it was tear gas. He'd had in-depth training at Quantico, she knew, but still. Bella wouldn't know the difference between tear gas and a heavy fog until her eyes began to water.

She'd escaped the effects of the tear gas, as had Holden and Delilah. But Marcie's eyes were still streaming tears and her skin was a ruddy shade. A fierce sense of protection welled inside her gut. Bella had only known these women, her competition, for two days and yet she felt they were part of a team.

Even Becky, for all her bluster and meddling.

"Look!" Delilah stood beside her, gaze glued to the scene at the open stage doors. EMTs were running across the small field, carrying a board. They disappeared into the building and Bella's stomach dropped. "They've probably found Becky. I hope she's okay."

"Me, too." But while she was concerned about Becky, Bella couldn't keep from worrying about Holden. What if he'd encountered the killer in the school's hallways and been hurt, or worse?

And why was she so invested in a man she'd met a little more than twenty-four hours ago?

You already know that answer.

She'd watched friends fall for someone they barely knew. She'd also seen her brother Spencer fall hard for his now-fiancée, Katrina, in a very short amount of time. When it came to finding the person you cared about more deeply than anyone else, time didn't seem to be a factor. One day or one year could be equal. But she wasn't falling for Holden.

No, Holden was the agent in charge of a special investigation. She was an undercover reporter hoping to avenge Gio's too-early death and to advance her career, truth be told.

It wasn't the time for even a brief fling, much less contemplating whether she'd met her match.

Bella was good at logic. It was all part of being a top-notch blogger and reporter. But logic and common sense blew apart into tiny shards that pierced her heart when she saw the EMTs emerge from the school with a woman, Becky, strapped to their board. At least Becky had color in her cheeks and appeared to be trying to talk, a good sign. Relief began to ease the tightness in her shoulders. Holden walked several steps behind, talking to Spencer as he led Boris to a spot to go to the bathroom.

The sight of Holden behaving completely normally lifted the rest of the tightness in her muscles. Was it normal to be this relieved, this joyous, that Holden was totally fine?

Probably not.

She was in trouble, and not just from a killer.

"It's important that we take twenty-four hours off to search the school and clear any remaining explosives."

Spencer spoke in front of the group of pageant officials, contestants and stage techs huddled under the stadium benches. "Seeing that you've all already been out here for too long, it's time to call it a day and go home."

"Wait a minute." Selina spoke up, her face flushed but otherwise not showing an iota of stress. Holden hadn't appreciated how she'd been so rude to Bella but he had to give the woman credit for composure. "You can't stop the pageant. We'll just have to move it to another venue until you declare the building safe again."

"I'm afraid that's not going to happen, either." Holden stood next to Spencer. They'd already gone over how to handle this expected reaction. "We've got the security in place here to monitor the pageant. It will take at least two weeks to find and set up security at another place in Mustang Valley."

"You're a security guard. I'll take direction from MVPD, thank you very much." Selina was back in full-blown pill mode.

"Mr. St. Clair is a qualified security expert." Spencer vouched for him, unable to reveal their ties or Holden's true identity. "He's right. Either take a full day off and continue the pageant preparations the day after tomorrow, or cancel the whole thing now."

Grumbles and complaints rolled through the small group but didn't last. Either they were all wiped from being out in the Arizona heat or frightened enough by the day's events to go along with whatever Spencer suggested. Holden watched them all carefully, and kept a hand on his phone in case his handler texted or called with information on Selina. Holden had asked him to check where she'd been during the two pageants that involved killings.

"What happened to Becky?" Marcie stood near

Bella, in the spot Holden wished he were—close enough to touch her.

"Becky's got a severe sprain, maybe a broken ankle." Spencer took his ball cap off and ran his hand over his sweating brow, then replaced it. He wore full protective gear, dressed in a tactical response uniform. Boris, his impressive K-9, was in the air-conditioned MVPD K-9 SUV. "She was regaining consciousness as the EMTs moved her to the ambulance."

"Fess up, Colton. Did you push her?" Laurel, a woman Holden had noticed seemed to stay quiet until one of the pot-stirrers like Becky spoke up, accused Bella to her face.

"I wasn't anywhere near the back stage doors all morning, in case you didn't notice." Bella held her own.

"Then it had to be you." Laurel turned to Selina. "You Coltons don't like being found out. There's no doubt you're going to give Bella extra points for being a relative. Becky had the ovaries to call you out."

"I've never been out of your sight all morning. Unless you weren't paying attention to the choreography?" One hundred and ten degrees in the shade and Selina kept her cool.

"That's enough." Mimi stepped in front of the group. "This isn't about the pageant anymore. It's about the safety of all of you, and the security of the school building. We're breaking until eight a.m. the day after tomorrow. I suggest you all practice the two routines Selina has already given you, and use the time to work on your talent portion."

"I can set us all up on videoconference. Anyone without a personal computer or laptop, talk to me and I'll have one sent to your home." Selina finally used her Colton bank for good. "I'll see you virtually tomorrow morning." Selina started for her car and a few of the contestants followed.

Bella walked up to Holden and spoke to him and Spencer privately. "I'm going back to my house to cool off. I can take Boris with me if you want, Spencer."

"You're going nowhere on your own, Bella." Holden tried to keep the growl out of his voice but he was working from a primal instinct he couldn't remember ever feeling before.

Heat flashed in her eyes, the visceral connection between them palpable.

"I can drive myself to the dang police station and wait while you two do whatever you need to here."

"Bella, go home with Holden. He's not part of the sweep." Spencer looked at Holden with understanding. He knew better than anyone how stubborn his sister could be. "We've ascertained your house is clear last night, and I've had a unit there all day, with two additional officers patrolling your property. Your house is safe as long as Holden is with you. I can't risk you going anywhere else, Bella. You could lead the killer to innocent people."

Bella's eyes widened, her cheeks pink with anger. "Wait a minute. You're blaming me for the explosion, for Becky's nasty fall?"

"Of course he's not." Holden knew he had to share in the line of fire with Spencer. "There's a criminal here, possibly a serial killer."

"You mean *probably*, don't you?"

"I can't confirm anything yet."

"Give Holden a break, Bella. Now's not the time to get all reporter on anyone."

"Oh, that's rich, Spencer. You telling me how to do my job."

"I just want you to be safe, sis." Spencer must have heard the hurt in Bella's tone. Holden wanted to take her away from all of this, to another state, another country. Anywhere but here, where the omnipresent sense of danger lurking wouldn't shake.

Bella's posture softened a smidge. "I know. But I have a job to do, too, you know. I can't do it from my house, no matter how safe. I have to figure out where the files from the Ms. Mustang Valley archive have been taken. I need to go through them, see if any of the suspects I'm looking at have evidence in them."

"Who are you looking at?" Spencer looked at Bella, then Holden.

Bella told him about Becky, Selina, Hannah Rosenstein, and Ben the lighting guy.

"You're right, sis—you need the information they contain. Someone on the committee knows where they are, and probably what's in them."

"Bella's already done a lot of the same background research that we did in our field office. But we still don't have motivation or corroboration on the suspects that are on the Ms. Mustang Valley committee."

Holden took a step closer to her and placed his arm around Bella's waist. He saw Spencer's brow raise. He didn't care. They were working a life-or-death operation and he suddenly didn't care what his best friend or anyone else thought about the nature of his relationship with Bella. His grandmother had told him that some connections were visceral, inexplicable. His attraction to—and protective instinct toward—Bella fell into that category.

Bella looked up at him, met his gaze and held it. If he was able to trust that it wasn't just wishful thinking on his part, he would say he saw a flicker of trust in her eyes. Trust in him.

"Do you think so?"

"I do. And if anyone can get someone to spill, you can. It just won't be over the next thirty-six hours." He turned to Spencer. "I've got your sister's back, Spencer."

Spencer nodded. "I know you do. I'll make sure the patrol remains in place regardless. For both of your sakes."

Holden had to fight the urge to keep his arm wrapped around Bella's waist and pull her to him as they walked across the wide field to the parking lot. He opened the door for her and then got in the driver's side of his non-descript sedan.

"Please try to see it from my point of view. This is my only chance to get this story right, and I'm coming up against brick walls in every direction." Bella spoke the moment his butt hit the car seat, and he had no doubt she was hyped up on adrenaline.

He put the car into gear and drove out of the school lot. "There are other pageants in the area, aren't there?"

"None is as important as this one, from all Gio told me. It's Ms. Mustang Valley where Gio got her start in the pageant business, and when she said her eating disorders began. I should know, as I tried to get her into a doctor six years ago, after that year's Ms Mustang Valley. For some reason, Gio's illness always flared around the time of this pageant."

"You never noticed she had issues before then?" She'd mentioned that she and Gio had been friends since grade school.

Bella sighed. "Not at the time. We did everything together, from summer camps to sleepovers. I thought Gio never ate differently than the rest of us, and she told me herself that her problems with body image and food began when she entered this pageant for the first time. Looking back, I suppose her problems may have began many years earlier than I originally thought."

"How many times did she compete in Ms. Mustang Valley?"

"Eight. Until last year, actually, when her physical appearance began to visibly suffer from the bulimia. There was a point when no amount of clothing or cosmetics could hide the toll of the bingeing and purging. It affected her mental health far longer, but it wasn't as physically visible until it was too late." He shot a look at Bella's resolute profile, the passing desert scenery serving as a colorful backdrop. The timelessness of her beauty struck him and he forced his gaze back to the road.

"It had to be incredibly difficult to watch that. When did she tell you she had a problem, or did you figure it out first?"

Bella shook her head. "That's just it. It was insidious. I had no clue at first, years ago. But gradually her symptoms began to add up to me. Her depression, bouts with anxiety, her obsession with food. Then I noticed her teeth were yellowed. Gio always had a bright smile and I asked her if she was smoking. She laughed and said no, it was from an antibiotic she'd taken as a kid. But I knew that wasn't true. Her mother spoke to me, as she was worried, too, as was her entire family. They thought I'd be able to convince her to go to the hospital. Gio had blown off their concerns. I begged her to get help, even offered to drive her to a clinic for treatment of eating disorders. Gio refused, said she'd fix it herself. Now I realize that we were both in denial of how lethal her illness was. Her mother called me a couple of months later and asked to meet me. She told me Gio had entered rehab and was in treatment. I couldn't visit her for the first part, but I did go several times to visit, when allowed."

"But that rehab time didn't do it for Gio?"

She let out a bitter laugh. "No. That's the hard part. Just like a drug addict or alcoholic, it can take several attempts to achieve a level of health that is sustainable. Gio went through treatment five times, and it looked like she was going to make it the last time. She gained weight and went back to work."

"But?" He turned onto her driveway, nodding at the MVPD officer in the cruiser on the street.

"It didn't hold. Less than two years later she was gone."

He turned off the engine and faced her. "You don't still blame yourself, do you?"

"How can I not? Sure, I've read the literature, spoken to my own therapist about it." She bit her lower lip as if regretting her admission. "I go to a counselor regularly, about once every other month. I used to go weekly after my parents died, and then again when my aunt died and my brothers and I were on our own. Despite our last name, none of the larger-than-life Coltons so much as invited us to dinner."

"That's rough. Let's go inside." He didn't want her to get warm again and the AC's effect was dissipating quickly.

"Sure, but Holden?"

"Yeah?"

"Thanks for listening. You have a lot on your mind with this case, and I'm sure the last thing you expected was to listen to a sad story."

"No problem."

No problem? He got out of the car before he said something equally ridiculous.

Bella was ahead of him and waited while he opened her door, following him only after he'd cleared the house.

As the front door closed she headed for the kitchen. Without preamble she opened the refrigerator and pulled out a pitcher of water and filled a large tumbler with an Arizona State logo. Bella gulped until it was empty, and immediately refilled it. Only after she'd finished half of the second did she stop and look at him.

"Do you want some?" Her face was flushed and large splotches of wet dotted her white tank top, dirtied from the explosion. Her breasts pressed against the light material and her skin glistened with perspiration. He rued the presence of her sports bra, which prevented him from seeing the outline of what he imagined to be perfectly round, rosy nipples.

He wished her sweat was from a long round of lovemaking, of bringing her to climax, and not from her being dehydrated.

"Yeah." He wanted "something" all right. But it wasn't anything he had a right to ask for.

She put the plastic insulated cup down. "Holden."

"Pour me a glass, Bella."

"Here you go." Bella handed him a glass and he carefully accepted it from the bottom, avoiding any physical contact. He was using every skill he possessed to keep an erection from becoming obvious.

But nothing was enough to dowse the fire Bella lit. If he did something stupid, like kiss her, how much would he regret it?

"I've got to get a shower." With no further preamble, Bella turned and fled toward her room.

Chapter 13

Bella was always mindful of water usage and made her showers short and functional whenever possible. But today had been a zinger and she needed to cool off. It wasn't from the hot sun, dance practice or running to escape the locker explosion, though.

Her body was on fire for Holden.

"Stay on course." After shutting off the shower she grabbed a towel and scrubbed herself dry. Nothing was enough of a distraction from her treacherous libido, though. Why hadn't she taken up with that pro baseball player who'd asked her out twice this past spring?

Because his brains didn't match his wallet, he didn't ignite the flame she wanted lit. Instead of regret at the road not taken, she was relieved that she wasn't attached to anyone. She was free to pursue any man she chose.

And for tonight, she chose Holden. May as well own up to it. Without further thought, she donned her silk robe that barely hit her upper thighs and belted it snugly around her waist, liking how the material provided just the right amount of support for her small breasts. Grabbing a condom from her nightstand, she slipped it into her pocket and went out into the kitchen and great room.

Holden lay on the sofa, stretched out to his full length. She placed him at six-three or six-four, as Spencer was six feet tall and Holden was taller than him. Padding across the wide-planked flooring in bare feet, she stopped no more than a foot from him. His arms were crossed and his head lay to the side, facing the back of the couch. She could make out the curve of his ear and the shadow of his short-cropped hair on the side of his head.

"Holden?" She whispered his name, her belly tightening as she anticipated his touch. Since he'd kissed her literally senseless behind the stage curtain, all Bella thought of when she looked at him was how it would feel to go beyond the kisses and into the full depth of Holden's lovemaking.

At first she thought she heard wrong, that maybe he'd said an endearment instead of her name. Until she leaned over him, straining to hear, and recognized that Holden wasn't talking.

He was snoring.

Holden woke to the aromas of coffee and bacon, two of his favorite scents. Second and third after the scent of female, which now took a place behind the scent of one particular woman.

Bella.

He looked at his watch, an antiquity he refused to give up even though most agents relied on their phones. He'd slept eight hours solid after Bella went back to her room, waking only when his alarm vibrated every two hours for him to do a house check. He trusted MVPD and the officers patrolling the yard to keep them secure, but he still wanted to check the inside regularly.

It'd taken every iota of bearing he had to not move when Bella came into the room. He'd started to doze off but immediately alerted when he heard her steps, then picked up her scent. A soft floral scent, belying the tough-skinned reporter image she projected. Mingled with what was undeniably her scent— musky, sexy, the epitome of feminine. Pure Bella.

It felt like it had been years instead of days that he'd had to keep his arms crossed, make himself not reach for her, grasp her waist, pull her to him, have her straddle him and allow him to press his erection against her until she writhed and they went back to her bedroom. Because he was going to make love to her in her bed, all night long.

Just not last night, or tonight, or anytime that he was on duty with the serial killer case. It was a rookie mistake to get involved with a civilian during an open investigation. He wasn't about to compound it by risking her safety.

"You're finally moving. Here's your coffee." She greeted him from the kitchen but stayed there, didn't come close to him again. He felt like a class-A jerk.

"I was up every two hours, checking around." He stretched, got up, walked to the counter. "Thanks."

"I'm making eggs, if you want some." She deftly cracked a brown egg against a clear glass bowl and looked at him.

"Sure, but only if you'll let me make lunch."

"Your job is to protect and serve, not cook." She added more eggs, tossed in salt, pepper, cayenne and whisked them into a frothy concoction with a fork. Her defensive posture reflected what he'd feared.

"You know I wasn't sleeping last night."

"Yeah. Got that figured out." She ignited the burner under a large pan, melted butter, poured the eggs. All without looking at him.

"It's not that I don't want to—"

"Spare me the integrity routine, Holden. My brother's a cop, remember? I know the rules as well as anyone. You can't get involved with someone during a case, especially one like this with the stakes so high. And you're protecting me, so you don't want to get distracted in any way, especially that way. Even if we did decide to pursue a connection it's pointless, in the long run. You live two hours away in a big city—I'm here in Mustang Valley. You're a big bad federal agent and I'm your nemesis, a reporter."

"You're a blogger." Wasn't that reporting light?

"A blogger and a journalist who is trying to get a job as an investigative reporter. Geesh, Holden, you still grimace whenever the word *reporter* comes up. What is your exact problem with the news media? It has to be more than what you told me in the diner."

"I don't have a problem with the media. The public needs information and it's the best way to deliver it. My problem is that I don't appreciate anything but the truth when it comes to reporting." He paused, then decided to just say it. "And I am not impressed with the dishonesty reporters utilize to get their story."

"Hmm." She moved a spatula around the pan, scrambling the eggs into fluffy clouds. He noticed the sexy robe from last night—he'd peeked—was replaced by yoga capris and a tank top. Her hair was up in a high ponytail and she had zero makeup on. And was more startlingly beautiful than ever.

Discomfort had him lean against the counter, eager to figure out what she was thinking.

After she dished up the eggs, she slid a plate and fork to him and took her plate around the counter. They sat at the same small table as yesterday.

Holden had no idea how it'd happened, but one day felt like years. As if Bella had always been a part of his life. What did Grandma St. Clair used to say? That it only took a minute when it was the right one? She'd say that whenever she told the story about meeting Grandpa in Paris right after World War II.

Was Bella his match?

"Stop it." She sipped her coffee, ate a few bites.

"What?" He decided to dig into the food before he said something more inflammatory.

"You're trying to figure out why I'm not exploding at your nasty dig toward reporters. I don't know a lot, Holden, but I do know that it's never smart to generalize or label. I'm not some jerk trying to get a story by hurting anyone or lying to them."

"You're undercover, though, pretending to be in the pageant."

She set her mug down a little firmer than necessary and her coffee sloshed over the edge. Her eyes were fire as she looked at him while sopping up the spill with her paper napkin.

"I'm not pretending to be anything, Holden. I'm in the pageant, a bona fide contestant."

"You mean to tell me you're going to take the scholarship if you win?"

She snorted, then giggled, then burst out into a belly laugh. "Holden, you are hilarious. Do you really think there's any chance of me winning this competition? Have you even looked at the other women who are close to my age? They've been doing this far longer and have the system down." She wiped her eyes with her hands. He'd made her cry, all right. To him, she was the clear winner in any competition.

"It's a fair question."

"It is. And if I won, I'd pass the scholarship on to my runner-up. But I have no reason to think I'm even in the top three. Gio used to say that by the end of day one it was pretty clear who the top five were. Trust me—it's not me."

"Who do you think it is, then?"

She tilted her head. "Marcie, because she's been around and has all the right answers, Delilah because she's Delilah, Leigh because even though she's odd, she's always on-brand, and maybe Becky. Do you know what's going on with her?"

He nodded. "Spencer said she's broken her ankle. It twisted when she was shoved down the backstage stairs. She's out of the pageant."

"Okay, so someone else is number four. And five could be any of the competitors, but definitely not me. The pageants haven't had a debut contestant final in the last ten years."

"You got this from Gio?"

She nodded. "Yes. Frankly, I have enough to write an exposé of the pageant industry in Mustang Valley, maybe even Arizona, from all that Gio's told me. But I can only corroborate it with her mother. It's not enough. And for the record? I think Leigh's a shoo-in to win. She's a little over-the-top with her positive-thinking preaching, but I sense she has a heart of gold. She has the enthusiasm needed to win." Bella's candor and total

One Minute" Survey

You get **TWO books** <u>and</u> TWO Mystery Gifts...

ABSOLUTELY FREE!

YOU pick your books – WE pay for everything!

See inside for details.

Dear Reader,

Your opinions are important to us. So if you'll participate in our fast and free "One Minute" Survey, **YOU** can pick two wonderful books that **WE** pay for!

As a leading publisher of women's fiction, we'd love to hear from you. That's why we promise to reward you for completing our survey.

IMPORTANT: Please complete the survey and return it. We'll send your Free Books and Free Mystery Gifts right away. **And we pay for shipping and handling too!**

Thank you again for participating in our "One Minute" Survey. It really takes just a minute (or less) to complete the survey… and your free books and gifts will be well worth it!

↖ We pay EVERYT•

Sincerely,

Pam Powers

Pam Powers
for Reader Service

"One Minute" Survey

GET YOUR FREE BOOKS AND FREE GIFTS!

✓ Complete this Survey   ✓ Return this survey

1 Do you try to find time to read every day?
☐ YES   ☐ NO

2 Do you prefer stories with suspenseful storylines?
☐ YES   ☐ NO

3 Do you enjoy having books delivered to your home?
☐ YES   ☐ NO

4 Do you share your favorite books with friends?
☐ YES   ☐ NO

YES! I have completed the above "One Minute" Survey. Please send me my Two Free Books and Two Free Mystery Gifts (worth over $20 retail). I understand that I am under no obligation to buy anything, as explained on the back of this card.

240/340 HDL GNPS

FIRST NAME	LAST NAME

ADDRESS

APT.#	CITY

STATE/PROV.	ZIP/POSTAL CODE

READER SERVICE—Here's how it works:

BUSINESS REPLY MAIL
FIRST-CLASS MAIL   PERMIT NO. 717   BUFFALO, NY

POSTAGE WILL BE PAID BY ADDRESSEE

READER SERVICE
PO BOX 1341
BUFFALO NY 14240-8571

NO POSTAGE
NECESSARY
IF MAILED
IN THE
UNITED STATES

unselfconsciousness tugged at something deep in his chest. A small part of the glacier that was otherwise known as his heart broke away. He couldn't hold back what he knew had to be a silly grin.

"What's so funny?"

"Aww, nothing. Just thinking about how glaciers calve icebergs."

"Some the size of small continents lately." She alluded to climate change, but like a true reporter didn't reveal how she felt about it. Which made him respect, and like her even more.

Like or lust?

He definitely was attracted to Bella—insanely so. But for the first time in forever, he was also impressed by a woman's sense of honor, integrity. Nothing like his ex.

"Now you're frowning, Holden." He liked how his name sounded on her lips. Crisp but a loving roll to it.

"I'm thinking I may owe you an apology."

"Why is that? Are you done?" She nodded at his empty plate, then carried it to the sink when he raised his hands.

"Thanks." He grabbed their mugs and glasses and set them on the counter. "Breakfast was delicious."

"You're welcome." She pulled out latex gloves and he took them from her.

"I'll clean up. You cooked—you're done."

"It's not necessary—"

"Please." He didn't budge, didn't let his gaze drift to where the tank top bared her shoulder and the lone angel drawn on it. An angel the size of a tiny fairy rested on her skin, its pink wings and hair unmistakably feminine.

"Fine. But tell me why you're so against reporters while you clean up."

She was so close, her scent teasing him as it had last night. Washing dishes was going to be his most difficult task to date on this case.

At least it kept his hands busy, and off Bella.

Chapter 14

Holden was looking at her with those bedroom eyes again. Did he realize it? Or was that expression purely a physical reaction to the chemistry that smoldered between them? Before she had a chance to consider asking him, he threw a dishtowel over his shoulder and went to work filling the sink with sudsy water.

"There's room for a dishwasher but since it's just me I haven't been in a hurry to get one."

"You don't need one. I'm here." He flashed his smile and she leaned a hip against the counter to keep from swooning toward him. Hopefully she appeared casual, not overly interested.

"Thanks. So, about your reporter hate?"

"*Hate* is the wrong word. My grandmother always said not to use it unless you really mean it."

"Is she still here?"

"No, she passed away a couple of years ago. Ninety-nine years old and still tending the same ten acres I ran around on as a kid." A wistful expression rolled across his face. "Funny, that's the second time I've thought of her in as many days."

"I've been thinking about my mom lately, too. Maybe it's the pageant, or having our lives threatened?" She tried to make it light but the words were heavy.

He finished up and faced her. "I've had one or two scary situations. Most of my work is actually pretty boring, much more than, say, Spencer's job as a sergeant and a K-9 handler. I'm not around the public each day, only when an investigation calls for it. It's easy for me to end up in the office every day, all day, for long periods as I do research and search archival evidence for clues. But the few times I've thought I might be facing death, yeah, I've had thoughts of my loved ones. I think it's natural."

"I can't say I've ever thought my life was being threatened until today with the explosion. The attack yesterday remains pretty much a blank still, other than what I already told you I remember. I'm not thrilled that someone planted surveillance equipment on my property, either, but again, that's creepy, not life-threatening."

He regarded her steadily. Not willing to look away, she allowed the heat to rise, to circle and settle in her most sensitive places. Was this when Holden was finally going to break down and do more than kiss her?

"About your question. Yes, I have a good reason for detesting reporters." At what must have been her annoyed expression he held up a hand. "Most reporters. Okay, some reporters. My ex Nicole Drew was a reporter. I went into the relationship knowing it, and ignoring it for the most part. I had no reason to judge her or her profession."

"Until?" She sensed his hesitancy to spill the truth. As if he was ashamed, or didn't want to betray his ex's confidence.

"Until I found out she was using me to get the information for an important story. The story? It involved another case I worked on. She tried to manipulate me to tell her classified information."

"I'm sorry that happened to you, Holden. That's rough."

"Rough isn't all of it, believe me. I am a total believer in free speech and the public's right to know where their tax dollars are going. But not when it comes to the security of an ongoing case, or an innocent civilian's safety."

"That can be a hard line at times." She thought about how her presence in the pageant might be what was drawing the attacker or killer out, but she didn't want to quit until she got her story. Was that what Holden was talking about?

"Yes and no, Bella. Would you put someone's life at risk for a story?"

"Isn't that what I'm doing? Putting everyone at risk in Ms. Mustang Valley because I have red streaks in my hair and I'm not quitting? Would you have to spend any time away from the pageant or school if I weren't still in the contest?"

"No, I'd be at the school for most of my time. Which isn't always the answer, to be at the event venue. Killers go for live bodies, not buildings. Today's explosion was an exception, a distraction so that no one would see Becky get shoved down the stairs. I'm convinced it wasn't an accident—she's been in Ms. Mustang Valley eight of the last ten years. She graduated from Mustang

Valley High, your classmate if I'm correct. There's no way she'd miss those stairs."

She watched him speak, saw the depth of emotion behind his words. Holden was the epitome of dedication to duty and if she wasn't already hot for his smoking bod, she'd be drawn to his honesty and intensity. Totally.

"Have you heard any more about what Becky remembers? Does she know who pushed her?"

He leaned back and picked up his phone, tapped and scrolled for a few seconds. "Yes. But no, she doesn't know who pushed her. According to Spencer, she was grabbed from behind, heard a scary voice tell her "Leave Colton alone," and then she was dragged to the stairwell. The last she remembers are hands on her back, throwing her into the pit. No one heard her scream because of the explosion."

Chills pricked at her nape. "That's horrible! And sounds exactly like the person who attacked me."

Holden nodded. "Agreed. But there's nothing we can do about it right now. Spencer and the rest of MVPD are all over the school, combing the area for evidence of any kind. The surveillance equipment we found here didn't have any prints but my officemate is searching for possible retailers."

"That's a needle in a humongous haystack." She couldn't imagine narrowing down what had looked to her like a standard surveillance camera to one particular retailer.

"Yes, but you never know. We catch criminals best when we're working all the angles."

"I'm sorry you can't be in the thick of it, Holden."

"But I am. I couldn't be at the school now, or I'd risk blowing my cover. Too many of the agents and local MVPD know me and might unwittingly reveal my true identity. I've got my laptop and I can access some sites, though not most of the ones I'd need. I'm okay with being here, Bella."

"Tell me the same in twelve hours. We're still not leaving until tomorrow morning, are we?"

"Nope. You are correct." The smoldering look was back in his eyes.

"Thanks for telling me why you don't like reporters. And I'm sorry about your ex. I can't tell you I'm not willing to do whatever it takes for the truth, though. I have done whatever I need to for a story before, and entering Ms. Mustang Valley is no exception."

He cupped her face in his hands. "You are nowhere near my ex." His breath was hot on her skin, making her lips tingle. He laughed and the chuckle vibrated through his chest, which she felt as her arms were braced against his torso. It was longing in the best way, this ache that wrapped around her. "I can't think about her when I'm looking at you, babe."

"Holden." She wanted to say something, let him know that she wasn't looking for anything other than to explore this insane desire between them. Instead she closed her eyes and wished for the stars.

Please don't leave me frustrated again.

"I haven't been able to stop thinking about kissing you again. Forgive me for overstepping my professional boundaries, Bella, but I have to have you." He lowered his lips to hers and just as on the back of the stage, her skin turned hot and her insides melted into liquid want. She reached around his waist, grabbed onto his T-shirt and tugged him as close as the embrace would allow.

Holden's tongue took every liberty with her mouth that she was willing to surrender. The moans in her throat were impossible to stem, and she almost cried out when he moved his hands lower to her hips and brought her snug against him. His need and response to her was evident and she moved her hips against his erection, needing the contact.

"Babe." He lifted her as if she was no heavier than the frying pan and placed her on the counter bar. Face-to-face, they looked at one another. His eyes were half-lidded. His hands rested on her thighs, heat searing through her workout bottoms.

"Are you sure, Bella?"

"Definitely." She leaned forward and pressed her lips to his, licked their outline with her tongue. "Don't tease me, Holden." His whiskers scraped against her skin and he fully opened his mouth to her.

Bella reveled in taking the lead, and loved that he let her. But kissing him wasn't enough. A deep part of her acknowledged that she'd never get enough of Holden St. Clair but she couldn't spend energy on the thought. Getting up close and the most personal possible with him was everything.

She wriggled her hips until her bottom was all but hanging off the counter edge, and lucky for her Holden let his arms and hands work again. He grasped her cheeks much as he had backstage, but this time, alone, certain of no intrusion by unwanted observers, he lifted her to him, his hands running the length of her hamstrings. She wrapped her legs around him as if they'd done this before, as if they already knew one another as intimately as she longed for.

Holden finally experienced what he'd suspected. Bella's skin tasted as sweet as it looked. He took his time, licking, kissing, teasing every inch of her lips and mouth. When she tilted her head back for his access, he buried his head between her breasts and one by one, kissed the very tops of them, to where her tank stretched across her chest.

"That's positively delightful," she murmured as he moved his hands over her, down her back, making circles in the two indentations he found at the base of her spine.

"You're the delight, babe." He wanted so much from her, wanted to drink from her lips and the hot spot between her legs.

"Mmm." She leaned up and gave him a playful bite on his neck, and when her tongue flicked out his erection became painful.

"I'm not going to last very long if you keep doing that." He captured her lips again and moved his tongue against hers until she whimpered her pleasure. Her nipples were visible under her bra and shirt, and it turned him on that he'd done this to her.

"I need to touch you, Bella." His voice shook with need and for the first time since he'd met her he didn't care what she thought, how he appeared. All he wanted was this moment, with Bella.

"Touch away." She trailed more kisses across his jawline.

Tracing the edge of her yoga tights he worked his fingers, then his hand, under her clothing. His pulse pounded in his ears as he felt the soft tufted hair, the heat under his fingers.

"Look at me, babe."

She opened her eyes and he thrust one, two fingers into her heat.

"Oh. My. Gosh. Holden!" She said his name with such intent he almost lost his control. Instead he focused on her pleasure, moving his fingers, exploring the newness of Bella.

Her gasps and moans led him to her pleasure points, to the rhythm that satisfied her.

"Let go, Bella. Take it."

She responded with a wiggle of her hips, a cry of passion. Holden had never held a sexier woman in his arms.

Bella gasped for breath, unable to do anything but rely on Holden's strength as he held her against the counter. The orgasm had rocked her, and he'd only used his fingers.

What was it going to be like when they were joined?

"Your room?" He kissed the base of her neck next to her shoulder and she melted against his erection.

"Yes."

"Condoms?"

"Yes."

They continued kissing as he slowly walked her across the kitchen and down the short hall to her bedroom. She slid down his body as her legs lowered to the floor, hanging on to his neck while his arms supported her, kept her from crashing.

With little fanfare they both disrobed until they stood in front of each other completely naked. Her gaze soaked in his muscular edges, the scars on his ribcage, the patch of hair over his sex. He'd driven her to an erotic point she'd never been before. There was nothing but this moment with Holden.

"I'll get, get the—"

"Wait. Let me look at you." He was breathing heavily, but stilled long enough to grasp her hands, to drink her in. His gaze trailed heat along her face, down her throat, across her breasts. As it lowered, her desire rose, and she didn't think it could become more insistent. "You're beautiful."

"You, too." Her voice was as hoarse as his, and they hadn't done a whole lot more than kiss yet. Her body shook with need, and she was glad the wanting was stronger than what lay under her passion.

Fear. Fear of the ferocity of their connection. No lovemaking had ever affected her like this before.

"Where are the condoms?" He was moving toward her nightstand, and at her nod he opened the drawer and took out her box of condoms, the box she'd only opened last night.

"Lie on the bed, Bella." He donned the condom with ease and waited for her to lie down, which she did with relief. Her trembling knees weren't going to support her much longer.

Holden knelt over her, his knees coming to rest between her legs, and his forearms supported him on either side of her head. She tried to think of something funny to say to break the moment but words failed her. She, the writer, blogger, investigative reporter, was at a loss for words as she was about to make love to a man she'd only met two days ago, yet didn't know how she'd lived without him until now.

When he continued to look at her, she smiled and reached her arms around his neck. "I can't take it anymore, Holden. Please, please take me." She tugged on his neck and she watched him lower his head, watched until his lids covered his eyes and she, too, closed her eyes.

It was all feeling now. Lips against lips, tongues wrapping and touching, skin against skin. The rough calluses on his palms ran paths down the outside of her thighs as he lowered his erection onto her, and then with one last deep kiss, plunged into her.

"Oh!" The intimate contact knocked the air from her lungs, sent tingling sensations across her skin down to her toes. It was so very, very good with Holden. Delicious.

"Hang on, babe." Holden began to move, first filling her fully and then pulling back no farther than he had to, to her great gratitude. She needed him inside her, to never leave, to keep the rolling wave crashing against the sands of her heart.

"Holden!" She couldn't stop the climax that hit her, but it wasn't enough for him. He kept moving, then reached his hand between them to touch her in the most perfect spot until she experienced an orgasm unlike any other.

"Bella." Holden cried out her name, joining her in the exquisite pleasure.

Bella wanted to hear him say her name again and again.

Chapter 15

Bella left Holden as he dozed atop her sheets and dove into the bathroom for a quick shower. It was enough time, though, to collect what was left of her thoughts. The sex with Holden had been so much more than she'd imagined, and definitely more than she'd bargained for. Electric, elemental, primal.

Life altering.

Do not go there.

She couldn't. There was the pageant, Gio's honor and a killer that Holden was after. Probably another criminal, too, if some of the attacks turned out to be those of a lesser villain. Maybe everyone who made it to be a contestant was put under surveillance. She'd have to ask Spencer about it later. He might not be able to reveal anything about an ongoing investigation but he could let her know what petty crimes had occurred during Ms. Mustang Valley in years past, couldn't he?

She opened the bathroom door and found Holden still stretched out on the bed in all of his sexiness. Her body immediately reacted and she forcefully focused on the exit.

"I'll be in my office." She gave Holden a quick smile before she left and went into the other bedroom that she'd converted into her writing space when she purchased the place over five years ago. She had to get out of her bedroom, away from Holden's naked bod, or she'd never check in to the videoconference session.

Would that disqualify her from the pageant?

"Give me a sec before you go." He deftly dressed, as if taking a woman to bed first thing was a daily occurrence. With a pang she realized it might be. How much did she know about Holden, really?

Enough to know that her brother wouldn't have become friends with him during his service, much less maintained the bond years later. And she'd watched Holden in action all day yesterday. He was a professional who put justice and safety of all civilians first. Otherwise he would have left her, Marcie and Delilah to get out of the building on their own while he tracked down the culprit.

"Hey." He was dressed in his white T-shirt and jeans again, and standing next to her. "Where did you go?" So he'd seen her drift off.

"I was thinking about how great you were yesterday. You made sure we were all safe. Don't you regret not going after the bad guy?"

He frowned, tilted his head. "I didn't have a bad guy to go after. At least, not in my face. It wouldn't have mattered though, because whoever it was had already made their way backstage and taken Becky. I want to point out that it's a good reason to eliminate Becky as the killer, but Selina and Ben might still be involved. I'm sorry Becky got hurt, but all three of you could have been gravely hurt or worse, if there'd been a connected fire. Then we'd have had four casualties instead of one."

"Said like only an FBI agent can." She tried to grin but her lips trembled and tears filled her vision. What the heck?

"Hey, come here." He pulled her to him, crushed her against the broad piece of wall that was his chest. "You've been through so much. You're a trooper—you haven't so much as complained. Let it out."

She wasn't one for spilling tears on a guy's shoulder, but it was Holden's shoulder and he was wearing a nice soft cotton T-shirt that felt so comforting under her cheek. "Sorry." She sniffed.

"Nothing to apologize for. The stress has to come out one way or another."

The meaning in his words took a heartbeat or two to reach her brain. She pulled back and looked up at him. This close she had to crane her neck back, he was so tall.

"Are you saying that, that—" she pointed at her bed "—was like a stress-relieving ball? I'm not sure how I feel about being compared to a squishy heart-shaped toy."

His eyes smoldered with a sliver of what she'd witnessed only minutes earlier.

"For the record, I don't hook up with women I work with, agent or civilian. And if I had any smarts I wouldn't get involved with my friend's sister."

"But?" She realized that it already had become second nature to coax details out of him that she was certain he'd rather keep close, private.

He looked away, and she saw the pulse ticking on the side of his jaw. Its visible, rapid staccato was incongruous to the air of total control and order he projected. When he turned back she saw the emotions that matched in the depths of his dark, dark eyes. Wonder. Passion. Regret?

"What happened did because we're both attracted to one another and have been through a heck of a lot of dangerous scenarios in the past forty-eight hours. But don't mistake me, Bella. I'd want you just the same, just as much, if we'd met on a tour bus to Smithsville." His mention of one of the oldest and most worn-out tourist attractions near Mustang Valley made her giggle. Smithsville was as corny as it got, with a fake Wild West ghost town and cheap souvenirs. Old-fashioned carnival games and rides completed the ridiculous ambiance.

"Smithsville? I haven't been there since second grade, on a terrible field trip with a teacher who told us she wanted to be a zoo keeper but couldn't get into vet school."

"How do you remember those details?" The lines on his forehead deepened with what she'd come to understand as his *Get out!* expression, when he found whatever she said incredible. Or maybe unbelievable was more like it.

She shrugged. "I've no idea. Spencer has the same talent, ever since we were little. He memorized all the commercial jingles and cartoon skits from our favorite shows."

"You're correct. Spencer was the best navigator to have in a platoon as he never forgot a landmark. We didn't need satnav during training when we had Spencer with us."

"Yup, that's my brother." She hoped her light banter hid how much she was moved by his reminder that he'd served the same time as Spencer. She'd always hated Spencer could have faced combat during his military stint. To know Holden, too, had served and risked the same chance of being sent to a war zone froze her insides.

She'd have never met him. And now that she had, she wasn't thrilled that his job was so dangerous, just like Spencer's.

Gio, girlfriend. Don't forget Gio.

"Is Jarvis like that, too?"

"In a lot of ways, yes." She missed Jarvis, even though he lived in Mustang Valley, too, but on a ranch in the crew quarters. His long days, every day, made him busier than even Spencer. She had a full schedule, too, but at least she had the option of working from home as needed. "Look, I've got to get in on the meeting that starts in five minutes or I could be kicked out of the pageant."

His gaze immediately shuttered and he looked like the security guard she'd met when she checked in. "Keep the door open so that I can have a bead on you at all times."

"Aye-aye, sir. Or is it *roger*?"

He didn't respond but for a growl in the back of his throat. It reminded her of how his voice had gotten deep and rumbly while they made love.

Yeah, she needed to make the video meeting.

Holden circled the entire inside perimeter of the house for the umpteenth time in an hour, waiting for Bella to be done with the pageant training session. He heard Selina's voice ring out from the laptop speakers, counting as he imagined Bella doing the coordinated dance moves. Holden wasn't a dancer or into performance art but he imagined it wasn't much different from orchestrating a takedown operation. Everyone in their place at the right time, knowing exactly how and why they would execute their moves. Plus have a backup plan.

He didn't look in on Bella because he didn't trust himself. After the best sex of his life how could he?

It's more than sex now.

Indeed. He looked through the living room window, saw the cruiser parked beyond a grove of cacti. Two MVPD officers patrolled the property, and he saw one or the other as he made his interior rounds, through windows. It couldn't last very long, the response from MVPD. They were overworked as it was, with recent events in town now including looters who'd taken advantage of homes damaged in the recent earthquake, investigating the attempted murder of Payne Colton and keeping tabs on the Affirmation Alliance Group. He knew from his background checks on each contestant that Leigh, the woman going out of her way to speak to Bella during the pageant practice, was a part of the mysterious group.

He had to find who was sabotaging the pageant before MVPD called the protection off Bella. Before the killer got to her, or any other contestant.

"Bella, your posture is totally off." Selina's voice blared out from Bella's office and he wanted to tell Selina just how incredible Bella's posture had served them both earlier. Making sure she was safe inside the house, he went outside to do a perimeter check. He knew that MVPD was patrolling the outer edges of her property, but Holden needed to see the house entry and exit points, make sure they were secure.

In case you want to make love to Bella again?

"Keep it in your pants, St. Clair," he muttered to himself as he again checked the bathroom's window locks. It bugged him that there was a high clear window in Bella's bathroom. He texted Spencer and asked him to bring either sticky opaque peel-on covering or curtains. He didn't care which, but he wanted to know that no one could see inside the house.

Be there in five.

His reaction to Spencer's immediate reply surprised him. Shouldn't he be grateful for the break from his position of constant vigilance? He could talk to Spencer while Bella continued her modified pageant practice, knowing that there was an additional LEA on-site in case the killer came back.

Instead he had a serious case of guilt. He and Bella were adults, and his decision to break his professional protocol to be with her was solely his. And Bella's decisions were her own, too. But—and it was a big but—Bella was his buddy's sister. No escaping that. And if Spencer caught a hint of what had gone down this morning, he'd be up in Holden's grill.

Which he totally deserved, but didn't want to have to deal with.

His phone vibrated and he answered his supervisor's call. "Holden."

"We've got DNA confirmation that it was the same killer in both previous pageants." His boss wasn't one to waste time on preliminaries, which Holden usually appreciated but this case had more meaning to him.

Bella.

It was as if his boss had punched him in the gut. He

sucked in a deep breath, fighting his nerves. Fighting the fear.

"Copy that. Any clues as to his identity?"

"We don't know if it's male or female, but the pattern seems to fit a male killer as he's always picking female victims who bear a resemblance to one another."

"He's making up for a lost love."

"Or nurturing pain from a loss that was never processed. Like a mother, or former girlfriend or wife. Both victims had red hair and green eyes, so we're looking at a mother figure with the same."

"Did anyone else get hurt at those pageants, contestants who survived?" Holden had to ask, even though it showed a hole he'd missed in his own research and investigation.

"Yes. In each case, anyone who had a visible problem with the victim was either assaulted or had other criminal activity that appeared aimed at them. One had a car stolen, abandoning her at a diner in the middle of nowhere. Another incident involved the death of a contestant's dog."

"What had the contestant done to warrant their pet being killed?"

"They criticized the victim. Apparently our killer is very defensive of his targets."

Holden breathed in and out in a steady rhythm as he'd learned to do to keep his anxiety at bay. The thought of Becky being shoved down the stairs on the same day she'd verbally sparred with Bella made him nauseous. "It sounds like positive confirmation that it's the same guy, then." He told him what had happened with Becky, how Becky had given Bella a hard time two days ago.

"We're close, Holden. Don't let up, and we'll have the killer before the end of this pageant."

"Yes, sir." After they disconnected, Holden took a minute to look at the blue sky, the small yard that backed up to pure desert beauty. No wonder Bella enjoyed living a little farther out from town. This spot had a quiet peacefulness he missed while living in Phoenix.

A treasured quiet shattered by a monster.

Chapter 16

Holden had suspected it was the serial killer that plagued the other two pageants, and now he had proof, or as close to definitive evidence as he'd have until he apprehended the bastard. The same DNA had been discovered at both murder sites, indicating the same killer. He didn't have DNA evidence processed from the Ms. Mustang Valley pageant yet, but he wasn't waiting on it. The fact that Bella was his next target was clear enough. From the camera he'd found on her window to the attack on first her and now Becky, the killer was following his or her own profile to a *T*.

Bella. He had no regrets about making love to her that morning, but it had been too risky. If anything had happened while he'd been distracted…

You knew you were safe, protected. MVPD had been there the entire time. Still, Bella was more than a woman he was attracted to in a very big way. She was his friend's sister. He owed the truth to Spence—that he'd let his dick run the show that morning. Of course, that put Holden at risk, because Spencer was likely to clock him when he found out he'd put personal pleasure over mission requirements.

Before he had a chance to come up with the best way to let Spencer know that he had made sure the other LEA were in place before he made love to Bella, he heard the crunch of steps on the crushed seashells and gravel.

Spencer rounded the far corner of the yard, his expression resolute. They were on the eastern edge of the house and property so there was still some shade thrown by the house, but it was rapidly narrowing as the sun traveled across the sky.

"Hey." Spencer nodded. He was alone, with no sign of his dog Boris or the curtain Holden had asked for.

"Good morning. Did you find something to block out the view through the bathroom-shower window?"

"I did—it's in my SUV. I wanted to talk to you alone first, without Bella hearing us. Is she inside?"

"Yes. She's busy on a videoconference for the pageant, in the spare room, so we can go inside if you want." It was at least twenty degrees cooler in the house.

Spencer shook his head. "Not right away. First, give me the rundown on what you have so far."

"Not as much as I'd like, but I do have some new information from my office in Phoenix." Holden outlined where they were so far, including the description of the explosion he'd gleaned from Bella and the other women. He told Spencer about finding Becky at the base of the backstage stairwell, and that she was expected to make a full recovery. "I'm waiting for you to tell me we can resume pageant activity at Mustang Valley High. Or do you think we need to move it?"

Spencer shook his head. "No, we're not moving it. My chief talked to your boss, too, and they're in agreement that this might be the only chance to catch the serial killer. At least it looks like we can take Becky off the suspect list. Although, frankly, I'm not ruling out anything."

"You think Becky threw herself down the stairs?" Holden knew it was possible, but considered it unlikely. It would have been too difficult for Becky to set off the bomb at the same time.

"It's always possible. No matter, we're going to go ahead with the pageant. We've got the high school locked down tight now. I'm concerned that if we move it anywhere else, it could leave a hole for the killer to sneak through."

Holden's gut twisted. "I don't like where this is going, Spencer."

"You think that I do? Bella's my sister, man." He didn't say what they both knew, he didn't have to. The killer had his target on Bella. She fit the profile perfectly with her green eyes and red hair.

"I can put a call in to get a substitute, a look-alike." But Holden knew that the FBI didn't operate as it was often portrayed on television or in the movies. Finding an agent who matched Bella's description wasn't easy, and they didn't have enough time. Plus it would involve letting the entire pageant know that Bella was out, some stranger that looked like her was in. Even if they cut in the contestants and board on the undercover op, it wasn't safe. It risked spooking the killer, too.

"We both know that won't happen in time, don't we?"

"Yeah." Holden crossed his arms in front of his chest.

"I have to think about how we're going to work this when we go back to the school. I'm pretty certain the killer is behind the attacks—who else would it be? But I don't like that he's actually a part of the pageant, and that we haven't figured out who it is yet. We've yet to confirm that any one person has worked all three pageants."

"I hear you. I'm working on a difficult case myself." Lines appeared between Spencer's brows.

"Yeah?"

"Are you aware of what's going on in Mustang Valley with the other side of the Coltons? The rich side?" Spencer grinned and it reminded Holden of the laughs they'd had downrange. Humor was imperative when facing life-or-death situations each day, and Spencer's had helped him through.

"I'm up to speed on the fact that Ace Colton was switched at birth, that no one knows by who or why. And the man he thought was his father, Payne Colton, remains in a coma, correct?" Holden had almost forgotten about that case, as he was so wrapped up in the pageant killer.

"That's right." Spencer shifted his weight, his concern evident. "We finally tracked the email sent via the dark web to Colton Oil that spilled the beans on Ace Colton not being a biological Colton. It was from a man named Harley Watts's laptop, and he admitted he sent the email, as ordered by his boss. He was about to tell us who exactly he worked for, but then he had a visitor and clammed up."

Holden's nape tingled. "Who was the visitor?"

"Have you noticed the contestant Leigh Dennings?"

"Blonde, pretty, always super nice—to a fault. Yeah, I've noticed her." He'd cringed as she'd spoken to Bella the other day. "She's with the Affirmation Alliance Group, right?"

"Yup. She's a big follower of Affirmation Alliance Group, AAG, one of their 'welcome managers.'"

"Right. I've heard of AAG, and have read quite a bit of backstory on them. I've been keeping an eye on her, but frankly most of my attention is directed at keeping Bella safe and catching the killer." He had two large interests that drew him to apply for the FBI: serial killers and cults. This particular case should be his dream LEA op, but instead he'd found himself more worried than intrigued.

It was a different way to work a case when he cared about someone he was supposed to be protecting.

He cared.

Did he care for Bella or would he feel the same about any woman he was attracted to right now?

"So you know that AAG is dangerous, Holden?"

"I do. I've warned Bella to be careful around Leigh, who seems very nice and welcoming, but—"

"But you know she'll suck the spirit out of you and she shares everything she's told and overhears with her superiors in the group. It's creepy at best, a cult at worst. I don't want Bella anywhere near her." Spencer sounded like the protective brother he was.

"Near who?"

Bella's voice came from the back patio, where she stood with two iced glasses of water.

"Is your rehearsal session over?" Holden smiled his thanks as he took the large tumbler, gulping down the cold nectar.

"Answer my question. Who were you talking about?" When Holden didn't reply, she focused on her brother.

"Spencer?" Their sibling bond was evident, as was her irritation at her brother for not speaking up.

Holden had served alongside Spencer Colton and trusted him with his life. He'd never seen Spencer as much as blink in the face of danger. Yet he appeared to have hit a wall—his sister.

"I can't talk about an active investigation."

"Holden?"

Green eyes he'd seen lit from within as he moved inside her, bringing her to a second climax, looked at him with exasperation. And a hint of warmth that hadn't been there a day ago. "Let me guess. You're talking about Leigh."

Holden exchanged a glance with Spencer.

Bella rolled her eyes. "I already know you're investigating AAG, Spencer. They've come up at *Mustang Valley Gabber* more than once. It's hard to miss an always-positive, be-your-best-you kind of group when it shows up in our small town. Spit out whatever else you know, Spencer."

"I don't know anything new, unfortunately. But that doesn't mean you can trust Leigh. I wish you'd quit this ridiculous pageant." Spencer wiped his brow and Holden felt the sweat pouring down his back. They needed to move this inside soon.

"As long as you intend to remain in the pageant, Bella, you need to be very careful around her. We don't know her motives." Holden knew Bella didn't like anyone telling her what to do, but he had to be honest with her.

"I used to think the way you both do, about Ms. Mustang Valley. About all beauty pageants. But they're not all about looks when they have scholarships available, and when there are more scores in relation to talent and essays and answering questions." A red blush highlighted her smooth skin, her determination etched on her expression.

"Sounds like you've been drinking some Ms. Mustang Valley drink that's brainwashed you, sis." Spencer wasn't moved by his sister's beauty.

"That's not fair, Spence, and you know it. I'm the biggest skeptic of all three of us." Holden instinctively knew she wasn't referring to him but to her brother Jarvis, Spencer and herself. "But since I've gone through the application process and have made it to the contestant phase, I've seen different sides of the pageant."

"Such as?" Spencer's incredulity was hilarious but Holden thought better of laughing aloud while the siblings were hashing it out.

"The women competing for the scholarship really need it. They are doing this to better themselves, Spencer. It's no different than when you and I fought like heck to get into college and then to find a way to pay for it."

"Except we didn't have to parade around in a bikini to get our scholarships, or suck up to a bunch of tight-lipped snobs."

"No, we didn't, but we knew we had other options, and it worked out for us the first time around. It doesn't happen for a lot of people, Spencer. Definitely not the initial time they apply." Bella's passion stirred a deep longing in Holden. For a partner, sure, but for more. Something lasting.

"You may be right." Holden couldn't tell if Spencer didn't want to upset Bella any more or if he really was believing her. He suspected it was a combination of both. "But you still need to be very careful around

Leigh. She's associated with a dangerous group, and that makes her a suspect."

"You don't think she's a murderer, do you? And are we sure there's a murderer or are we talking more of someone who gets off on scaring and injuring people? I know the DNA proved the other two murders are linked, but maybe we don't have the same person here."

"Murderer."

"Serial killer."

Holden's reply melded with Spencer's and he watched Bella's eyes widen for an instant before she regained her composure.

"Well, at least you two agree. Here I thought going after Selina Barnes Colton's backstory was going to give me an extra juicy piece to work on, next to my exposé."

"Both stories could get you hurt or worse, Bella. At least wait until we identify the killer." Spencer was on a roll. "What's so wrong with staying put at the *Mustang Valley Gabber*? You've built up a good readership and you like it, don't you?"

"I want more. I can do more. I'm going for a bigger job. If it were Jarvis looking to do something besides his ranch work would you be giving him such a hard time?"

Sensing a standoff between the two, Holden cleared his throat. "I don't know about the two of you, but I'm sweating bullets out here. Why don't we go inside?"

"You two go. I've got to get back to work. Let me get the curtain out of my car." Spencer stalked off and Bella shot Holden a questioning glance.

"Curtain?"

"Yeah. I asked him to bring me something to block the view through your bathroom window."

"The one with the camera." He saw her shudder. "You really think it's the killer, don't you?"

Integrity warred with the need to protect her from all harm, psychological as well as physical. Her vulnerability was guarded with her defensive posture, but he knew the softest parts of her, the treasure that the killer wanted to wipe off the face of the earth.

Bella's safety was paramount. She deserved nothing less than the truth.

"I'm positive it's the killer."

They thought they were smart, holing up at her house. The cops weren't going to make the job easier but the challenges were often the most exciting parts of the lifestyle of a professional killer. The only thing more fun was watching the girls die.

They were stupid, stupid girls for entering a beauty contest. The redheads rarely got as much attention as the blondes. Didn't Mommy always say that? She'd never been paid any attention by Daddy, who ran out when Mommy had a two-year-old to raise. The memories of lurid fights were still there, no matter how young the brain had been.

Mommy needed someone to help her die and that's where the best lessons were learned. Bella Colton would join the rest of the redheads that had died with love and affection, all because of what Mommy taught as she lay on her deathbed, unable to be cured of the awful disease that took her.

Soon, Bella, soon. I'm coming to save you from this awful life. Your death will be so, so peaceful. After I get you all to myself.

Chapter 17

"I'm craving a steak." Bella eyed the menu, her only protection between her and Holden. His aura wrapped around her as he sat across the Formica table on the opposite booth bench, his legs too close to hers.

"Get whatever you want." He'd already perused the menu then shut it without much prevarication.

"Are you sure? I mean, I don't want to take advantage of the government tab."

"It's not on the FBI—it's on me."

That made it sound like a date, except Holden wasn't playing the part. She'd angered him when she'd pushed to get out of the house late this afternoon, and she didn't blame him for being annoyed with her. If it were her guarding him, she wouldn't want him to leave a building that was surrounded by MVPD officers and wired with extra security systems that Spencer had Jarvis install today.

"I'm sorry, Holden. I know why you wanted to stay at my house, but after you told me that I'm definitely a target, that you know it's a killer, I couldn't stay there one more minute. The killer's been to my house, my home." She picked her menu up again. "At least he didn't get inside the house."

"No, there's no indication that he did." Holden looked at her with his dark, dark eyes and she wished they were back in her bedroom. Instead they were out of Mustang Valley and having a late dinner at an upscale shopping strip several miles away, hoping to get a mental break from the weight of the case.

"Thanks for coming here."

"Is it a place you go often?" He looked around at the southwestern-chic surroundings, the soft lighting even in the early afternoon, the linen tablecloth. She sucked in a breath when his gaze landed back where she craved it. On her.

"No, not really. I mean, I like it here, but I've only recently started to earn enough to come here whenever I want to."

"You seem very successful for a reporter. I'm told it's a brutal business."

Again with the allusion to his ex. She wished Holden had never met that woman. "All writing is difficult to make a living at. It's the way it is. But I hold my own, and if I can manage to get the kind of job I want, I'll be doing very well."

His face stilled and she saw it as a warning sign. A red flag that she was encroaching his offensive.

"You have to have a passion to do your job."

"A passion? I see it more as the desire for the truth. Always the truth, no more, no less."

"At any cost?"

"That's an odd question. It depends on what the story is. The pageant story, yes, I feel I'm willing to do whatever it'll take, because Gio gave her all to this system, in the worst way. Now, if I can glean some dirt on Selina in the process, you bet I'll take it and run with it. But Selina Barnes Colton isn't worth staying in the pageant for. Definitely not worth being stalked by a serial killer."

His face had turned to stone, reminding her of the sandstone cliffs she enjoyed hiking whenever she escaped north to Vermilion Cliffs National Monument. At least the cliffs reflected the setting sun. Holden revealed nothing. Wherever his thoughts had gone was a dark place.

The waitress took their orders and they remained quiet as their drinks—sparkling water for her and a cola drink for him—were placed on the bistro-style table that was covered with a white tablecloth, a nice touch in an otherwise casual dining atmosphere.

"Do you have any idea when we'll go back to the school?" She ran her fingers on her sweating tavern glass.

He shook his head. "It's up to MVPD to give the all clear. They're working with us, of course, and I don't anticipate it'll take much longer."

"I'd imagine it'll be a mess, from the explosion."

"Naw. It looked bigger than it was. The explosive was very small—it was how and when it was detonated that made it so scary, and loud. The tear gas was for added effect but didn't damage anything in the vicinity."

"Yet if any of us had been closer it could have killed us."

"Getting hit by the locker door, yes, technically it

could have injured you. But the tear gas was the real weapon. And surprise."

"Yes."

They changed the topic to less lethal topics, to include what each planned to do when the case was closed, the killer caught.

"I need some time out in the desert, under the stars." Holden had a dreamy expression on his face.

"You mean, away from Phoenix?"

"Yes. I enjoy being on my own, backpacking through state and national parks. There's too much light pollution in Phoenix to enjoy the night sky."

"I get that. I like to birdwatch, and the desert is a great place to do it. I'm lucky I can watch as much as I do from my back patio. But I hear you on the hiking— it's great to exercise while soaking up nature."

"Have you ever camped?"

"Out in the wilderness, like you? No." She met his gaze and his intent was unmistakable. Holden meant, had she ever made love in the night, under the stars. Heat pooled between her legs as she imagined sharing a sleeping bag with him.

"I'd love to take you with me sometime."

"Well, that might not be for a bit, considering we have a killer to catch, right?"

Holden didn't answer but kept his smoldering gaze on her, promising pleasure without even touching her.

She welcomed the arrival of their food, wanting a distraction from the memories. It wasn't enough that she and the other contestants, save for Becky, had made it out all right. She would not rest until the killer was caught.

"Spencer wants me to get an undercover agent to fill in for you."

"No way." She chewed her food, pointed her fork at Holden. "You know me well enough to figure out my body language. If I think I'm in trouble, I'm going to let you know. And this killer is smart, or they wouldn't have gotten away with two previous murders and all the crimes around them."

At his stunned look, she grinned. "I've been doing my own research, Holden."

"Clearly." He took a bite of his sea bass and she watched his Adam's apple bob with each swallow, saw the stamp of masculinity in his strong jawline. Her lips tingled with the memory of kissing that very line of bone, using her tongue to make him groan with desire.

They'd been incredibly compatible in bed.

"Tell me again about your ex. Why you hate reporters and have never changed your mind about them."

He set down his cutlery, sipped through the straw for a moment. When his gaze met hers, she noticed the fine lines at the edges of his eyes. Her fingers itched to smooth them. "You tell me, Bella. You're the one who's putting her life at stake to get the answers you want to avenge your best friend's death. A death, I might add, that was the result of her choices over the years."

"That's cold. No one chooses to be sick with an eating disorder or any other mental illness."

"You chose to write about it." He took a long swig of his soda. "Tell me you'll write anything other than what you've already decided will be the story."

Indignation rushed over her, and she was grateful for the semi-fancy restaurant or she'd recook his fish right here, with a votive added in for pleasure. "I do not pre-write my stories. That's the epitome of the worst kind of reporter. It's not reporting—it's creative writing."

"You mean to tell me you've never embellished story

details to get a better headline?" His derision scraped against the trust she had felt building toward him.

"No, I haven't. Sure, the *Mustang Valley Gabber* isn't the *Wall Street Journal*, but our, my work ethic and personal ethics have stayed the same."

"Yet you want to ask me what I know about Selina Barnes Colton." His lack of empathy was chilling. What had triggered him?

"Of course I do, if you know her or anything about what's going on with Payne Colton. You can see why I would, don't you? It could be foul play that landed him in a coma. How do we know it wasn't Selina behind it?"

"We don't. But I've found the press to be a bit rabid over a man who's been good to his community his entire life."

"Many wealthy people's companies have given lots of money to charity."

"Answer me this, Bella. If you found out that I knew the story behind Selina but couldn't tell you about it, what would you do? Would you try to force it out of me?"

"I'd do my journalistic duty to get the information from you, yes. You can't blame me for trying to do my job!"

"I can if it compromises an active investigation."

His resolute expression struck a chord with her. What had she been thinking, going to bed with him last night? She didn't know him. Maybe Spencer vouched for him, and Jarvis thought he was a good guy, but the side she was seeing now wasn't the man she'd thought she'd known.

How can you really know someone after only a few days?

"I need to use the restroom. Excuse me." Before he

stood up and tried to tell her he needed to follow her, as part of his protection role, she darted into the hall behind the bar, where the rooms were located.

Bella couldn't believe it but she had to get away from Holden before he saw what his words did to her. This wasn't like her, to get emotional over something a man said to her. She'd had a rough start in life, and she was thirty-one, not some adolescent being chastised by her first-ever boss. Still, Holden's words had stung, burrowed under her thick skin and found what she valued most.

Her passion for finding the truth and writing it into a succinct report.

After she splashed some cold water on her face and gave herself time to calm down, she headed toward the dining area. Laughter spilled from a room farther back in the café and she saw a big sign with gilded letters that welcomed a baby shower party.

Standing by the sign were Marlowe and Ainsley Colton, her distant cousins. She couldn't stop from staring. Marlowe's stomach was huge, and Bella vaguely remembered that she heard she was pregnant and engaged. But that had been months ago and Marlowe appeared near the end of her pregnancy, or maybe she was having multiples. Each of the women wore springy dresses and sandals—Ainsley's were high spikes while Marlowe's were lower and chunkier, offering her more support—and were laughing, their heads close together. A tight pang of exactly how alone she was when it came to the Coltons made her wish she knew them better. Why had her parents disengaged from the family? And why did Aunt Amelia keep up the same type of emotional walls that made Bella, Jarvis and Spencer the estranged cousins?

As if her presence drew their attention, they both looked over, spotted her and turned toward her at the same time. Panic gripped Bella but she found herself walking toward them, smiling.

"Bella! It's so nice to see you." Ainsley spoke first, and Bella couldn't help but notice how all three of them were petite.

"Yes, it's been so long." Marlowe's soft smile showed none of the malice she'd remembered as a kid, from when they'd be at a Colton reunion on Rattlesnake Ridge Ranch. No one had ever played with her or her brothers. Bella had used the time at the picnics to wander through the immense home, imagining she was a princess and it was her private castle. It had always been her, Spencer and Jarvis. Which had served them all well, and she loved her brothers with all her heart. But it would be nice to know more family.

"We were so sorry to hear about your friend Gio." Marlowe never lacked for grace. As the current CEO of Colton Oil, she was a consummate diplomat. But her sincerity felt genuine.

"You knew?" She let out a nervous laugh. "Of course you did, it's Mustang Valley, after all."

"I wanted to go to the funeral, to support you, but I never really knew Gio and it seemed the wrong time to reconnect with you." Ainsley's eyes were moist. Was she that concerned about Bella's loss?

"That's nice of you to say that." An unexpected and unusual shyness enveloped her. Maybe the events of the last few days were finally catching up with her. Deciding to run for Ms. Mustang Valley, meeting Holden, getting attacked, surviving the explosion—how had her life become an action movie instead of the usual steady one she'd built to support her writing routine?

"I mean it." Marlowe put a hand on her forearm. "We may not see one another very much but we're all still family."

"Agreed." Ainsley nodded. "As a matter of fact, wouldn't it be nice if we made this happen on purpose? Meeting each other, I mean."

"It'd be lovely to have you up to the Triple R." Marlowe pulled out her phone.

"That sounds good." Bella figured they'd never really want to hang with her. She was from the wrong-side-of-the-track part of the Coltons, the sister of triplets whose parents had left the clan years before their untimely deaths. Still, she went through the motions of exchanging contact information before they said goodbye.

When she slid back into her seat, she discovered Holden's plate was empty and her food cold.

"You okay?" His gaze was full of concern, and that muscle tic on the side of his jaw was jumping around. "I was about to come knock on the door."

"I'm good. I ran into two distant cousins."

"Oh? Did they have some dirt on Selina for you?"

And they were right back where the conversation ended, when she'd needed to leave the table.

"I have no idea. I didn't ask." She sipped her water. "I'm not against helping an ongoing investigation. In fact, I think that reporters and LEAs do their best work when it's together. Take the robberies we had in Mustang Valley a few years back. I usually am assigned to write fluffier lifestyle pieces, about homes and lives of the more affluent residents. But I was able to convince my editor that exposés on the victims of the crimes, detailing how hard they'd worked to get where they were, would be popular to our readers. Everyone wants to know about their neighbors, especially if it's perceived they're living the 'better' life. While interviewing one particular family, it came to light that the husband had an estranged stepbrother who was actively addicted to opiates. Since two bottles of painkillers were part of the stolen goods, it allowed MVPD to connect the dots and figure out who the thieves were."

"That's unusual, Bella. You know better than I do how rare it is for law enforcement to work with the media."

"You're wrong, Holden. Maybe with bigger agencies like the FBI it's not common, but at the local, small-town level, everyone works together to make things happen."

"You may be right." He motioned to her plate. "Are you going to finish that?"

She sighed. "I've lost my appetite, frankly."

"You need to eat if you're going to have another rehearsal later today."

"I'll get something at home." But the thought of returning to her house filled her with anxiety. It was usually her refuge and now, even with police presence and Holden, it was more like a prison. "Don't take this wrong, Holden, but I'm not keen on going back to the house."

"I don't blame you, but you're safe there, Bella. I won't let anything happen to you."

"It's not that. It's the reality of a serial killer, a monster, being so close to me, to where I live and breathe."

"We don't have to go straight back. When's your next video practice session?"

"Eight tomorrow morning." Selina had said she'd meet with them again after they had time to rest and study the routines she'd dealt out this morning.

"It's not even sundown yet. We've got some time."

"For what?"

"It's a surprise."

Holden liked how he'd gotten a smile out of Bella when he'd told her their destination was a surprise. She'd been far too serious when she'd returned to the table. Truth be told, he knew it was his staunch dislike of reporters that had put her in the foul mood.

Would it have killed you to go easier on her?

No, it wouldn't have killed him but if he wasn't on that sharp edge of awareness that a case like this necessitated, her life would be at risk.

He glanced at her as he drove onto the highway, heading west. She sat relaxed against the seat, her eyes closed. He hoped the AC and lull of the drive had put her in a decent nap. It was so hard to tell with Bella— her moods and bearing changed with the wind.

And dang it if he didn't love every bit of the challenge of keeping up with her.

"Why are you staring at me? Keep your eyes on the road," she murmured in a sleepy voice and he grinned.

"There isn't much out here but roadrunners and prairie dogs."

"We don't want to kill any innocent bystanders." She stretched and snuggled into the seat more deeply. "Don't wake me 'til we get there."

"Okay." He promised himself he'd keep his gaze on the flat highway, the mountains and blue sky in his peripheral vision.

Holden had never skipped out of an op before. And he wasn't now, not technically, as keeping Bella safe was his top priority. That, and luring in the killer.

At Bella's risk.

Guilt sucker punched him for the second time in a

day, but it had nothing to do with Spencer or their bond that would last a lifetime. His emotional discomfort had everything to do with the beautiful woman reclined in the passenger seat beside him, trusting him enough to keep her eyes closed and to nap on the way to an unknown destination.

Maybe he needed to learn how to trust, too. He could trust that Bella wasn't using him for information for her exposé. She hadn't sought him out, hadn't even known an FBI agent was undercover at the pageant.

The sun set as he pulled into their destination. He'd driven here without thinking, knowing it was safe as he was certain they hadn't been followed and he checked in with his Phoenix office and Spencer at MVPD regularly. His phone was connected to both to provide constant GPS location.

He'd reported that Bella needed a break from her house and it was a good security move to get her away from town for the night, until the pageant practice resumed at Mustang Valley High, as determined by Spencer. He'd received zero pushback on taking Bella away from either his boss or Spencer.

"Where are we?" Bella must have felt the road change and was sitting upright, peering through the windshield.

"My favorite getaway." He waited for her to register the other cars and people milling about with binoculars and cameras, each equipped with a long lens.

"Wait—is this Carr Canyon?"

"Yes. I'm a member of SABO." The Southeastern Arizona Bird Observatory was a favorite amongst locals and tourists alike, and it had provided him with much-needed respite from his heavier cases. He had a feeling he was going to need to escape into his birding after this investigation wrapped up, too.

"I've done so many articles on them over the years. Have you ever been to one of the hummingbird bandings?"

"Only once, but I'd like to do more. With the long drive from Phoenix I can't get here as often as I like, but it's always great when I do."

"So what are we going to see tonight?" She followed his lead and got out of the car and walked around to the back with him. He opened his trunk and handed her a ball cap, reflective vest and binoculars. He donned his birding vest over the black T-shirt, and retrieved his favorite camera.

"It's a long shot that we'll actually see anything, but we'll hear the owls. I'm taking my camera but it might be fruitless."

"I love owls. There's a family of screech owls in a clump of dead saguaros behind my house. I feel like they're my personal watchdogs at night—sometimes I hear them fussing when the neighborhood teens are playing flashlight tag."

"Are you sure that's all they're doing?"

"No, but I'm not their mother." They both laughed and headed toward the top of the trail, the walk steep as they were in the mountains.

Holden had tried to hang on to his belief that Bella had to be an opportunist because she was a reporter, just like Nicole, his ex. But as they headed into the canyon's depths it occurred to him that unlike his ex, Bella was all about grasping all the joy life had to offer. And she wasn't a martyr about being a serial killer's target.

Bella was the woman he'd dreamed of finding. Why did it have to be now, during such a dangerous op?

Chapter 18

Bella surprised herself with how easy it was to forget their acrimonious dinner conversation and allow herself to enjoy the nighttime walk with Holden. The moon was full and she was able to make out his features with little trouble. It was always a bonus when she could see a handsome, sexy man as he spent time with her.

"We lucked out with the moon." She looked at large white cactus blooms on the sides of the path. "The angel blooms are practically glowing."

"Yeah, they are, aren't they?" He moved his hand to her lower back, rubbed in soothing circles. It was a peaceful bubble, just the two of them. Until a family with several young children walked by.

"The full moon explains the crowds. I never realized how many folks would show up to hear owls and look at flowering cacti." She turned away and began to walk farther down the path.

"Birding's an early-morning and late-night sport during the summer here, as you know. We're lucky it's still cooler." Holden hopped easily over a grouping of rocks and turned to hold her hand as she leaped from the four-foot precipice back to the ground. When her feet hit the sandy, graveled surface, he didn't let go but instead intertwined their fingers and continued walking.

Bella knew she should pull her hand back, keep up staunch boundaries with Holden. He'd already proven to be the best lover she'd ever known and if she wasn't careful the end of the pageant was going to mean more to her than losing a crown.

"Tell me why you really signed up for the pageant, Bella."

"I already have. I want to find out the truth about what happened to Gio. And I believe this pageant board has skeletons in its closet."

"What if you don't find them?"

"Then I'll have to figure out something else to investigate."

"So your ultimate motivation isn't about Gio." Spoken quietly, his words held no judgement or criticism.

"It's twofold. I want justice for my best friend, yes. And I want to move on from the *Mustang Valley Gabber* and secure an investigative journalist position at a more prestigious publication."

"Is there a paper or news organization you're targeting?" His voice was low and sexy and she wondered if he realized how attractive he was. How many FBI profilers could switch from badass agent to serene birder all in the same day?

"Not really. I wouldn't want to have to leave Mustang Valley, and with most organizations I can work from home except for when I have to travel for a story. But I'm not opposed to leaving, either."

"I've stayed here, in Arizona, I mean, and a couple of times I was worried I'd thrown my career away with some of my job decisions. But so far it's all worked out. Unfortunately for all of us, there are enough cases to keep the Phoenix field office in business for the next decade. It's a good thing for me, personally, as I've been able to stay here and be closer to my family."

"Did you grow up in Phoenix?"

"I did, in a suburb of it. It was so hard to be away from my family and everything I'd known when I went in the army and then ended up downrange. That's when I met Spencer."

"Did you realize you were both from Arizona? And southeastern, to boot?"

"Not at first. I learned more about him after he shoved me out of the way of friendly fire during a training event."

"He never told me or Jarvis that."

"He wouldn't, would he? Spencer is that kind of hero."

Understanding dawned. "That's why you're so close—you were with him during that one training exercise." She mentioned the location and even in the dark, with the moonlight she was able to make out the grimace on his face.

"Yes." Nothing more was needed.

"Holden, I know it's awkward, but about this morning…" She halted on the path. They were far ahead of the crowds as their pace had taken them to a more remote location. Stars sprinkled the outer edges of the light shining off the moon and she suddenly wanted to come back here with this man and see all the stars.

"Hey." He tugged on her hand and she took the two

steps to be up against him, where the feel of his breath as it stirred the wisps of hair on her temple lit the fire that burned only for him. "It's fast for me, believe it or not. I never meant to make love to you like that, this soon. You deserve to be wined and dined first, at least."

"So you thought about it beforehand?" She'd feared it was a spur-of-the-moment decision for him, an opportunity.

"Touché." He wrapped his arms around her, their bulky binoculars and cameras the only items between them. "I just accused you of being an opportunist for doing your job—I suppose I had that coming to me. Yes, I've thought about taking you to bed since the minute you walked into the school."

She shivered with desire in the cool desert night, and wished there were no pageant, that the serial killer were made up, and that Gio were still here.

Gio.

Instead of feeling the usual guilt that she wasn't doing enough to search for what had really killed Gio, a wave of exhaustion swept over her. "I wish we'd met under different circumstances, too." But even if they had, he lived in Phoenix, two hours away. Was she ready for a long-distance relationship? Was he?

"We aren't going to figure out what's going on between us right now, Bella. There are too many things competing for our attention. I suggest we enjoy the moment."

"I couldn't agree more." She moved to continue their walk but he pulled her up short, cupped her head in his palm and lowered his lips to hers. As before, her body responded immediately to his caresses, and her lips tingled with the passion they shared.

As her breathing grew more rapid she held on to

his shoulders as tightly as possible. It was like floating in water that was over her head and Holden was her safety, his tall, lean length all she needed or wanted to stay alive.

When he stilled and lifted his head, she nearly whimpered from the withdrawal of heat from her mouth.

"Shh." His insistent order made her freeze, and fear began to shoot cold arrows through her heart. No, not now. How had the serial killer found them?

"What?" She trusted him implicitly. If anyone could save them, it was Holden.

"Do you hear it?"

She stilled her breathing and tried to tune out her rapid heartbeat. Fearful of hearing heavy footsteps, she almost missed it. But then, through her fears and reaction to this man, she heard it.

Hoooooot.

"A pygmy owl." She'd memorized the birdcalls years ago, for the article she had mentioned to Holden earlier.

"Yes. With juveniles. Listen." Sure enough, after the mother or father's long call, tiny, more "chirpy" sounds split the silence. Relief rushed in, followed by something she'd never been able to grasp no matter how long she'd ever dated a single person.

Trust.

It was too easy. Did they think they couldn't be followed, found, wherever they went? It would be easier if she were alone but no worries. He'd taken out other men who thought they were protecting the women, too.

They weren't in the house, which was a shame. He'd been able to break through the MVPD patrols with little trouble, once night fell. The feed from the camera he'd put over her bathroom window had disappeared, and he figured the police got it since he didn't see it from the perimeter of the property. He couldn't get close enough right now, but as soon as he knew they were back in the house, together, he'd get her.

And she'd pay for running away tonight.

The next morning Bella's phone woke her before dawn and she automatically answered, thinking it was one of her brothers. Holden had resumed his position on her sofa after they'd returned, assuring both of them that MVPD had her house under a basic lockdown. There was no safer place for her at this point.

"Hello?"

"Quit the pageant. You're in over your head." The same distorted voice that she'd heard before her world went dark in the staff room, backstage. Wide awake now, she bolted from her bed and moved in the darkness out of her room, into the hall and into Holden's granite physique.

"Who is it?"

She continued to listen, but the caller had disconnected.

"It was the same person as before. They hung up." Trembling began and, to her consternation, deepened in intensity. "It—it—it was him."

"Shh." He pulled her into his arms, held her tight. "You're safe. I'm here."

"I used to be so tough, but now I'm a puddle after a stupid prank call."

"Hey, you're not out of line to be afraid. This call wasn't just another crank call, but from a lethal killer. I'll have my handler see if he can get anything from the phone company."

"Thanks, that's reassuring me about now." She

smiled through the tears that ran down her face, her reaction to anger and frightening circumstances. She let his shirt absorb her tears, and didn't feel an ounce of guilt about it. It was safe, here in Holden's arms. "Sorry, I'm an odd duck when it comes to expressing my emotions. When I get really angry, I cry, which can come across as being overly emotional. The same thing happens when I'm afraid. But when Gio died, I couldn't muster a tear for days, weeks even."

"It was too deep. The hurt. I get it." He kept holding her and she heard his heartbeat since one ear was pressed against his chest. His breathing slowed, deepened. He let out a long sigh. "When Spencer and I were serving, we saw a lot. I'm not sure how much he's told you."

"Enough. He's told Jarvis more, I think, because both of them have always felt more protective of me than each other. They're not being jerks or misogynists, just good brothers."

She felt him nod, and his embrace tightened reassuringly. "If Jarvis is anything like Spencer, then yes, it's because they care very much for you."

"So during your work with the FBI, what have you seen that bothered you the most?"

He shifted next to her, as if seeking more contact. "Most cases aren't as bad as you might imagine. But when they are, they're rough. Anything involving kids is pretty much the worst. Sometimes I hit emotional overload. I know I'm there when I can't compartmentalize or shove down the horror. I've cried like a baby more than once."

"That's crying like a man, Holden. Accepting life on life's terms, even when it's awful."

"Yeah."

They stood in silence for several minutes, and to Bella it was as if they'd always been here. Together.

She pulled back. "I've got to get dressed. I imagine there's going to be another video session this morning."

"Actually, no. I was going to let you sleep a little longer, but I talked to Spencer about an hour ago. It's a go for the high school. Pageant practice resumes this morning."

"I didn't think Selina or the pageant board were going to give us Sunday off, not when all we'll have for the next three weeks are evenings." She was actually sorry that the pageant was only going to be for a few more weeks, with the final festivities at the end of the month. It meant she had only three weeks with Holden, before he went back to his life in Phoenix. Back to being an FBI agent, far away from Mustang Valley.

"You can ask for another agent to guard you if you want, Bella. You don't have to be tied to me for all three weeks."

"But you won't let anyone else have the final say in my safety, will you?"

"No."

"And we've gone past the point of acting as if we don't share more than this pageant and wanting to catch the killer. Right?"

He nodded. "Right again."

"Then I'm fine with you staying here. There's nowhere else I can go without bringing the threat with me, be it a hotel or even Rattlesnake Ridge Ranch, if I were ever invited there." She heard the self-pity in her voice and resolved to do whatever she had to do to erase it. Martyrdom had been Aunt Amelia's gig, not hers.

"I know it's scary. But you're right—wherever you go we'd have to start over again as far as your security."

"Then let's leave it as it is."

"I won't distract either of us again, Bella." His level gaze wasn't entirely convincing as there was a flicker of heat in its depths.

"It's a two-way responsibility, Holden. You didn't make or even convince me to do anything I hadn't wanted to since just about the time you opened my bag to check for contraband."

His color deepened and major dimples formed on either side of his mouth but he didn't widen it into a grin.

"We're only going to hurt one another in the end."

"I agree." She shifted on her feet, knowing she needed to get dressed or at least get a large mug of coffee. But she couldn't bring herself to walk away. As if it would truly mean the end of anything personal with Holden. "But, we can both agree that we're friends of a sort, can't we?" The plea in her tone made her cringe on her behalf but it didn't stop how she felt.

She needed to know Holden was her friend.

A flash of white in the dim hallway reassured her. "There's no way I couldn't be friends with my buddy's sister."

So she was back to being Spencer's sister. At least that meant they were still talking, and back on neutral territory. Away from the heated desire that threatened her heart as much as the killer threatened her life.

Except unlike her wish to see Holden apprehend the murderer, she didn't seem to care if her heart was on fire.

Holden knew he was being a jerk. No question. He'd just brushed off the woman unlike any other he'd ever known. But it was for her safety, the security of the entire investigation.

And the tightness around his heart every time he remembered why he was here, to catch a killer, served as a reminder that he was getting too close to Bella.

While Bella got dressed he took a cup of coffee out to the patio and placed a call to Spencer to pass on some information MVPD needed for the ongoing investigation against AAG. It was already hot, even in the shade of her terra-cotta-tiled roof, but he needed to be outside, to see the desert wake up.

"You're up early for a G-man." Spencer's teasing was a welcome relief after drawing the grim boundaries he needed with Bella.

"Don't worry, man, I'm going back to bed after this."

Spencer's silence had him replaying what he'd just said. "Oh, geez, Spencer, I didn't mean with your sister, for heaven's sake." Guilt slapped his conscience silly.

"It's pretty apparent that there's something going on between you two."

"I promise, I won't let anything happen to her."

"I know that. I trust you, always have." Spencer paused again and in Holden's line of work, he had learned that pauses were where trouble lay. "Bella's not had a lot of luck with guys, Holden, and I don't want to see a broken heart when you go back to your job in Phoenix."

"Copy that. I won't hurt her, Spencer." Holden couldn't say any more without betraying what he and Bella had shared. No matter how it ended, how it had to be now, what they'd made together was special, private. Sacred.

Sacred? He'd gotten in deeper than he'd thought.

"I wasn't referring to Bella, Holden. I meant your heart. Bella's been a heartbreaker since middle school." Spencer laughed. "In case you haven't noticed, she can hold her own against almost anything. I don't want her to have to do that, though, not with a killer."

"We're on the same page, then. Listen, I called to give you what our office found on the Affirmation Alliance Group and its leader, Micheline Anderson."

"You know MVPD got the charge to stick against Harley Watts, right? He's been charged with threatening the Colton Oil structure by sending a classified email over the dark web."

"Yes, my handler mentioned that. Another thing that's come up that I think you'll be interested in is that there are indications that Micheline might be planning some kind of mass-destruction event, like a mass suicide."

Spencer's low whistle pierced their connection. "You mean like a Jim Jones poisoned-fruit-drink kind of thing?" Holden wasn't surprised that Spencer recognized the reference. Law enforcement officers often studied the mass suicide orchestrated by the cult leader Jim Jones in Guyana, in 1978.

"Yes, exactly. And an eerie connection is that Jim Jones's spouse was named Marceline. It seems awfully close to Micheline, especially as neither are common names."

"You don't think she took this name on purpose?"

Holden sighed. "No clue. I've learned not to put much stock in coincidence, though. Not in our line of work."

"I hear you. Thanks for this, Holden, and please thank your office colleagues, and your supervisor. This saves me a lot of digging, and we'll be sure to keep Micheline and AAG under tight surveillance."

"Good to hear." He saw Bella walk back into the kitchen through the sliding patio door. "I've got to go. Ms. Mustang Valley waits for no one."

Spencer's chuckle reached him before he disconnected. Eager to get his head back in the game, he took a moment to remind himself why he'd come to Mustang Valley. To apprehend a killer. To prevent further murders. But Bella's safety had become priority number one. Long before Spencer had requested it.

Holden shoved aside anything that remotely felt like an emotional response to Bella and focused on the case.

Both of their lives depended upon it.

Chapter 19

"You're off by a half beat, Bella! Marcie, Delilah, stop letting her mess you up, ladies." Selina's voice cut through the soundtrack, a disco tune that required everyone to do three turns in a row, followed by a quick two-step. After their second week of evening rehearsals, it was the pageant's third all-day Saturday practice.

Bella clamped her mouth shut to keep from responding with some very unpageantlike words. But that made her even more out of breath, and she felt her face heat with the effort.

"Don't let her get to you. We're almost done with all of this." Marcie spoke through several more steps, her face flushed, too.

"She's not. Trust me." The number ended and Bella took the opportunity to walk off to the side of the stage to where Holden stood.

"How can anyone think I'm going to receive extra

points from her?" She gulped from her water bottle and didn't miss how his gaze drank her in. Her body reacted by sending heat everywhere she'd tried to shut down these past two weeks as he'd slept on her sofa each night. She'd had to deal with him being around all the time, including following her to the *Mustang Valley Gabber* headquarters a few times. It was fortunate from a security perspective that she was able to work from her laptop, and remain at home for much of her imposed "exile" from independent living. To be fair, she enjoyed Holden's company and they'd gotten to know each other better.

It wasn't a stretch to realize they'd indeed become friends, as she'd hoped.

But they'd avoided a repeat of their one night together. She was relieved and frustrated by their mutual agreement to avoid any further bedroom activities. They were adults, after all. Yet a big part of her wanted to bring that up, remind him that they could enjoy a physical relationship without worrying they'd expect too much from one another when it ended.

At least, that's what she'd thought before she got to know him so well.

"Keep your cool and remember to not let them see you sweat."

"Funny." Her clothes were soaked with perspiration and had been all day. "At least this is the last bit of today's rehearsal."

"Still, we can't take any chances. Be aware."

"Got it." She didn't want to be short with him but each night Holden had gone over what he thought she needed to do, to survive any possible attack by the killer. Stay alert, aware and always ready to run.

"I know you do." His confidence in her buoyed her

when she would have wondered just why she was doing this in the first place. So far she'd uncovered nothing nefarious about the Ms. Mustang Valley Pageant, and in fact had learned that it took a lot of work and dedication for the competition to continue year after year.

Was Gio's mother right? Had Gio's talk near the end been delusional, brought on by her advanced disease?

"You're frowning. Need to talk about it?"

"Not here. Maybe later." But what would she tell Holden? He'd take her admission that there was nothing the pageant could do to prevent Gio's illnesses as surrender. She wasn't going to ever claim being a reporter was in vain.

"Bella."

"Yes?"

"You're doing great. You'll get your story, don't worry." His smooth tone hid the depth of thought and intuition its accuracy required.

"How do you do that?"

"Do what?"

"Know what I'm thinking, what I need to hear?"

He gazed at her thoughtfully. "With you, it's easy."

"Break time's over!" Selina's command was her bidding, at least for another week. The ex-wife of Payne Colton still commanded a room as if she still was married to the state's richest man. Bella wondered how Payne's current comatose condition, affected Selina personally. It had to be difficult to be on the Colton Oil Board of Directors and not have the chairman present, knowing he might never return. Payne had been her husband once, after all. But as much as Bella had tried to talk to Selina alone, or asked others if they knew more about her, she hadn't been able to dig up any more dirt on the Colton Oil empire's current situation. Spencer had told her in the strictest confidence that there was big drama going on as to who the eldest biological heir to Payne's legacy was, but she wouldn't be able to use that for a report unless she heard it from a different source.

Which left her with doing what she came here to begin with—Bella needed to find the original records of the Ms. Mustang Valley Pageant that had been in the file cabinet.

"Okay, ladies, thank you for such a great day. I'm going to leave you with Dawn Myers, Mustang Valley's own winner of several pageants and the winner of Ms. Mustang Valley ten years ago. Please welcome her and follow her lead on how to get through your talent portion."

Crap. Bella had written on the original application that she'd be presenting a verbal essay on why reporting mattered in today's world of insta-news and social media. But she'd done nothing to prepare in the meantime. While many of her competitors were staying up late working on their talents, she'd been writing assigned articles for her paying job.

And lying awake too late, wondering what Holden was doing in the other room besides guarding her and laying his long, sexy body on her poppy-red sofa.

"Bye, Selina." Dawn was a perky blonde whose hair was in a twist, her figure still perfectly trim in white capris with a slinky sleeveless pale pink silk top. Bella wondered how she stayed looking so cool in the heat. Air-conditioning made life bearable in Arizona yearround, but it was still roasting outside in the sun.

For the next hour, the contestants were each grilled on their talent portion. Bella mentally prepared as much as possible, but when it was her turn to walk on and stand center stage without her colleagues she felt every bit the ingenue.

"Hello, everyone. I'm Bella Colton, and I am so fortunate to be able to earn my living doing what I'm most passionate about—bringing the truth to you, the reader, no matter how difficult it may be. Since I'm used to public speaking, I've picked poetry reading as my talent. I've chosen a poem—"

"Stop, stop!" Señora Rosenstein ran up to the edge of the stage, her cell phone in hand. "There's been a terrible accident!"

Bella looked around for Holden, and met his gaze with trepidation. Was this another distraction from the killer?

"What is it, Ms. Rosenstein?" Marcie stepped forward.

"Selina's car has flipped off the highway at the bend just out of town, on the way to Rattlesnake Ridge Ranch."

A collective gasp made the hairs on Bella's nape raise, and she fought to keep her feet planted. All she wanted was to run to Holden's arms as she had the night she'd received the crank call. It'd been easy to think the killer had changed his mind, that's how quiet the pageant had been.

"Is she okay?" Becky, who was still watching the pageant activities albeit with crutches and only as an observer, spoke from a theater seat in the front row.

Holden walked forward down the main right aisle. "I've just spoken to MVPD Sergeant Spencer Colton. Selina appears to be completely fine, just shaken up a bit. She walked away from the crash. She's being evaluated by EMTs."

"What caused the accident?" Bella asked.

"We won't know until a full investigation is completed."

Murmurs turned to panic amongst the women.

"This is crazy. No scholarship is worth this."

"What's going on, really?"

"I heard that there were murders at two other pageants." Leigh spoke up, her usually singsong voice shaking. "But remember, we can all be our best selves in the most trying circumstances. This is our chance to join together, to rise to be our best selves."

"Do you really believe your own lies, Leigh?" Becky, on crutches and standing next to the stage, was clearly not in the mood for fluffy sayings when they were all at risk.

"There's no reason to believe anyone here is a target." Holden didn't meet Bella's gaze. "I'm just pageant security, but we're surrounded by Mustang Valley PD, and the officers are conducting regular inspections. No one can get in here who isn't a part of the pageant."

"But what if there's a killer amongst us?" Delilah asked the same question that had given Bella nightmares all week.

"We're not going to allow negative energy to affect the positive motivation we all have to win this pageant, are we, ladies?" Dawn spoke up, her background in motivational speaking evident. "This is scary—I'll grant you that. But we've got MVPD on our side, and I'm willing to be here today to do the work. How about you?"

Bella was stunned at how quickly the panic turned to enthusiasm with the group. It wasn't the sticky-sweet platitudes from Leigh, either. It was genuine.

Pageant women were strong, and had reason to fight

for their privilege to compete. They all wanted to improve their lives, and education was a valuable ticket.

Later that evening, Bella faced what she thought of as her firing squad. Holden, Spencer and Jarvis sat on her crimson sofa and looked at her with a gravity she wasn't certain she could ever remember her brothers having before. Holden was almost always serious, especially about this case, so his granite expression didn't surprise her.

She sat in her recliner, a birthday gift from her brothers last year. It was one of her favorite places to write, but at the moment it felt more like an interrogation seat.

"What gives, guys?" Her brothers had already been in her driveway when she and Holden pulled up.

"Selina's brakes were cut." Spencer went for the jugular. "This matches all the information that Holden has on the killer. He goes after anyone who insults his target. Selina and Becky both criticized you. At the last pageant he cut brakes, too."

"And we're closing in on the time when he usually strikes. He likes to do scare tactics beforehand, but kills during the last week of pageant preparation, no more than three days out from the final performance." Holden's eyes held concern, but something else. An apology for not telling her these details sooner?

"When did you find this out?" She kept her focus on Holden.

"I found out about Selina's brakes while you were going through your talent portion this last hour. I've known about the killer's MO since I arrived in Mustang Valley but wasn't able to share everything."

"Yet you didn't mention it in the car. The part about Selina's brakes."

"There was no point. I thought you'd need your brothers here for support, and I wanted you to be able to ask Spencer any questions, too."

"What's different now? We know there's a killer, and he's after me because I made the unfortunate decision to streak my hair red." What had possessed her to do it? Not that it would have discouraged the serial killer, she suspected. He'd have found a target one way or the other. At least this way Holden could protect her, and she could protect herself.

"You should come stay with me at the ranch, sis. You can disappear until this blows over." Jarvis looked at her. "No one gets on or off the Triple R without having to pass their incredible security system."

"What, and stay with the other hands in the bunks? No offense, Jarvis, but I'm, we're thirty-one, not thirteen."

"Whoa, that's not nice, sis. And you'd be able to stay in the big house, that'd be no problem if I asked."

"I know you have to live in a bunkhouse as a ranch hand, but I wouldn't be comfortable there or in the Colton mansion. You know that, Jarvis. We're not from that cut of Colton. Why are you still working on the ranch, by the way?"

"Hold it." Spencer stood up. "This isn't about Jarvis and his career, or about me, or Holden. This is about you and your safety. I know you've already refused to quit the pageant, and we can't make you, but Holden and I agree that there needs to be an undercover MVPD officer working to distract the killer."

She looked at Holden. "You told me it would take too long to find someone. We only have days left until the pageant finals." Until the killer tried to end her life.

Shudders shook her but she crossed her legs, folded her arms in front of her, hoping none of them noticed.

"An FBI agent, yes, it would take too long. But Spencer has an officer who can do it."

"No."

"Bella, this isn't your decision."

"Hear me out, Spencer. I'm the one who entered the contest to get information, remember? And not just for Gio. I can help you close this investigation and catch the killer like no one else, being a contestant. I'm not quitting. If you let your undercover cop come in now, it'll spook the killer. Sure, it'll keep me safe but we won't catch the murderer and it will put more women at risk. That's the point with serial killers, right? Catch them or they're going to do it again. And again."

Jarvis shook his head. "I'm sure glad I've stuck to horses and ranches these past months."

Spencer looked at Holden. "It's your call, Holden."

Holden met her brother's gaze for a long stretch. It was impossible to tell his thoughts as his stone expression was back in place. She was once again facing Agent St. Clair instead of the Holden she knew and had come to care deeply for.

What?

Before she could analyze her thoughts, Spencer was pacing the room, shaking his head.

"Gosh dang it, Bella. You never, ever, can agree to do what's easiest for you! This isn't a race through the desert, though, or deciding on whether to double up on your majors." Spencer referenced her decision to major in both journalism and environmental science in college. All while working as a barista to keep her student loans to a minimum. Her brothers had been in school at the same time, of course, and had watched her work herself into a bout of exhaustion that had taken the first six months after graduation to get over. But she'd landed her degree and the job at the *Gabber* within a month of each other. It didn't feel like five years of work at the *Gabber*, though. It'd passed so quickly, because she really did love her job. But she'd enjoy writing more hardboiled reports even more.

"Don't throw it on me, Spencer, I'm not the killer!"

"We're down to the wire, folks." Holden looked at her. Did her brothers feel the connection between them? "You're not going to quit, so I say we do all we can to catch the killer before he does any further harm." He stood. "I'd rather you left the pageant, too, frankly. But you've already refused to, twice, and I have to catch this bastard."

"Tell me again—when did he strike the last two times?" Jarvis was clearly at a disadvantage, not being in law enforcement.

"Within the last few days leading up to the start of the pageant."

"Where we are now." Bella finished Jarvis's thoughts for him, wanting her brothers to accept her decision to stay. She needed them to leave, leave her alone. She had a pageant to prepare for, and *Gabber* work to catch up on. "I'm not going to lie to either of you. I'm scared. Of course I am. But it's not like I haven't been before, when I've been working on investigative pieces."

"I thought Gio's report was the first one you were going for?" Spencer challenged her.

She let out a sigh to give herself time. But there was no way around admitting her career failures. Except this time it was in front of Holden.

"I've tried to get information on a lot of different subjects. I want to move to the next place in my reporting, in my career. The *Mustang Valley Gabber's* been great, and it's certainly paid my bills for the last several years. But I've been doing investigative work, writing up draft reports, for the past year."

"So why didn't those articles get published already?" Jarvis stood, ran his hand over his head. "Do you really need this particular story, sis?"

"The other stories haven't published because I wasn't able to get relevant information. And at the rate this investigative piece is going for me, my exposé for Gio's sake won't publish, either. I'm at a stalemate until I find the pageant's archival records to verify which pageants each committee member served on, and if there are any indications that Ms. Mustang Valley really did cause Gio's illness." But even as she voiced her needs, she already knew the answer. There was no way one pageant, one event, could cause the kind of illnesses Gio suffered from. Not singlehandedly. And she'd learned a lot working in this pageant, enough to know that the majority of pageants as well as contestants were in it for the right reasons. Scholarship, community, empowerment. Still, for Gio's and her reporter credentials' sake, she had to close the loop. "Gio told me they were in a file cabinet in the staff room but I was attacked before I was able to look inside. When I returned, the drawers were all empty."

Jarvis let out a low whistle. "Is this worth your life, sis?"

"It's not about me. It's about Gio." And all the women who'd ever competed in a pageant, but especially the alumnae of Ms. Mustang Valley.

"You'll be able to write about the killer, once the case is closed." Holden turned to her brothers. "If Bella's not willing to quit, then at least she should have something for her sacrifice."

Bella was stunned by Holden's words. Sure, she could write about the serial killer investigation, and it would prove a promotion-worthy article. But he'd never admitted it to her, never gave her a clue he'd be willing to bend his FBI rules to allow her inside information that she'd be free to report on.

"I'd have to be careful, to protect the court case."

"Which I'm certain you will. You're a professional." Holden didn't hold back in front of her brothers. Not one bit. He closed the gap between them. "I completely trust you, Bella. I need you to trust me. It's the only way I can promise to keep you alive."

Chapter 20

Holden's gut twisted as he said the words, as Bella's brilliant green eyes widened and the blush on her cheeks deepened. Holding her hands, facing her, he knew what he had to say next.

"I'll protect you through every bit of this, Bella, as I have so far. But going forward, there probably aren't going to be any more warning signs or incidents perpetrated by the killer to throw us off his trail. The next move will be to take you out."

She nodded. "I know that. And I do, Holden. I trust you." She squeezed his hands and he squeezed back.

To their credit, neither Colton brother groaned or made a rude comment. Which appeared to move her more than the prospect of facing her attacker again.

Everyone knew this was a matter of Bella's life or death.

"This isn't a crackpot criminal, Bella. You're dealing

with an evil we don't usually find in Mustang Valley."
Spencer stood and looked at Holden. "I trust you with
my life, buddy, and know I'm trusting you with Bella's."

Jarvis didn't say anything and Holden didn't blame
him.

"I give you my word, nothing will happen to your
sister." He meant his words, but couldn't fight his own
worry over Bella's involvement in such a dangerous
pivot-point.

Holden had to keep it together, because zero FBI
backup was in the area and MVPD was spread thin.

"I'm going to walk your brothers out. Stay here until
I get back."

"I need a shower. Or is that off-limits?"

"Fine. Get one but make it quick and don't leave the
house, not even to go out on the patio."

"Got it."

He caught up to the brothers and fell into step next
to them until they were at Spencer's K-9 SUV.

"I'll keep you posted." He spoke to Spencer, as in-
forming Jarvis about the investigation wasn't protocol.
He knew Spencer would keep Jarvis informed.

Spencer nodded. "I know you will. I'll let you know
what I do, Jarvis."

"Sure thing. See you, Holden." Jarvis got into the
passenger seat and waited while Holden and Spencer
talked outside.

"Thank you for the extra security on-site at the
school and here." Holden couldn't do his job if MVPD
didn't do theirs.

"Yeah, well, whatever it takes, right? Let's get this
bad guy once and for all, Holden." Spencer looked up at
the deepening sky, the stars that were shining across the

earth's canopy. "It's not unlike the long hours we pulled waiting for the drill sergeant to ream our butts, is it?"

"Not much different at all. Except I've been managing some sleep each night, thanks to MVPD and you."

Spencer snorted. "I know you, Holden. You never sleep while the enemy's still on the prowl."

"Yeah, well, at least I can catch a nap here and there. That's more than we ever did in the Army."

"It is." Spencer opened the driver-side door. "Let's hope this doesn't go on for the rest of the week."

"If he does what he's done in the past, the next two days will be key." Holden had studied the timelines of each murder, the pageant preparations leading up to it. Ms. Mustang Valley was right on time for the murderer's schedule. He expected an attempt on Bella's life in the next forty-eight hours.

Spencer shifted on his feet. "Not to change the subject or make it seem like I'm not invested in my sister's stalker, but I have another case to ask you about. I need a favor."

"Anything. Shoot."

"You know about AAG, and that Leigh, one of the contestants, is heavily involved in it."

"Right. She's still ingratiating as all get-out, always telling Bella and the other contestants that they are all beautiful winners and can do it no matter what." Holden managed a short laugh. "We probably owe her, in a twisted way, for keeping the pageant going and the contestants coming back in the face of danger."

"I'd hold off on your praise. AAG is not right, I'm certain of it. And I've had reason to look into its founder, Micheline Anderson, after we talked about her. Turns out she didn't exist as a person until forty years ago." Spencer looked at him intently, clearly waiting for Holden to put something together.

"Okay, so she's forty years old?"

"No, nothing like that. Micheline isn't a day under sixty-five. But her birth date, or appearance on the planet, coincides with the disappearance of Luella Smith, the nurse at the hospital who likely switched her baby for the one we know as Ace Colton. Look, here's a photo of Luella Smith from forty years ago." Spencer tapped onto his phone and handed it to Holden.

"Wow. Save for the darker hair and glasses, this woman's the spitting image of Micheline." He'd observed the AAG founder at the pageant practices, sitting in the audience with the smattering of other relatives, friends and parents who stopped by to see how their loved ones were doing.

"Exactly. I questioned her about what kind of history she had, before forty years ago when it all goes dark for her. She told me that she was in the witness protection program until now, and can't talk about it. I thought that was odd, because you can't divulge if you've ever been in the program but I didn't want to call her on it right then. I want her to think we're clueless as to her motives."

"Good thinking. No, you're not supposed to ever reveal if you've been in the witness protection program." Holden referred to the Bureau. "I can ask a colleague who helps administer it to look her up."

"That'd be great!" Spencer's relief was palpable. "I appreciate it."

"But remember, I'm not privy to the protection's program information, not on an official level. Whatever you find out is yours—do with it as you need to."

"No, no, that's not a problem at all. I owe you, buddy."

Spencer's phone sounded and he looked at Holden. "I've got to take this. I'll be in touch."

"Same."

Holden turned back and was almost to the front door when he realized what mattered most to him in this moment wasn't the investigation and getting to his next rank in the FBI.

It was the woman in the modest adobe house.

Bella.

"Holden, hold up!" Spencer's voice shook him out of his revelation as he trotted up to him, phone in hand.

"What's up?"

"That was the head of the MVPD forensics team. The lab results are in and we have an ID on the prints that are on the file cabinet."

"Whose are they?"

"Becky's. She's voluntarily turned over several boxes of paper files from the pageant. She admitted that she didn't want the pageant to become fodder for tabloid gossip, which is what she said she considers the *Gabber* to be. She suspected Bella was reporting on the pageant the minute she signed up as a contestant." Spencer had a look of disgust on his face. "All Becky had to do was read the *Gabber.* She'd see it's a reputable news source."

"Those are the files Bella has been searching for." Holden felt a sense of pride. Bella had trusted her gut, and Gio's information, and she'd been correct. The pageant's archives had been in that file cabinet.

"We can have them to her as soon as we get through the red tape. Will you tell her?"

"Tell me what?" Of course Bella was standing in the

threshold. Holden tried not to glare at her. "What? I'm not outside, not completely."

As Holden repeated what Spencer had told him, she felt both men watching her, gauging her reaction.

"Becky?" Bella couldn't believe it. And yet, she'd never seen her attacker. "Holden, is it possible that Becky was the attacker you talked to?"

Holden frowned. "It's possible, yes, but improbable. I remember the assailant as wider, more muscular."

"This doesn't explain how she fell, or who pushed her, or how the explosion was set off at the same time, or even why she'd want to kill the victims."

"If she was pushed. It's possible she jumped, faked being pushed. But I've never had a case where someone intentionally hurt themselves, to distract from the real crime. Becky really wanted to win the pageant." Spencer shook his head. "Nothing is as it seems in this case."

"That's exactly what the attacker said to me." Holden's mouth was a straight line, white around the edges from pressing his lips together.

Chills assailed her. Holden was the one person she counted on to know what the heck was happening.

"Spencer has an officer at her place now, questioning her. She's already turned over several boxes of pageant files. Spencer said you'll have them as soon as he takes care of the administrative and legal details."

"Is it possible that we don't have a serial killer, but a woman who is for some reason bent on keeping the history of Ms. Mustang Valley a secret?" She had to ask the obvious.

Holden expelled a breath. "Possible, yes. Probable? No."

Spencer shook his head. "I'm a local cop, you're the serial-killer expert."

"The majority of participants are really just trying to get ahead. It's often their last hope. We have no reason to think Becky didn't want the same. So of course she wanted to protect the files, and the pageant—she didn't want it shut down." Bella blurted out her thoughts before she thought twice about it. Both men turned and faced her. Standing on the threshold, she saw Jarvis sitting in the SUV with Boris.

"That wasn't your opinion when you signed up for this." Spencer's exasperation made her wish she'd kept her mouth shut. He had enough on his shoulders with Payne Colton still in a coma from a gunshot and the shooter still on the loose. Not to mention the other everyday myriad petty crimes that kept MVPD busy on a slow day.

"It's my job to keep my opinion out of it. I'm learning as I go along." She paused, afraid to ask the next question. "Can you get me the files as soon as possible? I'm willing to come in to the station and copy them myself."

"I'll see what we can do, but my first priority isn't an old stack of paperwork, Bella."

"That's fair. I get it." Still, if she could have the files, her exposé would be complete.

"Keep us informed, Spencer." Holden looked distracted.

Spencer nodded and walked back to the SUV.

As soon as she shut the door, Bella followed Holden into the kitchen where she watched him start a pot of coffee.

"Isn't it a little late for caffeine?"

"Normally, yes. But it's going to be a long night."

"Again." She rounded the counter and stood next to him. "I'm sorry that you haven't been able to get much sleep."

"It's my job. This isn't the first time I've had to go without. It's always worth the final results."

"It seems a high price to pay, your health."

"Lack of sleep is manageable, short-term. But most cases aren't solved as quickly as we're hoping this will be. It's not like on television or in the movies. I've worked as long as three years on a single case before connecting the dots well enough to not only get the criminal, but to ensure the case is solid for the prosecuting attorney."

"I know it's not like the movies, trust me. Spencer is my brother, remember? I also know that you're being modest. It takes an incredible amount of tenacity to hang in there, day after day." She knew; reporting was often the same.

"You're trying to show me that you do the same thing, Bella, but it doesn't equate." His tone was cooler than it had been since he'd first made it clear he wasn't a fan of reporters almost three weeks ago.

The most revelatory few weeks of her life. Not that she had time to process it all right now.

"I'm not trying to manipulate you into believing something you never will. If I have something to say to you, I'm direct. You should know that by now, if nothing else." Heat rushed her face and she turned away, damning the tears that threatened to fall. Anger at herself for falling for this unreachable man combined with frustration at reaching the end of the pageant with not a heck of a lot of exposé material, save for whatever the archival files Becky turned over might have, had made her a hot mess. Plus the fact that maybe it was time she faced some hard facts about Gio's illness and its causes. She might never have that answer, and she had to figure out what to focus her reporting on, besides Ms. Mustang

Valley pageant wrong-doing. The pressure of it welled inside, adding fuel to her tears of frustration.

Think.

There was plenty to draw from with all she'd learned as a contestant, albeit undercover. The scholarship award was particularly noteworthy, as the motives for each contestant to win were deserving of their own story. The other topics she'd inadvertently learned so much about were eating orders and mental illness. There was never enough light shone on them, as far as she was concerned. She'd figure out a story topic, even though her emotions were making it seem impossible at the moment.

"Hey, hang on." Holden reached for her and she dared herself to look up at him. "We're at the tough part here. It's normal to feel like it'll never end."

"Stop it with your constant stream of FBI platitudes. I know what I'm feeling and while it's probably hard for you to believe, you can't read my mind." She watched his face as she challenged him and where she expected an answering anger she saw heat…of a different kind.

"Bella. When are you going to get it that much of my—what did you call them, oh yeah, *platitudes*, are my way of staying on the straight and narrow, where I have to be to do my job?"

"Your job is to catch a killer and you've given yourself the additional assignment of protecting *me*. Unless you see me as the ideal lure for the murderer."

"Never." He pulled her up against his chest, her breasts flattened by the sheer masculine wall, and lowered his mouth to hers. Hadn't she just told him she was direct with communication? Holden had the direct part of physical communication down.

His kiss turned into their kiss as they didn't waste

time on preliminaries. Mouths opened, tongues swept, breathing hitched. Desire rose and pooled in the most delicious, torturous way as Holden's hands caressed her cheeks, her throat, then grasped her breasts with unabashed need.

"Holden," she moaned against his mouth and he began to kiss her jawline, her throat, as his hands moved over her belly and down to the molten hot spot between her legs. Her knees felt as impermanent as the desert sands, the quaking he caused making her hang on to his massive shoulders. "I can't take this much longer."

"Then don't, babe." He lifted her into his arms with zero fanfare and walked into the living room where he deposited her on the sofa. Her question must have been in her gaze as she looked at him, marveled at how her fingers had tousled his hair, her kisses had made his lips fuller, his eyes half-lidded. "It's safer out here."

"Okay." She sat up. "Let me get—"

"This?" He pulled a condom from his jeans front pocket and grinned.

"Were you expecting this?" She'd thought she'd never experience his lovemaking again, not during the investigation and definitely not if he really couldn't stand her profession.

"Never expected, but hoped." His words were as hot as his tongue and fingers, setting her already flaming want into a full-raging inferno.

Unlike the other time they'd made love, she wanted to undress him. He shucked out of his T-shirt and she got on her knees, the sofa cushions buckling underneath. "Let me." Kissing his chest, licking the skin through the tufts of his chest hair, she heard him sigh, groan. She unbuckled his belt, unbuttoned the single jean fastener. Unzipping his jeans was the single most sensual moment she'd ever had. Her reward for going slow, slow, slow was grasping his erection and freeing it, pushing the pants down with her other hand.

"You next." He sucked in air as he spoke, and the huskiness of his voice made her aware of how wet she was, how ready to be one with him again.

"Holden, I want to—"

"I know, babe, but we're short on time here." He pushed her back to her feet, lifted her top up and over her head, peeled her leggings off. She stood in front of him wearing a sports bra and lacy thong.

"I do have matching underwear, I swear."

He chuckled but it was strained. Never had she been with a man who so clearly wanted her as much as she did him.

"Babe, I'm not interested in your bra-and-panty sets." He squeezed her breast through the thin stretchy material, lowered his head and sucked on her nipple. As she cried out with need he lifted the bra up and off, then kissed and suckled each nipple, the feel of his tongue against her bare skin driving her close to the edge. And she still had her thong on.

"Holden, I—"

"Come here." He grasped her thong and pushed it down, his fingers doing what she was certain was some secret move to her most private parts. As soon as she was naked, he sheathed himself then lay on the sofa. "Come here."

His hands on her hips to guide her, she propped her hands on his shoulders and leaned over, her knees on either side of his pelvis. He moved his grasp to her buttocks and pulled her down atop his erection. The sudden heat and fullness sent her into preorgasmic miniquakes, her body shaking beyond her control.

"That's it, babe, take it, take it." He spoke as he gyrated underneath her, moving the way that made her gasp, sigh, and with a definite swirl of his pelvis, scream.

He didn't wait for her climax to end before he began moving hard and fast inside her, forcing her to cling to him, holding on for what she thought an impossible second orgasm.

His forehead was bathed in sweat and it turned her on more to know she'd made him feel like this. She'd helped drive him to this point, the same place she was. Where whatever it took, they were going to come together.

"Holden, I'm going to come again." She couldn't stop moving against him, meeting every thrust with a downward swing of her hips, the swell of her climax surging, threatening to take her down with Holden's next move.

"That's it. Babe!" He thrust up and shouted as she screamed. But the intensity of their mutual climax didn't drag her down at all—it lifted her to the highest places imaginable.

Chapter 21

"We can't stay like this all night." Bella spoke against his chest as he moved his fingers through her hair, brushing it off her damp brow. They'd taken a full fifteen minutes to come back to Planet Earth and he'd reveled in every second of it.

And silently thanked MVPD for having the outside security down pat.

"We could, but it might get sticky." He laughed and loved that she let out a little giggle, too.

"Ewww." She rose to look at him and he'd never seen such a beautiful shade of green. "Now you sound like a guy and not—" She stopped.

"What?" He helped her off him and then stood next to her.

"Let's finish this in the bathroom."

"The guest shower." He didn't want her near her shower until they either caught the killer or were certain Becky had been the criminal all along. They padded, naked, down the hall. Holden took his gun with him, his only concession to the reality of their situation. His thoughts were on getting into the shower with Bella. Two minutes later they were under the cool spray.

"What were you going to say, when you said I sounded like a guy?" He was massaging her scalp as he washed her hair and the way she leaned her head completely back let him know that she trusted him. It was a sacred space and he didn't take it lightly.

"You are bigger than life. It'd be easy to think that, that I'll never meet someone like you again."

His hands stilled and he turned her around.

"Babe, it's not me, or you. It's what we become together. Us."

"But you don't like reporters."

"And I live two hours away."

"We have different career goals."

"We do."

They remained quiet as they stood together under the spray, then took turns drying one another off.

"So this was it?" Her voice was steady and he admired how pragmatic she was. He felt like he'd been kicked in the gut multiple times, except the memory of their lovemaking made it impossible to feel much of anything besides completely content.

"Bella, I—"

Suddenly, the sound of gunfire rang through the night, coming from the other side of the house wall. He pushed her down onto the floor, covering her with his body. He listened, but silence descended. Reaching up to the sink while still protecting Bella, he grabbed his phone and called Spencer.

"Inside the house, we're under fire. Where's MVPD?"

"We're on it, Holden. Take cover until I find out where your patrol is." Spencer's frustration bit through his words.

He left the phone on speaker and placed it on the sink, next to his weapon, which he grabbed and flipped the safety off. "We're in the guest bathroom, northern side of the house. I've got my weapon and we're going to stay put until you tell me it's clear."

"We have to get dressed." Bella's voice was low, meant for him.

"Quick, let's get clothes from the bedroom." He'd left a bag in the guest room and knew she had her workout and out-of-season clothes in there. The bedroom was between them and the center of the house, where they'd have the most protection from bullets. "I think the MVPD patrol was disabled. There's no other way a shooter got past them."

They were dressed in thirty seconds flat, and as he zipped his cargo shorts and Bella tugged on bicycle shorts, gunfire again rang out.

Bella didn't need him to push her down this time— she was already flat on the floor, between the bed and closet. He'd been in only one other live shooting and he'd relied on what he'd learned in Quantico at the FBI Academy. "Stay down, and let's get into the center of the house."

"Do you think it's the killer?" Bella spoke as she shimmied on her belly down the hallway.

"Don't go any farther. Stay between the two walls." He sat, his back against the wall, weapon loaded and aimed at the ceiling until needed.

Bella copied his posture, and he again was impressed with her composure under duress.

"What do you think is going on?"

"I don't know." Spencer hadn't, either, which was a red flag.

"What if—" She was cut off by a loud, splintering sound. "The kitchen door!"

"Stay here." He ran up to the edge of the wall, weapon first, and peered around the boundary. It was dark and he was unable to see anything but a large shadow of a person on the other side, kicking in the door. The motion-detector light had been shot out, no doubt.

"Stop or I'll shoot!"

A barrage of bullets through the shattered door window was the only reply. Holden's only recourse was to fire back. As he held his hands steady, he got off six, seven shots, waited for the attacker to either drop or flee.

Rapid footsteps faded into silence, and he waited. The front door was one hundred and eighty degrees behind him, so he positioned himself to be able to answer fire from either entrance.

Sirens sounded in the distance, the wails soft but persistent. He had at least five more minutes before the house would be surrounded by responding MVPD. What had happened to the patrol unit in front of the house, and its officers, remained unknown but experience screamed at him that the killer had owned up to his role tonight.

"Holden!" Bella's scream had him turning to the left, looking down the hallway. She was scrambling to her feet, trying to run to him, as a figure similar to the one he'd seen in the staff room stood at the end of the hallway, weapon aimed at Bella, who was now behind Holden.

"Stop or I'll shoot!" Holden kept his weapon aimed

at the killer. The intruder seemed to consider his options before he leaped sideways and disappeared into the master bedroom. Holden shoved Bella back, into the kitchen. He saw she held her handgun, which he'd asked her to keep by her side when at home. "Keep your weapon out—watch both doors."

He was down the hall and cleared into the bedroom, where all he found was the window wide open, gauzy drapes hanging both in and out of it, billowing into the night. Running to the open window he knew what he'd find—nothing. As he peered out, he spotted a MVPD officer in tactical gear as they rounded the corner of the house.

"He took off into the desert!" Holden yelled, pointed at the heavy brush that made it easy for the killer to disappear. The officer nodded and Holden heard mumbles through their helmet as the officer spoke into his or her microphone. The officer ran to the back of the property, followed by another, who'd entered the backyard. Bella's garden backed up to the desert and the perfect escape for a criminal who knew their way around the southeastern Arizona scrub.

Holden swore, the words inaudible to his own ears as the sirens roared and cruisers screeched to a halt, surrounding Bella's house. The killer had eluded him once more.

Bella.

Running out into the hall he let out a huge breath when he saw her standing in the apex of the entryways and short hallway, her defiant posture underscoring what attracted him to her in the first place. Not her beauty, nor her sensuality, but her strength.

Bella was the strongest woman he'd ever met, and

that was a big deal, as until now he'd always counted Grandma St. Clair as the toughest.

Beams of light splayed across the living area from the windows and partially-cracked-open door. Bella was safe.

For now.

"You can stand down, Bella." Holden's voice reached her ears but she couldn't stop from standing on alert, her arms raised with her weapon ready to fire. Only when his hands touched her shoulders, ran down her arms to hug her from behind, did she lower her arms and engage the safety. "You're safe."

She leaned against him, not caring that it was only minutes since she'd promised herself she wouldn't so much as touch him for the remainder of the pageant, no matter how much longer she had to rely on his protection. There was no hope for them past what they'd already shared, and she wasn't about prolonging her own agony. Her resolve seemed trite in light of the shoot-out, and while her brain registered that she'd been intimate with Holden for the last time, her body needed the physical reassurance of his hold to confirm that they were both alive.

They'd survived.

"That was wild." Her words came out higher pitched than usual, not unlike a cartoon character. Giggles erupted, joining the trembling that shook her.

"You're going on adrenaline. It'll pass." His voice, his warm breath, was against her left ear and she had to fight to keep from turning her head the few degrees it needed to put her mouth to his. To escape into the heat they alone shared, far away from the threat of immediate death at the hands of a determined monster.

"This will never pass, Holden."

He didn't respond and she sensed he knew what she meant. Their combined attraction and connection wasn't trivial, and was made of the fiber that bound couples together for a lifetime.

But their lives were too different, too separate. Even if she were willing to choose a career he'd be more accepting of, and she wasn't, not for any man, Holden had made it clear that he wasn't about long-distance relationships. The two hours between here and Phoenix wasn't impossible to manage but she knew he wasn't talking about mere miles.

Holden meant their worldviews and values were too far apart to navigate. To make holding on worth it.

"Listen, Bella, if the intruder is the killer, if he'd captured you—"

"He didn't. You were here."

"But I might not always be. Do you know what to do if you're taken hostage?"

She looked up at him. "Stay alive."

"Yes, but there are some techniques we know are worth employing. Keep the kidnapper talking, try to draw them out. And don't let them take you to a different place if you can at all help it. Promise me you'll do that." He wanted her to promise not just for her, but for him. Because he wasn't sure he'd be able to live without her.

"I'll do it, promise. But with you around, no killer is getting to me."

He wished he was the man she thought he was. With Bella, he felt invincible.

Footsteps stomped outside, and someone pounded on the kitchen door.

"MVPD. We're coming in. Stay still with hands up."

The female voice that sounded from the other side of the kitchen wall, on the patio, was Detective Kerry Wilder, whom Bella knew well through Spencer.

"Kerry, it's Bella Colton. I'm with—"

"FBI Agent Holden St. Clair." Holden's voice was loud and commanding next to her, and she started to relax. "The shooter took off through the desert, heading toward the edge of the neighborhood."

"Roger." Detective Wilder's next commands were rapid and Bella imagined Kerry was telling the team with her to disperse into the desert. "Stay put until I come back." Kerry's voice reached them from the other side of the kitchen door. Bella saw several shadows swipe by the window as the tactical team ran for the desert.

Holden and Bella stood in the quiet of the kitchen, and she reveled in the strength she drew from being in his arms. It was almost possible to believe they might be near the end of this nightmare.

Until the shadow of a police helmet passed the kitchen window. "It's Detective Wilder, I'm entering your kitchen through the door."

When Bella took full stock of Kerry in full tactical gear, her nerves forgot about relaxing. It was impossible to tell it was Kerry, as she couldn't see the woman's flaming red hair, obscured by a dark helmet complete with night-vision goggles. Kerry reached a gloved hand through the broken kitchen door window, turned the dead bolt and opened the battered door. She carried an automatic weapon and Bella registered the magazines of rounds clipped to her body armor.

Kerry lifted her helmet visor, sending the NVGs above her head, too. The flash of her familiar blue eyes sent waves of relief through Bella. Followed immediately by quakes of nausea. Where was Spencer? Had one of the bullets hit her brother?

Sweat beaded her upper lip and she forced breaths in and out of her mouth, not sure if she was going to pass out or throw up.

"At ease, folks. We've cleared the outer perimeter, and we've got several officers chasing on foot. You won't be staying here for the rest of the night, though."

"Is, is Spencer okay?" Holden wrapped a firm arm around her shoulders and she shrugged it off. Whether she got sick or crumpled to the floor, she had to do it on her own. Holden wasn't her personal support system.

"I'm good." Spencer walked in from the backyard and stood next to Kerry. "You're going to need a new kitchen door, sis."

Chapter 22

Three days later, Holden and Bella arrived at the school together for what would be the last pageant practice. Against her wishes, Bella had to stay at different places each night after the break-in to thwart the killer. The assailant at her house had knocked the police offers out with tear gas, similar to what happened after the high school locker explosion. So they knew it was most likely the same person but exactly who was still a mystery. They couldn't rule out Becky as a suspect, even with her admission of not wanting the pageant to end if the files were examined by a reporter or the police. It made Bella nervous, knowing Becky might try to hurt her mid-finale.

Holden had remained at her side the past few days, but like her, never crossed the romantic involvement line that they'd silently laid down before the killer injured two MVPD officers. Bella kept telling herself it was for the best; it would make the last time she saw Holden that much easier.

If only her heart dealt in logic.

"This is really heavy, and hot." She wore body armor under the evening gown she'd chosen. The short-sleeved, round-neck blue dress was the simplest and most modest style she'd ever worn, but it did the job of hiding the Kevlar vest. And also made her look twenty pounds heavier, in her estimation, but she had no illusions of winning the pageant.

"You've got tonight and then the pageant tomorrow to sweat it out. After that you'll be free." Holden strode next to her, his looks heightened by the tuxedo that he wore. The pageant board and Selina in particular had requested everyone be in the same attire they'd wear for the actual pageant. Since the final event was being live streamed via the *Mustang Valley Gabber*'s website, Selina and the technical-production team wanted the optics and blocking to be perfect.

"When do you go back to Phoenix?" She bit her cheek as soon as she asked. So much for keeping it platonic and easy between them.

"As soon as I catch the killer."

"What if you don't?"

"It's my job to. What I came here for."

She caught the undercurrent. He hadn't come here to meet her, get involved with his buddy's sister. Irritation that had nothing to do with the Kevlar armor made her chin rise, her anger sharpen.

"As I came here to get my story. I'm still waiting for MVPD to turn the files over to me." She'd tried to get them released sooner but Spencer had made it clear that his team had to go through them first. With the demands of the pageant security, plus chasing the assailant at her house to no avail, there hadn't been time to read several decades' worth of pageant files. Bella didn't doubt Gio but she also had to face facts. Gio's mind hadn't been operating at one hundred percent near the end. Her memory could have been faulty, but again, Bella needed the files to verify her theories. She'd done further research on the women who'd come forward with their eating disorder and mental illness stories, and while they'd all competed in Ms. Mustang Valley, none of them blamed the pageant. To a fault. They all stated that they'd had a tendency toward mental illness or eating disorders before ever joining a pageant, and the sometimes frenetic activity and perceived pressure may have triggered their illnesses. But none would state that the pageants, or any one thing, had caused their disorders.

"Bella, do you have enough for your story?" Holden stopped short of the front steps. The lowering sun cast streaks of violet and fuchsia across the Arizona sky and reflected a light in his mahogany eyes and made her heart hurt. He'd had the same spark when he'd looked at her naked.

"Maybe. But not really, no. Not until I read the files." A clump of hair fell in her eyes and she shoved it aside, ignoring the crackle of too much hairspray.

He chuckled. "You never did figure out how to get your hair to stay up, did you?"

"I like to wear it down. It's not my fault the pageant requires more than one hairstyle throughout the night." Straightening her spine, she squared off with him, ignored the devastating contrast between his skin and the white crispness of the tuxedo shirt. Or how the black jacket material made his eyes appear impossibly seductive.

"You haven't answered my question." Spoken as

softly as the endearments he'd whispered in her ear before he made her come in full technicolor splendor. Yet the current of his dislike of her profession remained.

"I will have a story at the end of this, yes. It might not be what I'd hoped for or expected, but I don't have a choice. If I want to go further with my career, become a bona fide investigative journalist, I need to produce. If this isn't the story to move my career needle, there'll be another."

"Let me guess—you've finally found some dirt on Selina and the hold she has held over Payne Colton for years?"

Did he know his words were like an owl's talons? Cutting deep, causing irreparable damage?

"Maybe." She had no such thing, but wouldn't admit it to him. Holden had gone back to being her adversary. "And just think, I didn't have to pry it out of you with more sex." Without further comment, she turned and bolted for the entrance. It was too agonizing to see if her words had landed anywhere as soft as his had.

Right in her heart.

Holden fought against pulling Bella up against him, holding her and kissing her until they both forgot why they had to throw down their respective gauntlets. Why they had to so effectively deny each other the pleasure they'd found in one another's arms. And more—they'd found friendship, understanding, agreement between them. An intimacy he'd never experienced. And it wasn't due to the intensity of this case, the constant threat of a methodical killer.

It was Bella.

He had no time or energy to spend on a failed relationship. She'd made her position clear. Bella had her entire life here in Mustang Valley, and would only ever leave for a new job. Judging from her diligence to meticulous research and the articles he'd read under her column in the *Gabber* and on its website, she'd receive offers from all over the country, if not the globe after her pageant story published. No matter what she chose to write about, Bella had a voice that demanded to be heard and stories that deserved the readership a major newspaper would bring.

"Okay, ladies. You all know what we're here for tonight. We'll take it from the top, with the opening number." Selina, garbed in a sparkling, formfitting multicolored dress, stood onstage with a gold microphone, her bright red nails like talons on its neck. Holden wouldn't miss this woman's drama, or the pageant itself.

You'll miss Bella.

He scanned the stage as the music began and the lights focused first on each contestant as she walked across the stage. He followed the beams to where the lights were affixed to scaffolding brought in just for the pageant. The school's theater lights were manually operated from a control booth in the audiovisual room above the theater seats. The scaffolding lights were remotely operated, too, but he knew there were two techs up in the rafters affixed to the metal structure, there to maneuver some of the special effects, to include a net of balloons that would drop when the new Ms. Mustang Valley was announced.

He counted one, then two of the techs, in place as prescribed.

"You're looking awfully dapper for a G-man." Spencer stood next to him in the theater, grinning as if he'd discovered Holden's deepest secret.

"It's for the pageant. Selina demanded it."

Spencer guffawed, the noise swallowed by the loud music booming through the theater as the contestants moved through the opening dance routine. Holden's gaze never left Bella's form, and he didn't see why she was so unhappy with wearing body armor. To him, it only made her look more the warrior that he already knew her to be.

"Do you really think the killer's still even in Mustang Valley?" Spencer spoke from the side of his mouth as they both watched the stage.

"I wouldn't be here if I didn't."

"It seems stupid. If he really wanted to kill Bella, he would have."

Spencer's comment was salt to the self-inflicted wounds he'd been nursing the last few days. And the long nights in three different hotel rooms around the area, where he'd slept on a bed next to Bella's, while the entire place was in lockdown with plain clothed MVPD officers and two rookie FBI agents who'd been sent in to help out.

"Aw, crap, Holden, I didn't mean to say—"

"Yes, you did. I left your sister in the hallway and never thought about the fact the killer had disabled two officers and would enter through the master-bedroom sliding door."

"You're not perfect, Holden. You kept the killer from coming into the kitchen. If you hadn't, you'd both be dead."

He shoved his self-loathing aside, spoke out of the side of his mouth as he kept vigilance on the stage.

"We're both still here and I have a killer to catch. Bella can defend herself as needed." Not that he'd ever let it get to that point. "I'm certain he is still here, a part of the pageant. His MO is to take his time, draw out the actual murder. You've read the same reports I have."

"No, I haven't. You have more access than I do with the other two murders—they're out of my jurisdiction."

"Trust me on this. The killer is still here."

And he was going to catch him.

Bella squatted down behind stage left to adjust her ankle holster. Her dress was long enough to not reveal the weapon, but she didn't want any of the leather to show, either. Holden had watched her affix it to her leg, and it had been difficult to keep her mind on the investigation and the killer who was after her with him looking at her so closely.

"You holding up okay?" Holden had materialized as if from her thoughts.

She stood and even in her heels only came up to his chin. "I am. To be honest, I'd really like this to be over once and for all." She was tired of fighting her fears, and the knowledge that the end of the pageant meant the end of ever seeing Holden again was getting to be too much for her already-worn-out emotions.

"I'm sorry it's not already finished for you."

Was he referring to the killer or their unrelationship?

"Everyone center stage, please. Last call before the final number." Señora Rosenstein was filling in for Selina while the woman changed into what she said was *the best costume this pageant has ever seen*. Someone needed to tell her that she wasn't a contestant.

"Do you really think the killer is still even in Mustang Valley?" She and Holden spoke in hushed tones as they stood on the stage, under the lights, waiting for the last instructions.

"Yes."

Holden's grim expression told her what she dreaded. The killer was that cold, that measured in his attack plan that he'd do anything to get his way and have the murder be to his liking. His depraved needs.

Funny, she'd willingly entered a contest she didn't believe in, only to find she had more in common with all the other women that not. Bella understood how Gio had seen the pageant community as an extended family.

The memory of Gio reminded her that she'd not gotten far at all on her exposé. Suddenly it didn't matter. What mattered was the safety of these women, of all the future Ms. Mustang Valley contestants. Anger flared and lit a flame she'd always carried but had never allowed to empower her like this before.

"Holden." Her voice was loud, and not only did Holden turn to her but so did the entire pageant.

"Excuse me!" Selina had returned.

"Shut up, Selina." She turned back to Holden and lowered her voice to a whisper. "Look, we have to make this happen on our terms, not the bad guy's."

Holden opened his mouth to probably tell her to be quiet and let him do the find-the-serial-killer bit, but she saw the opportunity for what it was. Bella leaned up and wrapped her hands around Holden's nape, pulled him to her and kissed him with all her might.

He stiffened, and while he didn't push her away he didn't tug her in close, either, as he had before. Bella paid it no mind—she was after one thing.

To entice the killer.

The other pageant participants tittered, gasped and *awwwwe*d until they all broke out into a loud round of applause. Only when she was certain no one involved in the event could have possibly missed the kiss did Bella pull back.

Holden's eyes glittered with cold fury. He leaned in, though, and for a moment she thought he was going to kiss her again.

"What the hell, Bella?" His voice low and lethal, he asked his question against her ear.

"The killer wants me. This is the surest way to draw him out." She felt Holden's breath hitch as she whispered back. "I'd rather have him come for me tonight than tomorrow during the actual pageant finale, with a few thousand civilians in the audience."

"I don't know how you got the impression that the stage is your personal rendezvous spot, but it's not. Please do your job, Holden, and Bella, you've come too far to get disqualified now."

She stepped back but Holden's hand still had a grasp on her wrist. She turned and looked at him. "What?"

"Don't forget what I've taught you."

He released her and disappeared behind the stage, where she knew he'd be on alert, patrolling, waiting for the killer to make his move. As she walked to her spot to wait until her time to give her talent portion— the recitation of a poem written by a reporter two centuries ago—she wished she could hang with Holden in the dark. Just one more time before they parted ways and never saw one another again.

Chapter 23

Holden looked under the stage, and through the entire backstage, with zero evidence of a killer or anyone else. Becky moved through the routine of the pageant numbers like any other contestant, and she never once appeared to be doing anything but what everyone else did. She didn't have a weapon on her—every contestant had been searched and put through the metal detector as part of the extraordinary security measures. Everyone, it seemed, was either on the stage, in the orchestra pit below stage front, or up in the lighting scaffolding. The pageant board members were all seated in the audience seats in rows one and two, save for Selina. She continued to cue each contestant to come forward to answer their questions and then perform their talent portion, just as they would on finale night.

Marcie began to sing the Broadway tune he'd heard at least twelve times during the previous practices, and he felt his insides tighten with adrenaline-fueled anxiety. He was always wound tight before an op went down, if he was aware of it. This time it was so much more than an op, or taking out a serial killer, no matter how hard he tried to believe it wasn't.

This was all about Bella and saving her. Sure, he'd catch the killer in the process, and while it wouldn't hurt his career progression to do so, it wasn't what mattered to him most.

He wanted Bella at his side all the time, not just as the woman he was ordered to protect through the investigation and eventual apprehension of a serial killer.

Holden watched Bella walk across the stage when it was her turn but didn't allow himself the luxury of appreciating her beauty or grace, even in the cumbersome body armor. If the killer attacked before he had a chance to react, it would mean Bella's life.

He cursed himself, wished he'd insisted she drop out of the Ms. Mustang Valley Pageant. It was beyond agony to know that at any moment she might be hurt, or worse.

The only thing keeping him sane was that the level of security imposed by Spencer and MVPD was the best it could be. He prayed it'd give him enough time to save Bella, if and when the killer struck.

When Bella finished the poem, which he hadn't paid attention to, intent on observation, she walked offstage toward him, before turning to go to the staff room. He knew she was going to change for the last number, as were all the other contestants.

He scanned the light scaffolding and his heart stopped. Only one tech was atop the metal structure instead of the two who were always present throughout the entire pageant. A movement in his peripheral vision made him turn to the left. He immediately spotted a man dressed in jeans, black top, and most chilling, a mask. He recognized the clothing as that of one of the lighting techs, Ben. Ben stood with his hand on the main stage light switch. Holden hit the comms unit on his chest and alerted MVPD, already surrounding the building as a precaution.

Precaution had turned to deadly intent.

"Stop!" Weapon drawn, he ran toward Ben, perpendicular to his course, planning to cut him off before Ben got any farther. Before he reached Bella.

The stage went black and Holden was plunged into darkness.

A piercing scream split the air.

Bella.

"Shut up or you're dead now, bitch." Ben's voice was so close, above the cacophony of screams from the contestants. Holden reached for his phone, intent to use the flashlight function. As he enabled it a heavy blow to his head made everything go dark.

"You're mine now. Stay quiet and I won't kill your boy toy." Ben, one of two lighting techs, had her by the hair, the barrel of his gun pressed painfully to her temple. He was forcing her to walk through the school's dark, empty corridors. He didn't falter, as if he'd practiced this escape route. As if he meant business.

Keep him talking. Do not let him move you.

Holden's words were her guiding light, gave her a sense of purpose.

"What did you do to him? And why do you want to hurt me?"

He yanked hard and she saw splatters of light across her vision. Sirens outside and the school fire alarm inside sounded; the emergency lighting came on, giving the hallway a dim but serviceable light.

"I said for you to. Shut. *Up!*" He pushed her into the wood shop, forcing her to land on her knees. His foot landed on her lower back and she almost passed out from the agony.

Stay conscious. Don't worry about your kidney.

Scrambling to move away from him as he turned and locked the door, then hauled a workbench in front of it, she looked around the room. The only other exits were the windows, an entire wall of them, through which she saw the blue-and-red lights of the LEA surrounding the building. The only other way out was a bay of double doors where the lumber was delivered. She recalled that it was a loading dock in the back of the school.

Ben didn't seem as worried about her escaping at this point, as he focused on fortifying the door. Which meant only one thing.

He was going to kill her here and now.

Please, please, Holden. I need you.

"Holden, where did he take her?" Holden opened his eyes to his best friend standing over him. Spencer's voice came through a deep fog. He ignored the monster headache that originated from the back of his head. Groggily, he stood, and was ready to make for the staff room.

"She's not onstage, Holden." Spencer put his hands on Holden's chest, stopped him. "Think, man. Where would he take her? We've got the other contestants and judges secure in the breakroom, but since the lights went out no one saw where he took her." Spencer confirmed the safety scenario they'd practiced with the contestants earlier this week, just in case, which had them gather in the breakroom if it was too dangerous to risk exiting the building. "The entire school is surrounded. He's not going to get out of here alive."

"Then he'll kill her, if he hasn't already. I need you to make sure no one gets out of this building. I'm going to find her." Holden felt like another person was saying the words. It couldn't be true. He couldn't lose Bella. His head cleared and he had to move, had to save her. He began to run.

There was no sign of Bella or Ben anywhere, and he strained to listen for a scream or voice but it was impossible with the school's emergency alarm clanging. The hallways seemed like one long row of tiled floors after another.

Until a sparkle caught his eye.

Several sequins lay scattered across the floor, in front of the industrial-arts-classroom door. Bella had sequins on her evening gown.

He paused, not wanting to risk barging in and forcing the killer to do anything stupid out of surprise. There were two doors, and he knew that one opened inward, the other swung out into the corridor. It was to allow for maximum-sized furniture and equipment to move through it with ease. The door that swung inward had a window, and as he peered inside he saw the door was blocked by a pile of wood—and he saw Ben's back, turned to pick up more wood to pile on. Bella lay crumpled at the base of the teacher's desk in the front of the room.

Please be breathing.

He quickly texted Spencer what he saw and then made a decision that would mean Bella's life or death. If she was still alive.

She's alive.

She had to be.

* * *

Bella wanted to scream for Holden to run away when she saw his figure through the classroom-door window. But she had to move very, very slowly, while Ben continued to pile wood atop the workbench. She noted that the bench had wheels, and she hadn't seen him lock them.

He wasn't such a smart killer, after all.

Slowly, inch by inch, she got to all fours, then her knees, then when Ben went farther back in the classroom to get more lumber, she surged forward and with all her might pushed on the workbench. It didn't move an inch.

A sob escaped her, a fatal mistake. Within a split second Ben had her by the hair again, and was screaming in her face. His spittle hit her skin, his face flushed with rage. But his eyes remained flat. Cold. Unemotional.

He was going to kill her.

A loud *crack* stopped Ben in his tracks, and like an automaton he dropped his hold on her hair and kept his arm around her neck as he turned his head toward the noise.

Holden leaped into the room sideways, the bench now at a sidewise angle, his weapon pointed at Ben's head. But Ben had already pulled her around in front of him as a shield.

"Don't make a move or I'll kill both of you." Ben's voice was full of rage and intent. "Put your gun down."

"Drop her. I'm an expert shot." Holden's hair was mussed, his tuxedo a mess; he was her avenging angel. But it was too late.

Bella didn't make a sound, but her gaze never left Holden's. He was focused on Ben, never wavering.

"You won't get her. She's mine. You don't deserve

her. You don't know how to treat a woman." Ben yanked on her hair, rubbed his cheek against hers. She wanted to close her eyes tight but everything depended on this moment. On how she and Holden communicated.

An explosion, then the back cargo door blew open. She felt Ben startle next to her, not as much as she was sure she had, but it was enough. She dropped to her knees, giving Holden a clear shot.

Holden fired.

Holden watched in slow motion as Ben dropped his weapon and collapsed to the ground. He wouldn't be getting back up. Without hesitation he ran over to Bella as MVPD and EMTs surged into the classroom. She stood halfway up to meet him.

They clung to one another for a brief, endless moment until Spencer burst into the classroom, followed by several other MVPD officers.

"Stay here—I've got to get his confession." Holden kissed the top of her head and walked over to where Ben lay on the ground. Spencer had already kicked his gun out of arm's reach but Ben was too weak for that. Spencer had just finished reading Ben his Miranda rights. Holden had to act fast. He looked at Spencer. "Be my witness."

"Got you."

Holden knelt down next to the man who'd terrorized three pageants, killed two women, and almost killed Bella.

"I'm FBI Agent Holden St. Clair. Do you have anything you want to say?"

"I only did this for my mother. She didn't want me to love anyone but her, but it was so lonely after she died."

"What did you do, Ben?"

"I just wanted my mother closer."

"Did your mother have red hair, Ben?"

"Yes, and her green eyes were so beautiful. Just like the beautiful women in the other two pageants, and Bella." A sneer moved across Ben's face as he focused on Holden, seeming to remember that Holden had stopped his efforts to take Bella. "I was so close. You ruined my chance with Bella. She looks the most like my mother did."

"Did you hurt Becky and Selina, Ben?"

"It's their fault. They went after the prettiest in the pageants. I had to protect my women from them. Becky and Selina were mean to Bella. I wanted them dead for what they said to Bella. But they lived. If I had more time… They tried to kill my mother." Ben's voice was whisper thin, his breathing very shallow.

Holden and Spence exchanged glances over Ben's prone form. They'd caught the killer. He'd somehow looked at each victim as "his," and while they were alive, conflated them with the memory of his mother.

"Let us in, officers." Two EMTs swept in, and started to work on Ben. Holden stood, as did Spencer. They'd gotten what they needed from the murderer. Ben stopped breathing and CPR was administered, but after several minutes it became clear that Ben was no longer a threat to anyone.

Holden's work was done. He needed only one thing now.

Bella.

"Babe, you did it." He lifted her to her feet and hugged her tight. Then pushed her back, looked at her face, her body. "Are you okay?"

She nodded slightly. "I am, but my scalp's going to be sore for the next few days."

"That bastard will never bother you again."

She went back into his arms, rested her head gingerly on his shoulder. "No other woman, either. We'll be able to have the pageant finale in peace, at least."

"Bella!" Spencer was next to them, and Bella turned to him. Watching the siblings hug, a sense of deep longing hit him. He wanted to be part of Bella's family. He wanted to be her family.

But she needed room to finish her exposé, and he had his own work to do. He'd disabled the threat but there would be a long after-investigation and reports to fill out. Law enforcement learned from each case and relied on accurate documentation.

More EMTs showed up, and escorted Bella away to check her over. Spencer turned to him. "You okay, buddy?"

"Yeah, why?"

"I've never seen you cry at a scene, man."

He wiped his eyes. "There's a first for everything." Including the realization that what you've been working for isn't everything. Not even close.

Chapter 24

One week later Bella scanned the audience from her vantage point on a stage bleacher, during the opening number. MVPD had asked the pageant committee to delay the final night of the competition until the following weekend to allow for cleanup and investigation closure. She fingered the tiny owl charm on the silver bracelet that had arrived two days after the shootout. It had been gift wrapped with a note in bold print.

> **Hope you find peace again. Gio would be proud.**
> **Thanks for being such a great partner.**
> **Holden**

It was the last she'd heard from him. As each day passed she came to accept that it signaled the end of whatever they'd shared.

"Welcome to the thirtieth annual Ms. Mustang Val-

ley Pageant and our final night of exciting competition!"
Selina's voice boomed over the sound system and the
funky music she'd insisted upon and the crowd roared.
As much as Bella had signed up for this for such different motivation than to win the crown of Ms. Mustang Valley, she couldn't help but react to the adulation
and enthusiasm from the audience. She waved from her
bleacher spot onstage toward where she saw Spencer
and Jarvis sitting, both hooting and hollering as they
clapped. They still didn't know what kind of exposé
she was about to publish—no one did. She'd written it
all last week. The pageant files from Becky had told
her nothing about the pageant committee, except that
they'd handed down nutrition and fitness plans to the
contestants.

Becky had been afraid Bella would misconstrue the
diet plans and make it look as though the committee had
told Gio personally to starve herself. Bella wasn't surprised by what she found and didn't find. It had been a
hard won conclusion, but the plain truth was that eating
disorders and mental illness were complicated, rarely
caused by one event or instance. Triggered, yes, but
from what she'd read in the archival files, Ms. Mustang
Valley hadn't remained in the dark ages about beauty
pageants and in fact had always called itself a scholarship contest. Bella had to admit she'd been too ready to
find fault when she started this investigation, and had
learned a valuable lesson to always keep an open mind,
even when trying to justify a beloved friend's untimely
death. Bella knew she was lucky to be healthy and alive,
and once she accepted what she'd really learned through
this entire ordeal, the Ms. Mustang Valley pageant's
files had ended up fortifying the article she did write.
There would never be enough attention given to eating

disorders or mental illness. This report gave her a platform to shed more light on both, from a personal angle.

Holden remained MIA the entire time she worked
on finishing her report. "He has so many loose ends
to wrap up, you know," Spencer had told her. But she
knew there was more to Holden's absence. Her worst
fear was substantiated by him not showing up at all.
She figured Holden realized that what had looked like
a budding relationship wasn't going to go any further.

Still, she searched the faces of the crowd, as many
as she could see from her vantage point on the bleacher
step and through the stage lights. Hoping against hard
reality that Holden was here.

Leigh Dennings had her own cheering team in other
Affirmation Alliance Group members who sat together
in the first several rows. Micheline Anderson was in
the center of the group and Bella wondered if Spencer or Holden had seen her. Holden didn't appear to
be present, but she knew Spencer would let him know
Micheline had shown up.

The grief over losing the relationship she'd never had
a chance to appreciate or enjoy without threat of immediate death threatened to make her sob onstage, in
front of several hundred of her best friends.

Only for Gio did she hold it together. She may have
lost Holden, but she still had her life to live. This wasn't
the time for self-pity.

Holden had the pageant streaming on his laptop as
he took care of all the personal business he'd neglected
over the past month. A month spent searching for, and
finding and ultimately taking out a disturbed serial
killer. Ben's musings about his mother, before he'd died
on the high school classroom floor, had proved true.

She'd been a redhead with green eyes, and according to Ben's elementary school records his mother had abused him repeatedly. He'd been in and out of foster care, always returning to her side and no doubt more abuse. He had no regrets about that, except for the surviving victims' families who would never see justice carried out in a court of law.

Streaming from unclassified, insecure internet at the Bureau was strictly prohibited, so he'd saved his bills and personal correspondence until tonight.

The stream wasn't as clear as he'd wished; while he knew which tiny figure was Bella onstage it was only because he'd witnessed all of the practices.

No, he had no regret over the case and how it had worked out. But he did wish he'd been able to express to Bella what she meant to him. It didn't make sense to begin something he couldn't follow up on until he closed the case.

Until he knew he was worthy to ask her to consider to be his partner.

The television sound was background as he double-checked utility bills, caught up on laundry. Vaguely he registered that the talent portion had begun. When he heard Selina's voice, unmistakable even with a shaky internet connection, announce the next talent portion, he stilled.

"Ms. Bella Colton tells us what matters most to her in a very special personal essay." Selina's intro revealed none of the acrimony she'd shown to Bella during the rehearsal period. He had to give the ex-Colton credit; she earned her PR director pay grade in spades.

"Good evening, everyone." Holden sat down in front of his laptop, unable to move as Bella spoke.

"It's been a dark journey for our pageant, and for

all of Mustang Valley, as well as Arizona, as we've endured the threat of a vicious criminal. But unlike the sad endings we're seeing too much of these days, there is a happy ending for Ms. Mustang Valley. For all of us. And there is peace of mind for the surviving victims of this awful killer."

Bella went on to talk about how she'd entered the pageant looking for information on her best friend's struggles with bulimia and major depression, but instead found a community of strong, intelligent women who fostered empowerment she'd never felt before.

"I've picked a poem to read for my talent. Some of you might know it; it's by a journalist from a long time ago but still holds true today. Its title is 'To Jennie' but for me, it's 'To Gio.'"

To Jennie

Good-bye! a kind good-bye,
I bid you now, my friend,
And though 'tis sad to speak the word,
To destiny I bend

And though it be decreed by Fate
That we ne'er meet again,
Your image, graven on my heart,
Forever shall remain.

Aye, in my heart thoult have a place,
Among the friends held dear,-
Nor shall the hand of Time efface
The memories written there.
Goodbye,
S.L.C.

"S.L.C. was Samuel Langhorne Clemens, also known as Mark Twain. I want to add that I've learned one other thing these past weeks. True love comes in many forms, but when it does, it's unmistakable and always worth fighting for. Thank you.

She looked straight into the camera as applause boomed over the audio and while Holden couldn't make out her exact expression, dang the low-quality feed, he didn't have to."

He heard Bella. He'd figured out some things himself over the course of the pageant investigation. Bella wasn't his ex, and she was a woman of integrity. Her reporting reflected that.

And he realized he'd never make it without her. But he had to get this case wrapped, and see if he could get moved to the Tucson Resident Office. If not, they'd work out the commute between Phoenix and Mustang Valley. Whatever it took.

"Trust me, babe. I couldn't agree more." He knew it was silly, speaking to Bella's image on the television, but it made him feel that much closer to beginning the rest of his life with her.

The last remaining piece of the puzzle would be to see if she agreed to his plans.

Bella waited onstage with the other contestants while the finalists were named. She wasn't surprised to not be amongst the final five, and waited with anticipation as it came down to Marcie and Leigh, who held hands center stage.

"And this year's Ms. Mustang Valley is…" The winner of last year's contest stood at the podium, hands shaking as she tore open the sparkling, large gold envelope, another Selina touch.

"Leigh Dennings!"

Marcie smiled graciously and hugged Leigh, who smiled wide and accepted her crown, placed on her head by the previous winner. Leigh walked to the microphone.

"This wouldn't be possible without knowing I can live my best life today, and every day! If you want to know how I did it, you're welcome to the next meeting of the Affirmation Alliance Group. Find us on your favorite social media platform."

Bella looked out and tried to meet Spencer's gaze, but he was already on his cell, no doubt reporting what he witnessed to Holden. Her breathing slowed, almost stopped as she faced her truth.

Spencer and Holden would always have their friendship and working relationship. Bella wasn't in the picture at all any longer.

"Congratulations, sis." Jarvis and Spencer stepped out from under the school's front awning as she exited. Jarvis handed her a large bouquet of sunflowers. "These are from both of us."

"Thanks, Jarvis." She hugged him. "It was sweet of you to come tonight."

"Hey, what about me?" Spencer gave her his classic bear hug and she hugged him back, too.

"We want to take you out. To congratulate you for making it through the pageant alive." Jarvis kept a straight face until Spencer laughed and Bella punched Jarvis on the shoulder.

"Funny. I appreciate the offer, but I'm beat. Can we go out for something to eat next week?" The reality that Holden really hadn't come to see the last night of the pageant finally hit her and she was bone weary. If she couldn't be with the one person who'd made a major difference in her life these last weeks, she wanted to be alone and reading a novel.

"Are you sure? There's sure to be a big party at the diner." Jarvis grinned and she smiled back at her brother.

"You've been quiet through most of this, Jarvis. Except when you kept telling me I was crazy to sign up for the pageant. What's going on with you? Have you dug up the old family secret you think is at Rattlesnake Ridge Ranch? Or are you going to admit it's for naught and go back to being your businessman self?"

"It's not for naught, but I can't talk about it yet. Let's just say I'm close. Besides, I like ranch life more than I realized I would."

Bella turned to Spencer. "Do you believe this?"

Spencer shrugged. "I didn't believe you'd signed up for Ms. Mustang Valley, but you did. Anything's possible."

"You didn't think I'd make it out alive, did you?"

"I never doubted you would. You had the best man watching you."

Tears threatened but she didn't want to let her brothers see how deeply Spencer's words affected her. Not yet. Maybe not ever.

"Thanks for your belief in me. I'll catch you both next week."

All she wanted to catch tonight was sleep. If it was an escape from facing her true feelings, and the grief over losing something that had never taken off, then so be it.

It was one thing to have the right man next to her, to guide her and protect her through a tough situation. To expect he'd be around afterward was pushing it.

But she refused to blame herself for feeling how she did. Holden had been a special chapter in her life. She'd come too far in life and in this past month to accept anything but the truth from herself.

Two weeks after the pageant, Bella made her way through Mustang Valley Hospital with a huge bear balloon and an arrangement of chocolate-dipped fruit. The pageant and its aftermath had brought her both joy and sorrow. The sorrow she wasn't ready to face just yet, but figured she had a lifetime to mourn losing Holden to his career, and hers.

The text that she'd received as she pulled up to the hospital helped buoy her steps. She'd been offered an investigative-reporter position with the county paper, the *Bronco Star.* She'd been so excited she'd immediately changed her job status on all of her social media accounts. If Holden wanted to find her, to see what had happened with her career, thanks to the pageant, he could. The county publication, still in print but with a robust online presence, fed into several major national news outlets. After years of hard work and an especially brutal previous month, Bella had realized her dream.

If it wasn't as great as she'd expected, because she'd lost a lot to get here, too, then so be it. She couldn't allow herself to be sad over Holden leaving her life. If she started down that emotional path, she wasn't sure she'd ever find her way back to the joy she'd thought she'd lost when Gio died.

Today she found joy in being reunited with her extended Colton family. As Marlowe had suggested, she'd met up with her and Ainsley for coffee a few days ago. Marlowe had been very uncomfortable, and Ainsley said they all thought the baby was going to make an appearance at any minute. When Spencer let her know that Marlowe was in labor and had been taken to the hospital from her work office, Bella had experienced a radiant sense of quiet happiness that she could only attribute to family.

Another reason to work on letting Holden and her feelings for him go. Their connection had no "quiet": part to it. It wasn't all sexual passion, either, but an intense bond she couldn't explain.

The hospital-room door was open and she walked into a world of flowers, pale blue ribbons, baskets chock-full of baby needs and a radiant Marlowe sitting up in the hospital bed, the newborn at her breast.

"Oh, I'm sorry!"

"Don't be silly. We're family. Have a seat." Marlowe's mother, Genevieve, smiled and moved over, offering Bella the easy chair closest to the new mother. Bella was struck by Genevieve, Payne's third and current wife. The woman's grace while enduring so much personal suffering thanks to her husband's shooting and coma was awe inspiring.

"I wasn't sure what to bring, so I opted for food." Bella placed the balloon arrangement on the crowded bedside table and held out the platter of bright fruit.

"OMG, let me finish this side with him and I want one of those chocolate strawberries."

"I thought you had to avoid caffeine when you nursed?" Genevieve spoke up, her gaze glued to the baby. Her grandson.

"One little bit won't hurt." Marlowe grinned at Bella.

"He's so beautiful." She looked around the room again but as she'd first determined, Bowie wasn't here. "Where's the happy father?"

Bella watched as Marlowe lifted her son from her breast and proceeded to burp him. The little peanut complied almost immediately and all three women laughed. A warmth of belonging and peace filled Bella. This was living life to the fullest, as Gio would have wanted her to do. Enjoying each and every moment.

Marlowe laughed. "I sent him to get a shower, and to bring back some real food. Would you like to hold him?" Marlow held out her bundled babe and Bella tried not to blanch. "Um, I've never really been around such a new baby."

"It's fine. Here." Genevieve took the baby and handed him to Bella as she sat in the chair. "Keep his head supported, yes, like that, and just enjoy his precious little face." The grandmother love radiated from her.

"Thank you." Bella stared at little Reed Colton Robertson, and allowed herself the simple pleasure of holding him.

"We read your piece in the *Mustang Valley Gabber*." Marlowe spoke as she readjusted her bedclothes. "It was fantastic, and what an honor to your best friend. Gio would be so proud of you, Bella."

"Thanks. I appreciate that." She'd decided to write about why she'd initially joined the pageant, her change of heart about the lack of pretentiousness, save for Selina, and why pageants that offered scholarships and ways for women to improve themselves were important. "I've learned a lot from volunteering at the MVED clinic. They're always looking for volunteers, if you're ever interested."

"Thank you. I like how you gave all the resource links for people seeking help for eating disorders and how you explained that while Gio had suffered from an awful disease, it wasn't possible to blame it on pageant culture per se. It was so wonderful how you presented Ms. Mustang Valley as an opportunity for every woman. You handled it so well, Bella." Genevieve's sincerity made the lump in her throat grow.

"It's my job to tell the truth." She adjusted Reed so that she could look into his sweet, tiny face. "Right, little dude? Truth and trust. It's the only way."

"You forgot one thing there, cuz." Marlowe lay back on the bed, beginning to wind down.

"What's that?" Bella handed Reed to Genevieve. It was time for her to depart. New moms needed their rest where they could get it, she'd read.

Marlowe smiled, close to drifting off. "Love."

Later that night, Bella opened the front door to her two brothers, each wearing dress shirts and jeans.

"This is a surprise. What's going on? Come in." She walked back into her living room and shut off the crime series she'd been bingeing. It was too difficult to watch her favorite shows, mostly romantic comedies. The happy endings were still hard to stomach.

"We've been trying to reach you for the last three hours, sis." Jarvis took the lead while Spencer tapped on his phone. Police business was never over.

"Oh, sorry. I turn my phone off when I get home. It's the only way I can unwind from my job." And stop obsessively checking for a text or call from Holden.

It hadn't happened in over three weeks. It wasn't going to. Why torture herself more?

"Do you want something to drink?" She noted that Jarvis had a cooler in hand. "Or did you bring your own?"

He smiled enigmatically. "This, dear sister, is a surprise."

She mentally checked the date. Not their birthday,

not a holiday she'd forgotten in the flurry of the previous weeks.

Spencer shoved his phone in his back pocket. "That was Katrina. She and Boris will be by in a bit."

"Okay…" She looked down at her old T-shirt and jean shorts. "Do I need to change? Oh wait, is this about celebrating for you and Katrina?"

Spencer slowly shook his head. "Nope."

"It's about you and I, Bella." The voice reached to her core and she turned toward the figure who walked up behind her brothers.

"Holden!" Confusion and a tiny flicker of something else—hope—rained on her. "What are you doing here?"

Spencer and Jarvis stepped aside to allow Holden a clear path to her. He wore a pale blue dress shirt, black jeans, cowboy boots. With one hand behind his back, he looked everything and nothing like the FBI agent she'd fallen for.

She'd fallen in love with. Tears began to spill down her cheeks and she sniffed.

"I wanted your brothers to be here, because I know how important they are to you." Holden pulled his arm around and handed her a huge bouquet of multicolor flowers, with a single spiky creamy bloom in the center.

"Thank you." She touched the center pale yellow flower, smiled. "An angel cactus. Just like—"

"The ones in Carr Canyon." He looked over his shoulder at Spencer, who stepped forward and took the bouquet from her hands so that Holden could grasp them.

"Holden, I—"

"Bella, it's my turn to talk. I'm hoping we'll have all the time in the world to work out the details of where we'll live, how we'll handle two careers—congratulations on your new job, by the way, I couldn't be prouder—but right now, I have one question to ask you."

Holden bent down on one knee, still holding her hands. She was vaguely aware of her brothers standing behind him, giving their silent blessing to the event. But all she could see were Holden's dark, dear eyes, looking up at her with complete trust. And the truth.

"I love you, Bella Colton. Will you marry me?"

"Yes, Holden St. Clair. I will marry you—I will!" She tugged him up, and to the applause of her brothers she met her fiancé's mouth and let herself fall into the most delicious kiss of her life.

* * * * *

Don't miss previous installments in
The Coltons of Mustang Valley miniseries:

In Colton's Custody *by Dana Nussio*
Colton First Responder *by Linda O. Johnston*
Colton Family Bodyguard *by Jennifer Morey*
Colton's Lethal Reunion *by Tara Taylor Quinn*
Colton Baby Conspiracy *by Marie Ferrarella*
Colton Manhunt *by Jane Godman*

And be sure to read the next volume in the series:
Colton Cowboy Jeopardy *by Regan Black*

Also available in April 2020!

#2087 COLTON'S UNDERCOVER REUNION
The Coltons of Mustang Valley • by Lara Lacombe
Ainsley Colton hasn't seen Santiago Morales since he broke
her heart years ago, but he's the best defense attorney
she knows. To get him to agree to defend her twin brother,
though, she has to pretend to be Santiago's wife while he
goes undercover to save his sister—and they reignite their
passion in the process!

#2088 DEADLY COLTON SEARCH
The Coltons of Mustang Valley • by Addison Fox
Young and pregnant, Nova Ellis hires PI Nikolas Slater to find
her missing father, who could make her a Colton. They work
together, uncovering danger and mutual attraction—and a
threat that's after them both.

#2089 OPERATION SECOND CHANCE
Cutter's Code • by Justine Davis
The only one who blames Adam Kirk more than
Amanda Bonner for her father's death is Adam himself. And
yet the tragedy brings them together to uncover one last
secret. Can the truth of what happened that night bring
forgiveness to them both?

#2090 INFILTRATION RESCUE
by Susan Cliff
FBI agent Nick Diaz enlists Avery Samuels, a former cult
member turned psychologist, to help him take down the
cult—undercover. She's just trying to save her sister, but the
unexpected attraction to Nick is proving to be more than a
mere distraction!

She ended up on his lap. And the first thing he saw when
he caught his breath was Cutter, standing right there and
looking immensely pleased with himself.

"He bumped me," Amanda said, a little breathlessly. "I
didn't mean to…fall on you, but he came up right behind
me and—"

"Pushed?" Adam suggested.

She looked at him quizzically. "Yes. How—"

"I've been told he…herds people where he wants
them to go."

She laughed. He was afraid to say any more, to explain
any further, because he thought she would get up. And he
didn't want her to. Holding her like this, on his lap, felt
better than anything had in…at least five years.

"I'd buy that," she said, as if she didn't even realize
where she was sitting. Or on what, he added silently as

he finally had to admit to his body's fierce and instant response to her position. "I've seen him do it. But why…"

Her voice died away, and he had the feeling that only when she had wondered why Cutter would want her on his lap did she realize that's where she was.

"I…" she began, but it trailed off as she stared down at him.

He could feel himself breathing hard, felt his lips dry as his breath rushed over them. But he couldn't stop staring back at her. And because of that he saw the moment when something changed, shifted, when her eyes widened as if in surprise, then, impossibly, warmed.

She kissed him.

In all his imaginings, and he couldn't deny he'd had them, he'd never imagined this. Oh, not her kissing him, because sometimes on sleepless nights long ago he'd imagined exactly that. He'd just never known how it would feel.

Because he'd never in his life felt anything like it.

Don't miss
Operation Second Chance *by Justine Davis,*
available May 2020 wherever
Harlequin Romantic Suspense
books and ebooks are sold.

Harlequin.com

HRSEXP0420

**IF YOU ENJOYED THIS BOOK
WE THINK YOU WILL ALSO LOVE**

HARLEQUIN

INTRIGUE

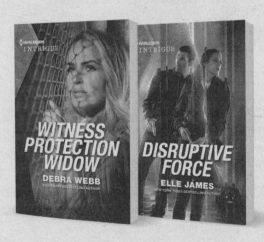

Seek thrills. Solve crimes. Justice served.

Dive into action-packed stories that will keep you
on the edge of your seat. Solve the crime
and deliver justice at all costs.

6 NEW BOOKS AVAILABLE EVERY MONTH!

Love Harlequin romance?

DISCOVER.

Be the first to find out about promotions,
news and exclusive content!

Facebook.com/HarlequinBooks

Twitter.com/HarlequinBooks

Instagram.com/HarlequinBooks

Pinterest.com/HarlequinBooks

ReaderService.com

EXPLORE.

Sign up for the Harlequin e-newsletter and
download a free book from any series at
TryHarlequin.com

CONNECT.

Join our Harlequin community to
share your thoughts and connect
with other romance readers!
Facebook.com/groups/HarlequinConnection

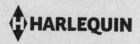

HARLEQUIN

Heartfelt or suspenseful, inspiring or passionate, Harlequin has your happily-ever-after.

With new books published
every month, you are sure to find the
satisfying escape you know you deserve.

HNEWS2020